EARLY PRAISE FOR GETTING BETTER

Will Carter's searingly honest look at his recovery from a life-changing accident is a welcome reminder of our shared humanity.

~ Jessica Handler, author, *Invisible Sisters, Braving the Fire,*
and *The Magnetic Girl*

Will Carter's memoir of his healing from brain injury is a blueprint for hope for anyone who faces self-doubt and a seemingly insurmountable challenge. It is a testament to faith and to the love of parents and teachers. Poignant and powerful, it captures with humor and optimism the routines of the sophomoric teenage years that most people take for granted.

~ Anthony Grooms, author of *Bombingham* and
The Vain Conversation

GETTING BETTER

WILLIAM CARTER
(12/29/2022)

Running Wild

Getting Better
Text copyright © 2025 William Carter
Edited by Angela Andrews

Published in North America and Europe by Running Wild Press. Visit
Running Wild Press at www.runningwildpress.com. Educators, librarians, book
clubs (as well as the eternally curious), go to www.runningwildpress.com.

ISBN (pbk) 978-1-960018-47-2
ISBN (ebook) 978-1-960018-31-1

I dedicate this book to my wonderful parents, Bob and Debbie Carter, for loving and supporting me through my healing journey, and my wife, Ashley, for giving me the encouragement and support to write this memoir.

CONTENTS

ON MEMORY: AN INTRODUCTION

This is not a story about what happened or how things were.

This is not a story of things corroborated or cross-referenced.

This is not even a story that attempts to be accurate.

This is my story as I remember it.

Honestly, no one's story is ever about what happened. We only have our experience of events; we can only access how something happened to us, how we experienced it, or how we saw the moment through our specific lens of perception.

Our only access to life is through our experience—each person's story told by a different narrator. So, who cares what actually happened? Who cares how things really were? Who cares if that is what he was wearing, or if that's what she really said, or on and on and on.

My story is *my* experience of it, and no one can tell me otherwise.

I, for one, have a unique perspective on this.

On October 7, 2007, I was involved in a car accident,

suffered a brain injury, and was put in a medically induced coma.

Funny thing about coma drugs is they make you forget.

This, of course, is a good thing. You don't want to remember the accident, remember the blood, the pain, the twisted metal, the shattered glass, all the hospital lights, and desperate operations that followed. Nobody needs pain like that taking up valuable space in their memory.

Coma drugs are nondiscriminatory though. They take a swipe at everything around the event that put the person in the coma. They don't care. Even if an event happened several months before the coma, the memory of it is either fuzzy or gone.

My car accident, my injury, my recovery, this pivotal moment in my life, is a foggy, misremembered collection of stories I have been told and ones I have unintentionally made up.

See, years after my accident, when I was working on my thesis play about a couple dealing with their son's brain injury, I told my parents things I remembered from the hospital—stories, people who came, or things that were said—and I was told it didn't happen, or it didn't happen like that, or they didn't come by, or they didn't say that.

I am an unreliable narrator.

I do not fully remember waking up from a coma, and to be frank, I don't really remember a good bit after. I hardly remember my first year of college, the summer that preceded it, or even the months of my senior year of high school before the accident.

There are colors and faces, but they're in streaks or underwater, visible yet completely unclear, wispy grasps of moments, snatches of memory, nothing tangible.

It's strange to have a recollection of almost two years like this, a memory that feels like a chipped and peeling mosaic on the wall of an old Italian church.

This is not a story about what happened because it cannot be. I cannot trust what I remember, and there are gaps; oh, there are gaps.

No one has an objective take on the past. Experience is clouded by one's own bias. Things get deleted, repeated, mistaken, misremembered, and on and on. There is no truth, of the kind we are comfortable with, that exists.

But what good is that? Your story is what you have lived with; your story is the one your conscious and unconscious mind teamed up to develop in order to steer you through this confusing thing called life.

This is not an invitation to throw out the idea of truth.

This is only to say, when it comes to our stories, I don't know how useful the idea of truth is.

However, this question of the truth of narrative is something we all face. If you've had someone correct your story, you understand. The frustration of another human being telling you what happened is almost unbearable. Even if you're wrong, it takes reminding yourself of every terrible prison movie, TV show, and documentary in order to not murder them right then and there.

You don't say, "Oh, I'm sorry. I apologize for my error. It seems some of the details of my story are not what some might consider correct." No! If you have even a drop of humanity, your mind screams, blood filling your face red, "It's my story! Butt out!"

Because, it is your story, and if you've remembered something wrong, okay. Somebody else can give their story, as long as, of course, it is not in the middle of your story.

My memory is an imperfect thing, but the story I have lived

and created myself to has been crafted by this strange, uncertain thing.

What are we to do?

Pick up the pieces and let our story take the lead, falling and failing all the while.

I cannot remember correctly, but I can hand you a raggedy quilt of stitched together, mistaken, and fraying versions of events and hope it will do you good.

My story is unreliable, but it's the only one I have.

Enjoy.

1

THE COMA

Who is Will going to be?

Beep. Swish. Beep.

Beep. Swish. Beep.

Dad bows his head, his shoulders forward, his chin on his gut. He rests his goatee on his blue and grey striped button-up, wrinkled, faded. He looks down, taking in the music on the stereo next to his son's hospital bed as the ventilator and heart monitor offer a steady tempo.

Beep. Swish. Beep. "God, give me peace." Beep. Swish. Beep.

"Give me peace for who he is when he wakes up." Beep. Swish. Beep.

"Whenever he wakes up." Beep. Swish. Beep.

Then, the light taps of the xylophones at the beginning of Sufjan Stevens's "Chicago" filter through the stereo. As the violins kick in, my heart's beep gets a little faster.

"God," Dad drops his head, defeated.

Eyelids flutter. My mouth moves ever so slightly as the drums pick up. I can't talk with the trach in. I'm not fully conscious, drugged up and out of it, but, for the first time in two and a half weeks, I am awake. I am awake. I am confused at the pain in my head, but I am awake. My parents cry, hugging each other as the nurses and doctor rush in, and the music of Sufjan Stevens fills the room, "All things go, all things go to recreate us; all things grow."

With a new lease on life, raised from the dead, brought back from darkness, I cannot think of a better song to reenter life to.

And now, the recreation begins.

Here I am, brown and yellow spots on my chest beneath my blue and pink hospital gown, IV drip still active, my buzzed scalp itching beneath the foam on the inside of my plastic helmet. My feeding tube is still pumping life into my stomach, catheter still plugged in. I can't really lift my head up. My eyes are only half-open. I don't understand what's happened. I just keep looking at Mom and Dad and saying, "I love you. I love you. I love you." With their knuckles intertwined, both of them are crying softly, not messy and dirty tears but, rather, soft, gentle tears of joy, as they look upon their dazed boy.

I imagine my mom releases the knot of tension that's been coiling and recoiling inside her stomach when I say, "I love you," to her for the first time. She's been crumbling every day since I first came to the hospital, but now, I can see she's rebuilding. You know those moments in movies when characters are in an altered state of consciousness, and it's like there is Vaseline rubbed on the camera lens? It's just like that: shiny, fuzzy, blurred moments of realities that bleed and bend while you experience them, but even more so when you remember them. The family all came. Granny leaning her short, large body on her walker, my Uncle Roland in his paint-stained flannel and green pants, Aunt Linda with her cardigan and silver cross around her neck, Aunt Nancy,

2

green pants and a copper top—everyone came in and out. Then, the close friends, Peter, Stephen, and Anna came too. Everyone is standing near my bed as I just listen. I can see the shape of them, but their words float away.

I am lying in my bed, almost asleep, without a ventilator, hours after waking up, and Mom's on the phone with someone from Shepherd Center, "Yes, he has a brain injury. Mhmm. . . subdural hematoma. . . Yes, we can do that. . . Please, let me know. . . Thank you. . . Bye."

I know I'm in a hospital room. I know I am alive. My head and throat hurt. Yellowish-brown spots speckle my body, and I am here, no identifiable pain, but I feel the lightness in my head, see the blurry shapes in front of my eyes; I know something is different. A knock on the door, and my mom nods to my dad. He pushes down on the black plastic of the chair legs and heaves himself up with a, "Ugh."

Once Dad sees who it is, he lets out the tension in his shoulders and smiles.

"Joe." My dad lets out a happy, "Hey, come on in."

A tall, bald, heavyset figure enters. His smile can light up a stadium, and my mom announces gleefully, "Will, look who it is!"

I see the wrinkles and the bald head, and. . . I turn my head, "Granddad?"

Laughter rings out among the room, my parents breaking into the laugh they have been unable to capture for a long time, loud and reverberating, mouths open, teeth showing. During times like these, it's the letting the air out of the balloon that keeps you going. Still with a grin, Mom leans her short body to my bed, glasses falling to her nose, side pressed against the side railing, "No, Will, not Granddad. Granddad was here yesterday."

Yesterday? Why do you use these words? What is yesterday?

Dad slaps Joe on the back, "How does it feel old man?"

Joe smiles, stepping closer to my bed, hands on his hips, "Well, I am a granddad."

Patting my hand, Mom locks her brown eyes on to mine, "Look again, sweetie."

I peer forward, voice raspy, soft, "Joe?"

He moves his large form over, a man in his fifties dressed in jeans, Converse, and a button-up. He actively decides to dress differently from anyone else his age. He definitely stands out among the other parents at church, which is why it's not strange that I saw him as a mentor. He comes in close, "Yeah, buddy. Joe here. How ya doin'?"

I want so badly to be present, to be there, to be a part of the conversation, but all I can do is breathe out, "O-o-okay. . . just tired."

He touches his goatee as he laughs his usual big-gutted laugh, "I bet! Always tired after a long nap!"

And there is laughter in the room as my parents exchange sweet, happy looks, while I only feel the itch of my scalp under my helmet. What are we laughing about? What was the joke? What am I doing here? I don't know why, but my cheek bones poke up into a smile. All the bounce in my body is gone. Whatever I've been doing here has caused all of the fat to drip out into the IV, and I have become a frail version of former myself: pale-yellow skin, wrists you can easily wrap your fingers around, a bruised up, skin-wearing skeleton. Joe does what he's supposed to; he stays. He stands, and he eats away the awkwardness with my parents and me as with a knife and fork. There is a beauty of the staying, of love, and of true friendship. I never truly knew its value, but I am learning it now. I see Joe is carrying something in his hands. He holds it up, "Well, I brought you something."

He picks up a CD and puts it in my lily-white fingers. I look at it, with the track of a smile, "What. . . what is it?"

"A mix. You might know some of them, but I hope you don't know all of them."

The track of the smile grows, a glimmer of teeth under the chapped lips of an exhausted boy, as Joe touches the top of the CD player to open it, places the mix in, and [1]Rufus Wainwright's "I Don't Know What It Is" lights into the room.

I nod my head, eyes staying level, slits bringing in light but not much else, "Is good."

I don't really understand. I know who this is; I know I'm in a hospital; I know who Mom and Dad are and the rest of them, but it's a weird thing to have your mind, your memory, your perception, your experience of the world, and yourself completely altered. I don't understand what now is, or why I am here. I don't know what life was like before my injury. Whatever happened caused me to have memories of the past like a movie reel, but I don't have any idea what it was to experience those events, how life was, who I was. It's kind of beyond words to think about, but there was a me before this; there was a way life was, a person who experienced that life, and then, there was the beep-swish-beep, and it was like a reboot, but the computer started differently. I know that I am different: I am received differently, looked at differently, that people lower their eyes and bring up their lips in pity, soften their voices, and I just can't stomach it. Call it a sixth sense, call it existing as a human being, but I know that things are different. I know this is not the way it had been, even though I can't access how I experienced life before. For the first time, I am starting to realize there is a different me.

As my eyes open and close, as I look through the bleary

current state of my life, I see Mom on the phone confirming my spot at Shepherd Center, Dad hugging Joe Kirk, Anna Shults touching my arm. I hear my brother talking with Uncle Roland —and my body—I can't really even feel my body. I am flitting and flying in and out of focus, zooming in and out of reality, but I know that I am here. For the first time in a long time, everyone in the room knows I am here. At least for a little bit more of life, I am here. I hear the words *coma* and *brain injury*. I don't know what they mean. I guess they relate to me, but I don't know how. I hear my mother. "Yes, well, you understand. With his brain injury, we are trying to get him into Shepherd. It's been hard with the coma because Will had to be awake before I could even get him, but we just got him in."

"That's great!"

Mom holds Dad, "It is one of the best brain injury rehab centers in the country."

"That's great that it's in Atlanta."

I don't know where this spot I'm at is or what Shepherd Center is. I'm tired. What's a rehabilitation center? I guess I have a brain injury. Maybe? Was I in a coma? I see everyone's tired eyes. I see the hugs. I hear the sobs. That must be true. That must be me they are crying over. Then, the track changes, and there is the slow, soft plucking of an electric guitar, the familiar chords, and at first it's unclear as the guitar slowly and quietly strums on, but then, Buckley's haunting voice, sings "Hallelujah."

Joe really created a mix to capture this moment in my life beautifully.

The Hebrew word *hallelujah* is simple; it means, "Praise Yah," with *Yah* being the Old Testament name for God. It doesn't mean, "Today is great," or "Happy day." It means, "Praise God!"

Praise God for today. Praise God for now. I mean yeah, it's

hard, sure. But, today, I am awake. Today, Mom and Dad know I am alive. Today, they believe I will have a tomorrow. They must grapple with having a son with brain injury and understand what it means to have me go through this. I'm sure they are anxious and scared, but right now, all anyone in here can feel is hallelujah. The problem is that we've used this word so much. We've used it so carelessly that we've forgotten what it means. Even used it sarcastically: Coming back from a restaurant to a parking ticket on our windshield, we'd throw up our hands, "Hallelujah!" But hallelujah is "Praise God!" Their boy is alive. I am awake. I have a bed at one of the best brain injury rehabilitations hospitals in the country. Praise God!

Hard times are coming as they do, and tomorrow might be hard too, but they know they are thankful for right now. And with that, they kiss and hold each other as she speaks in his ear, "We got him in, Bob. He's going to Shepherd."

He tightens his arms around her, enveloping her in a hug, "We did."

They linger like this, warm, sweet, loving, smiling, "That's so great."

It is great.

Hallelujah.

2

SHEPHERD

Getting my feeding tube, a gross, brown little tube, taken out of my stomach is the last affliction I will suffer at the ICU. It's the adult equivalent of an umbilical cord, which, of course, you can't take with you once you leave.

Dr. Weaver is by my side, his reassuring voice, "You're going to feel a little pressure."

And I swear, Understatement 101 must be a required class in medical school.

There is a suction pop like opening a bottle of wine as my eyes go wide, and I offer a "Guggh!" This is the noise you make when you're in so much pain you no longer have access to human language. A hole just opened in my body, and yeah, that's a little pressure, yeah, sure, like the meteor that killed the dinosaurs was an unexpected visitor.

Dad laughs, "You looked like Roadrunner[1] for a second there."

I look up, dazed, thinking, "What is happening?"

Mom puts her hand on me, "You just got your feeding tube out. You were in a coma."

8

What? This seems familiar.

"You were in a car accident and suffered a brain injury. You were in a coma, so you could heal. You just got your feeding tube out."

Car accident? When was this? I put my hand up to a foam helmet on my head, "What's this?"

Mom looks into my eyes and pauses. I don't know if she's said any of this before, "They took out part of your skull because of the swelling in your brain."

Coma, brain injury, broken skull, I feel like I've heard these things. I have snippets I draw on. I think on my hospital room, white, yellow, and blue, and I remember cards and medical equipment, and as these nurses take out my IVs and unhook my oxygen, Mom holds exercise pants and a black T-shirt, "Honey, you ready to get dressed?"

Ready? I haven't been ready for any of this.

After helping me undo my gown and helping me with my shirt, she then slides the exercise pants over my diaper. The diaper is a new normal for me. It's from the coma, but I'm also not in a place with my body where I can really control when I can get to a bathroom either.

A knock on the door, two nurses come in, pink scrubs, smiling faces, "We're sad but happy to see you go."

Mom nods, pats my back, "We've been here so long. Thank you for everything."

Dad goes for a handshake, met by a hug. Mom hugs the other nurse, and then, hugs are equaled for everyone. Before they leave, one of the nurses leans down at the bed, the white of her teeth shining bright against her caramel face, "You must at least come back and visit."

Mom grips my shoulder, "He'll be back in December."

A dazed look, I turn to her, "Back?"

Everyone smiles, pity in their eyes. Tapping the tan foam of my helmet, Mom reminds, "Remember honey, you're missing part of your skull."

I put my fingers up to my skull. Thank God the helmet's there because I want to touch it. The nurse smiles big as another, older nurse comes in with my new means of transportation: a wheelchair, black back, blue stripes outlining the seat, black wheels. The nurse parks the chair and holds up a tan, cloth belt, which she then straps around my waist.

It's on tight, bringing my ribs almost together, "What's. . . what's this?"

"This is a gait belt." The nurse's red fingernails shine against my thigh, "Gait, like, you know, walk."

Then, she helps me up, and the older nurse steadies me with her lily hand, pink veins showing. The nurse looks to my parents, then back at the other nurse, "One sec, Cheryl. I need to talk to the parents."

The nurse hugs my parents then pauses, bends down to me, "My name is Shani. You don't really know me, but I've gotten to know your parents very well."

I look up to see them beaming at me, and Shani continues. I appreciate how she is meeting me at my level.

"And I know you will do very well at Shepherd. You're going to recover. You probably won't remember me when you come back, but I want you to try. Okay?"

I nod. To be honest, I have already forgotten her name. I don't want to acknowledge that. I'm lost. I don't really know what's happening. Shepherd Center as a concept has already vanished from my mind. It's a horrifying thing to have such bad short-term memory. I get why some older people in nursing homes always look so scared. You know there's something to remember; you know you've forgotten, but you can't keep asking, "What's happening? What's going on?"

So, you just keep pretending. You nod, give a soft casual

laugh, but inside, you are spiraling. You're in the deep end after the pool's closed. Lights are out; it's pitch black, and you keep pushing your foot down, trying to find the bottom.

"Will?"

Even though I went to that place inside my head, where I'm thinking about something else, I reply, "I'm listening."

Shani smiles, "I hope you enjoy Shepherd Center." I nod. Shepherd Center? What the heck is that? "We'll see you in December, Will."

And with that, the wheelchair's moving. My mouth is almost open, and my head bobs like an infant learning to sit up —weeble, wobble, weeble, wobble. The foam helmet is sliding down, so Mom stops pushing the chair and tightens it. The automatic doors open as Dad waves to the receptionist, and then, the breeze hits my face as I see the blue, white, and yellow of a Georgia November morning. It's almost nice to get that chill, Mother Nature's way of reminding you that you are still alive: that early morning first-day-of-school sting in the air that bites at your skin, but it's not so cold you shiver. Maybe, it's anxiety, maybe nerves, maybe you haven't been out of the house since May, but there is the slightest chill. The car ride goes by like a movie, the feeling of living life as a passenger, as an audience member. It's not from grief, depression, or the simple choice to vacate the space of an internal struggle, but rather, it is my mental awareness, and I vacate both involuntarily and often.

Shepherd Center is a big hospital as you get to Atlanta. On a busy road, up a hill, the blue and gold sign stands tall. What is this place? Why am I here? Once you enter, there's the paperwork, always paperwork. Mom sits in the chair next to my wheelchair, and she does most of it. Dad sits in the chair next to her with my green Adidas bag by his feet.

A nice middle-aged man with a streak of grey in his black

hair and a bit of gut, struts up in khakis, a blue Shepherd staff polo, and Sketchers. I don't say anything; I don't notice much these days, but the footwear stands out. He bends down, with an enthusiastic smile and the voice of an overeager dad, "Hey, I'm Greg. Nice to meet you! You are?"

And Mom's hand on my shoulder, "This is Will."

Greg has the demeanor of a man who smiles for a living. Polished, a repetitive kindness that's genuine, but it's also routine. He starts the walk with us, "Welcome to Shepherd Center! This is one of the best brain injury rehabilitation centers in the country. Glad you could get in so soon! It's really a miracle, so glad you could get in when you did."

Dad gives Mom's a hand a tight squeeze. Worn hands in worn hands, as they walk the brightly lit blue hallways of Shep herd seeing nurses busying to each room, patients in wheel-chairs, on walkers, and with canes. An old man with a pale skin and two tufts of white hair shooting out from either side of his speckled scalp wears the same tan woven belt with a hook on the front as I do, and a nurse holds him from behind. He gives me a wave. The nurse tugs, "Gerald, focus please." A snarl from the old man with a look back at her, as his cheek turns up in annoyance. Greg gives Gerald a wave as we keep moving down the hall; brown, plastic railings shoot down the sides of both ends of the hallway. Pictures of patients and doctors splatter the walls, giving the walkway a little bit less of a hospital feel compared to the hand sanitizer dispensers, call buttons, room numbers, and a white linoleum floor that reflects all this in addition to the oppressive fluorescents that beam down in place of the sun.

Greg has been talking this whole time, but I'm not there. I'm taking everything in, a passenger as we move down the hall to my room. It's a weird space to be in, to be somewhere and also feel not there. The only other way you can do it is with a fistful of Vicodin. I'm just a bobblehead on a broken body in a chair bumbling down the hallway to my room, but it's not really my room, is it? I'll be here for a bit and then, onto the next place. It's not like the nurse is going to scream, "Will, go to your room!"

And after a brief pause on the elevator, we are there: Room 203, almost at the end of the hall. There is a big, white hospital bed, a TV on the other side, and by the window, a wooden desk and a wooden chair with a green cushion that looks like it feels as comfortable as sitting in the tree it was made out of sit next to a plant against the wall. White floors, a lamp near the desk, one of those trays on wheels off to the side of the bed complete my new home. Home. Ugh. For now.

"Here you are!" Greg says enthusiastically, and as if he's our real estate agent, "Home sweet home!"

He says this to every patient coming to Shepherd Center, always to the same half-hearted smile and tired, polite chuckle.

"Now, the nurse will be in soon, and then, the therapy team will make their way in."

Mom and Dad nod as I look around the dark room. The window provides little light as the other side of the hospital blocks out the sun from truly entering and lighting the room. The lamp has a soft glow. Like the one in my granny's den, this one offers a soft orange light that makes the room feel sleepy, and with some help from Dad, I get in the bed, lower the arm rest, and find a big plastic remote, one so enormous that if you hit yourself in the head with it, you might double that brain injury. Part of it is the typical hospital bed up and down controls and nurse call button, but there are also buttons for TV volume and channels.. It's like my old ICU home but with a window.

Mom takes the bag from my dad and sets up my CD player on the dresser across from my bed and unloads some clothes in the drawers, exercise pants, pajama pants, black T-shirts. Before, with the teenage obsession to be cool, I acquired so many band shirts because I needed to let everyone know the music I listened to was better than theirs. Mom stands up cards from my hospital room to show that people were thinking of me. Then, they pull the chairs from the wall and sit. Two middle-aged boomers sitting across from me like a high-powered interview panel, but they're just concerned.

"What do you think?" Mom asks.

"I think. . . I think it's. . . nice."

Mom nods. Dad nods. Stillness. I like it. It's nice when I don't have to ask questions, when I can simply enjoy the moment and not be confused. I don't need to ask, "Who's that?" or "Where are we going?" It's a beautiful thing to not be confused and just sit in a moment of quiet.

But it's not for too long as a small man with a gut rattles a knock and enters. Blue scrubs, a black mane, lugging a machine behind him, he smiles wide, "Hey everybody! I'm Guy."

Dad smiles and points, "You don't mean a guy?"

Finger guns and a fake laugh (he's heard this his whole life), "No, just Guy. And I'm assuming you're not the guy?" Looking past Dad to me, "This is the guy, right? The man?"

Dad laughs, shakes Guy's hand as the linoleum shines in the soft glow of the lamp.

"Need to get the man's vitals."

"Okay."

And he gets the numbers, normal. Good. I wish I was normal too. For someone who spent his whole high school career trying to prove how different he was with long black socks under camo shorts and a Ramones T-shirt, all of which said, "Look at me," I just want to disappear now, to be like everyone else. Get me a polo stat! Guy tells Mom and Dad about the hospital, but me, I'm barely there. I'm trying not to make it clear that I'm lost, so I nod. Nod and no one will call you out.

Guy adds, "Well, hang in there, buddy. I think you're gonna like it here!"

I nod, "Huh, yeah."

Mom smiles sweetly, "Guy, thank you. Hope to see you soon."

Guy unholsters the finger guns, "I'll be back with some food."

And he leaves as Dad checks his watch, "Food?"

I am hungry, hungry and tired.

Mom is just looking at me, "I think it will be good here."

I nod as my tired head swivels around. This room is so small, and the pale blue and white walls remind me of the hospital. There is a little couch under the window, but it's the couch you see in doctor's offices and hallways, the kind of couch you have never seen in a person's home in your entire life. Mom is teary-eyed. Even through her black-rimmed glasses, I can see her eyes are glassy. Dad pats her hand as she fills the silence, "I think the therapists are coming in soon."

I can feel my eyes falling, the headache, "I'm. . . I'm sleepy."

Dad nods, one hand to his goatee, "Okay, you want to nap?"

"Yeah."

Dad stands, "Okay."

Soon, they leave, and I bobble my head around the room, eyes half closing to see a sink and cabinets, a chest of drawers, my CD player, and an Adidas bag next to it, a TV above the drawers, a desk next to the sink, the soft glow of the lamp, the window, the couch, the chairs with the faux wood and blue backs, the nightstand, the tray on wheels, all existing on the white floor of a hospital room. It's weird that there could be this much stuff and the room could feel so empty. I'm used to being alone, but this room feels lonelier. Thoughts jumble through my brain, but there's no clear directing them; there are a number of pictures from the day, but there is no context to set them in. I know I have a brain injury. I don't really know what that means, but I know I can't walk. I know I'm wearing diapers, and I know I want to be better, to get better. When you're in this position, where your mind is a word scramble, you look for something to hold on to, something to grab and know is true, some kind of direction: get better.

3
FIRST DAYS AT SHEPHERD

After getting woken up by the nurse, getting my diaper changed, and falling back asleep, I crack my eyes and scratch my face to Mom and Dad sitting on the couch, Dad holding his morning cup of coffee and Mom downing a Diet Coke. Mom in her turquoise fleece jacket, my dad in his blue one, jeans, both look so tired.

Dad tips his coffee my way, a morning cheers of sorts, "Morning, buddy. How'd you sleep?"

My mind is looking for shore, "O-okay." My brain has lost its mooring as the rope slithers down into the lake, green water devouring that last bit of string. Where am I? "Where's Dr. Weaver?"

Mom bites her lip, light pink, no lipstick, "Honey."

Waves roll against the wooden hull, no land in sight. I turn my eyes toward her, "What?"

She gets up, comes over to me, "Sweetie, Dr. Weaver's at North Fulton."

This tracks. I remember that.

"And you're not at North Fulton anymore."

The boat felt like it docked, but never mind, it was just a sand bar. "What?"

Her eyes are glassy; I know this is hard for her. Her face looks pained. but I don't know where we are.

"You're at Shepherd Center now. They're going to help you recover from your brain injury."

As I am capturing what's going on, an overweight nurse in blue scrubs enters, clearly sporting a weave with a short, straight cut, "Here to get the vitals."

I nod. I don't really know what's going on, but I know the boat is sinking, and I'm not finding shore. The nurse wraps the blood pressure cuff around the skin and bone that is my left arm, "Going to get your pressure, pulse, and oxygen," she says in a soft voice as she hooks up a little device to my index finger.

I nod. What is this place? What happened? What day is it? What time is it? What's the last meal I ate? Who is this nurse?

"All good," the nurse assures.

My mom confirms this as she peers over and looks at the numbers on the white rolling screen.

The nurse smiles, "I'll be back later on," cracking the tan, wooden door to the sound of a patient in the hall.

"AHHHHHHHHHH! FUUUCCKKKK!"

Dad smiles, pursing his lips, "Well, isn't that nice."

Mom gives him a look, but she can't help but crack a smile.

The nurse, taking her cart, offers, "That's Chad. He's cursing up a storm. Got here yesterday, and he is angry."

Dad's head goes to the side, "Angry?"

A sigh as her shoulders go down, "See, he has a spinal cord injury, and then, something got mixed up with the anesthesia, and now, well, boy's got a brain injury too."

Mom touches her hand to her mouth.

18

"God, that's awful."

Oh. So, this is both a rehabilitation center for those with brain injuries and spinal cord injuries. The nurse came and went; we learned about Chad, and we were told the therapists would be in soon. My mind swims for a long while. I don't really know how to describe it. I have forgotten so much, but I feel like I'm always wondering what I'm supposed to remember. Life is in Monet, streams of little dots of existence.

At some point, I doze off, only to be woken up by a knock at the door. Mom projects, "Come in."

The door cracks, as five bodies come in and make their way over to the bed, two blondes, two brunettes, and one medium-sized man. Their features are shaky, but the man stands out, a button-down shirt and grey pants, while three of the women are in exercise pants and Shepherd T-shirts.

One of the women with long brown hair in a bun, in her thirties, and sharper facial features that become clearer the closer she gets, comes to me so that she can tell I am focusing on her.

"Hi Will."

She stops, waits a beat; my mom is about to nudge me when this woman says in a clipped rhythm, "My name is Sara. I am going to be your speech therapist. I know your speech was not impacted, but there is still a great deal we can do."

I smile. I don't know what speech therapy means, but I'm glad my speech was not impacted. The light-brown haired woman, younger, softer features but still slim comes up, a foot or so shorter than Sara.

"My name is Caitlin. I am going to be your occupational therapist. I look forward to helping you out with your left hand and any visual challenges."

Visual challenges? I just smile. I am barely able to keep

track of anything, much less add anything to this conversation. A blonde woman, a larger build—not heavyset, but a bigger build—pale skin, takes a step to me.

"My name is Ashley, and I am your physical therapist. I'm going to help you get back to walking."

I smile at this. I like this thought. Walking sounds really nice. I don't even have a concept of what it was like to walk before my accident, but I know walking means independence, and I like the thought of that. The other blonde is a little bit more heavyset, just as pale though, with a little bit blonder, brighter hair.

"My name is Ashley as well, and I am your rec therapist. We're going to be playing games and having fun. Do you like sports?"

Dad runs his hand straight across his neck, "Abort. Abort."

Mom laughs, "Not really his thing."

Ashley's not phased, "I'm sure we'll have fun either way." The man in the collared shirt, a nice pattern of green, grey, and black, comes forward, possibly the oldest, late thirties, short hair but a shining smile; he moves up, "Thomas here, and we're going to add some music to your life. You play any instruments?"

Mom jumps in as I look for my response, "He played piano. He was in a band."

Thomas looks at me, with an exaggerated expression of inquiry, "A band? We will have to get you back on the keys."

And I smile, a nod, a hand to my yellowish-brown colored helmet, "Yeah."

Sara pivots, a practiced smile, "Any questions?"

Dad, one hand on his gut, the other to his goatee, adds, "Greg said something about a mee—"

With a quick gesture to indicate understanding, Sara

answers, "Yes, we will meet with you once at the start of every week to go over Will's progress."

"Okay. That sounds good."

At the moment, with the battalion of therapists on one side and me and my parents on the other, I don't really get who they are or what their point is, but I know that this is the start of something.

Another short smile from Sara, "If there are no questions, we'll see you later today, Will."

They smile, say goodbye, offer a wave, and go off to the next room to say hello. I don't have anything but questions, Sara. I have nothing but confusion and a fuzzy static I'm trying to decode. All I can offer is "What? Who? Why? Where? When?" So, I nod at their leaving. Mom and Dad look at me. I want to say something; I want to make them laugh again; I want to be the entertainer, the center of attention in a good way, but I don't have the energy or ability.

"How do you feel, Will?" My mom smiles at me, her glasses down on her nose.

I answer with all I can offer, "Tired." The boat is completely away from the mooring, and my body is begging for rest. It's a weird feeling to be so tired when you've just been asleep for three weeks, but I think I've been told it's the coma drugs in my system, and I am exhausted.

"Okay."

Dad nods. "You want to nap?"

"Little bit."

Standing up and running his hands down his jeans, he picks up his coffee cup and tugs at Mom, "We'll let you sleep for a bit."

Mom looks to him, "But."

"What?"

"Anna will be here soon."

Dad lowers his head, "Right." Then, a look to me, reassuring, understanding, "We'll let you sleep until Anna gets here. Then, we'll wake you up. Okay, buddy?"

I run my hand slowly under my helmet, the sprouting hairs on my scalp itching, that feeling of a wound healing you just want to pick and scrape at, unbearable.

Mom's eyes go wide, "Careful."

"It itches."

The helmet always itches. It's the foam against the back of my scalp and the top of my head. Maybe, it's my hair growing in or my scar healing, but whenever I have this helmet on, it feels like insects are crawling on my scalp and the back of my head. I hate this clump of foam. Not only does it make me look like I am playing football in the Special Olympics; it is a constant reminder of how broken I am. I mean, I am missing a chunk of my skull. Now, I see myself in the mirror, and I don't see myself; I see the person I don't want to be: the disabled guy in a wheelchair, the guy people give sad eyes and sympathy to, the one strangers call "sweetie." Sure, yes, I am from the South —well, wait, let me correct that—I am from the Atlanta area, which is more South adjacent, but it's not really the South. The "sweetie" people offer to those with walkers, wheelchairs, or canes is a yardstick between the person saying it and the one with the assistive device. Though, I try not thinking about that or anything else as I close my eyes over my paler than ever cheeks. I'm drifting, and I'm dreaming, ever so vividly. I don't know what prescription I am taking that makes my dreams like nighttime movies, but I can remember my dreams more vividly than ever before. Perhaps, that's what some of this is. Maybe, this is just a stitched together series of dreams.

At some point, Mom and Dad knocked on the door and brought Anna in. I am always happy to see her. She is a little bit like the anchor from my earlier life. She's my girlfriend, but it's not like I think about her in this way right now. She was always at the hospital and is always at the rehab center, but she's my friend who didn't let go, the friend who keeps coming, regardless of the awkward silence. This day, though, she's here to be with me and my parents, and we go out for a walk in the garden. It's cloudy as November in Georgia always is, and there are no leaves on the trees, and we don't walk too long—I mean, I don't walk at all. I'm in a wheelchair. I've got a blanket on my legs, a jacket, and, of course, that dang helmet.

There's a little pond close to my room, and Dad, Mom, and Anna sit on the benches and I'm in my chair, and we just enjoy the fresh air.

Today, I can see the visitors, these older people who wear blue fabric vests, and they talk to the patients. They are older people, and they all have smiles upholstered all over their faces. Khakis, jeans, sweaters, they look like they are from a catalogue. They made so much money in their careers they now spend their free time being nice to the disabled.

A sweet lady with a tall, skinny body and curly, white locks, comes over, "Hello, my name is Judy. What happened to you?"

My sense of humor is coming back a bit, so I simply offer, "Got in a fight with a bear."

An upward lilt in her voice, as she steps back, eyes up, "Ooohhhh."

Anna chuckles as Dad quickly looks to her, serious, "He's joking. He was in a car accident."

She opens and closes her lips, almost chewing and, then. with a real forced Christian sweetness, "I'm sorry to hear that, sweetie. I hope you get better."

Mom and Dad smile at her as I smile at my own joke. Even with the fog of a brain injury and coma drugs wearing off clouding my brain, I feel like I've bested someone. They tried to make me feel less than, but I won. Dad rests his elbows on his knees, looking at me, my head falling forward, "Will, you can't say that to people."

"What?"

"You can't tell people you were in a fight with a bear."

"Why not?"

"They don't know you're joking."

I'm silent. I don't really have a response. I made the lady feel uncomfortable for making me feel awkward. I feel satisfied.

Anna smiles and grabs my hand, wrapping her fingers in mine, "It was funny though."

I smile, proud of my accomplishment.

As the clouds get darker, the kind of dark weather that spells trouble in Georgia, we start heading in. It's time for lunch in the cafeteria, bright lights, round tables, and trays of food. Anna and I sit at a table, while Dad and Mom go to get us food. Anna brings her skinny body as close to my chair as possible, "How are you feeling?"

"Still tired. But. . . I feel a little better now."

"That's good."

There's a bit of a silence as I try and think of what to say. It's funny because I never had a shortage of words before my accident. People were always telling me to be quiet, calm down, let someone else talk, but now, I'm so tired with nothing to say, and everyone wants me to share. She talks some more, but I'm not really paying attention. It's not that she's boring, but I'm not really paying attention to anyone at this point.

Mom and Dad arrive with the trays: chicken, green beans, and bread, but it looks like hospital food on hospital food trays, so how excited can you really get? Dad's got on his black Nike sweatshirt and jeans, while my mom is in jeans and her grey Mini Mouse sweatshirt; I think a hospital is the only place no

24

one judges you for wearing a sweatshirt. In fact, gloriously, it's the only place where, unless you work there, no one questions your attire at all. Dad looks at Anna, paler than she's ever been, skinnier than she's been—and that is saying something because Anna was always petite, so thin she was made fun of in middle school for being skinny.

But she's sitting there, looking tired and worried, and my dad jumps in, "How's school?"

Anna slumps, her long brown hair falling in her face a little bit, which she removes with her long, skinny fingers, "School? They're really relaxing on me. I'm not having to do much."

Eyes wide in interest, Dad is in the midst of stuffing in a fork full of salad, so Mom, sipping on her Diet Coke, offers, "Really? They're not making you do anything?"

A laugh, her pink lips wide, a break for happiness she needed, "Ogle's not making me do anything, and my other classes, I mean, I get the major work done, but my AP lit class," turning to me, "You remember Ms. Colvin?"

A french-fry covered in ketchup in one hand, I nod.

"Yeah, she's completely understanding. Some days, she understands if I can't make it, and as long as I'm working on the stuff for the exam, she doesn't care at all. Rumble's fine. I think he might want me to take a final, but all of my teachers have been really understanding."

I know these names. I know these people. I want to join in, but all I can muster is, "Wow. Awesome."

Scraping to get the last croutons of her salad, Mom asks, "And Dr. Spurka? Is he supporting you?"

Another laugh, another smile as Anna's pink and white fingernails cover her mouth, "Spurka's been great. I know we used to trash him, but he's actually been amazing. He really wants to help, and I don't get in trouble for leaving school early or missing classes."

Mom nods; she's thinking about me going back to school, anxious about that, what it looks like, when it will happen, and her brown eyes are now looking at me, nodding as Anna talks, and I look so much less than I used to.

I don't want to make it sound like my seventeen-year-old pre-accident self was amazing, like the star athlete of Roswell High School or anything, because I was not prom king or class president, but I was driven, outgoing, energized, and full of potential. It's kind of hard to describe, but my parents and teachers all said I was "going places." Now, I can't even go anywhere without someone pushing me. With one hand, Mom covers her mouth, and with her other, she rubs her hair, thinner now and with a grey splotch at the top. Who can think about root touchups at a time like this?

Anna crosses her legs, grabs my hand, which I offer easily, and she strokes my fingers; hers are cold, but the feeling is always nice, someone running their hand over yours. Dad looks to Mom, his glasses on the brim of his nose as seems to happen slowly over the course of any conversation, "Have you talked to Dr. Spurka about a plan for Will?"

A look to me, then to him, "Yeah. We've talked about at-home tutoring, and then, we'll get him back to school after inpatient." She looks to Anna, "I know you said he didn't support the theater, but he's a really nice man."

"Yeah, I know. We were kinda hard on him."

"I guess you didn't know his side."

"No."

There's a lull in conversation, and then, Mom offers, "Will's going to get better."

Then, when Anna leaves, Mom wants to read to me, *Much Ado About Nothing*, and I am okay with this. I do not want to go back to therapy. I don't know the schedule, but I don't want to ask; I don't want to disappoint anyone. I am happy to listen to this play. I wanted to be Benedict; I know that the theater department is going to do it this year, and I know I won't get to audition. I just want to get better. Then, I can worry about not being cast.

As we sit in the garden, I see Gerald, small, wrinkled, bent over like all men seem to be once they're over seventy, and he's opening his mouth, but he's not saying words, just making noises that sound like talking without a tongue. He has a tongue of course, but he had a stroke, so he's making noises, and I think, "Thank you, God. Thank you that I can talk." Yeah, it's kind of a selfish thought, kind of a jerk thought, but it's so easy to get lost in feeling sorry for yourself—wish you could walk, wish you could remember, wish you could go to the bathroom and sit on a toilet—that it's important to find moments to be thankful for what you do have. I can talk. My mind drifts to people who are in a vegetative state, and I think of how hard it must be to have thoughts they can never express, to dream up speeches, to want to scream but be unable to make a sound.

I see Chad being pushed by Ashley, the physical therapist. He's a seventeen-year-old in a grey North Face fleece and sweat- pants, and she is in a blue Shepherd sweatshirt and jeans, but mostly, she's wearing her current emotion: pissed off. She's trying so hard to be nice, doing that thing where she's so angry that she enunciates every syllable precisely, "Chad. Do not call me shawty."

A smile from the buzzed head of the former footballer, "Why not, shawty?"

Ashley's smile is not working as a cover for her anger, "Because Chad, I went to graduate school. I have a medical degree."

Mouth open wide, Chad's smile can be seen from space as he looks up, "Sure thing, Dr. Shawty."

Looking down, Ashley's blonde hair is in the tightest ponytail, "Do you want to go back inside?"

"Lead the way, Captain Shawty!"

A huff and a hurried push, and I smile as I think the same thought about Chad as I did about Gerald, "Thank God."

No, not because Chad is being a jerk (That part made me laugh.); it's his spinal cord injury. Me, I can heal; I can get better. I believe I can get back to who I was, but Chad and the others with spinal cord injuries never will. They will never get to experience who they were, and maybe, I never fully will either. But. . . I will be able to walk at some point. I will be able to drive at some point. I will get out of this wheelchair. . . I hope. I won't have to feel like a prisoner forever.

As I see Chad go back inside, I am grateful and sad. I am sad that, right now, I can't be the person I want to be; I can't be the guy who is writing, directing, and acting in plays; I can't be the guy winning debate tournaments; I can't be the guy writing applications to the top schools; I can't be the guy who is going places. But there's this shiny coin in front of me, tempting me all the while: better.

If you're someone who has ever spent a good deal of time in the hospital, you understand the allure of better. There's this future you believe exists, but you can't quite see it; it's foggy and half-formed, but you see it truer than anything: better. There is a moment when I will be better, when I will say goodbye to wheelchairs, hospital beds, diapers, nurses, therapists, doctors, when I won't get woken up to get my vitals taken, and I will be better. I will be a version of me I am satisfied with, and I will be at a place where I enjoy the life I'm living. It's not here; it's not now, but it's coming, someday soon. . . better.

I keep praying to this idol; I can't help myself. Better.

No, it's not always physical healing, but isn't it something we all kind of have in our minds that helps keep us going?

Tomorrow will be better. I need to keep going because tomorrow, when I have this job, make this much money, have a spouse or partner, have a child, have a house, have another kid, have this promotion, live in this area, have all my debt paid off, and on and on and on. Better is what keeps us all getting up in the morning, keeps us struggling through, slogging through every boring email, every soul-numbing work meeting, through every morning when we wake up to heavy shoulders and a sore back; we get up because, after today, tomorrow will be closer, and tomorrow will be better. And if not tomorrow, the day after or the day after or the week after or next month or next year and so on and so forth we go.

At Shepherd, in my wheelchair, padding too firm that it never quite felt comfortable, puke-colored cloth gait belt around my waist, I can't even define what "better" is. Obviously, it's walking; definitely, it's going back to school, but it is also more nebulous than that. It is something intangible; better is who I was before, the goal I cannot yet reach. At the end of the day, I want to want to be me. I want to like being the me of today.

At night, when Mom reads the Bible to me, she asks, "Do you ever get sad?"

I always reply, "No." I don't feel sad. I think "better" is keeping me from sad. The hope that one day I will be better keeps me from being sad. It doesn't keep me from being frustrated or upset, but right now, it keeps me from the weight of sad. I can survive Shepherd Center because I can see the Will of tomorrow waiving at me. He's standing on his own, and he's smiling, laughing, telling jokes, being the life of the conversation like he used to, and I think I might even see him driving to school, going to a good college, making friends, and enjoying life. This is what I dream about. As I go to sleep that night— with Anna gone, with Mom and Dad gone too, back home for an actual, good night's sleep—as I lay in my bed alone, hearing only the slow hum of the air conditioner and the beep of hospital machines, I believe, deep down in my heart I will get better. Not today, not this day, not later but definitely soon, I will be better, and I can see the Will of tomorrow. I just need to work to catch up to him.

4

VISITORS

My Shepherd room is becoming more crowded than my room at North Fulton: flowers, balloons, stuffed animals, coloring books, and other things that I do not understand. Things like the coloring books or the children's toys that made my mom sad. My brain injury impacts my memory, vision, reflexes, ability to walk, the strength of my left side, and my balance, but it does not mean I have regressed to the mind of a nine-year-old. As Mom holds a coloring book, left by someone from church, she breathes out.

"People don't understand brain injuries."

She pushes up the sleeves on her blue fleece jacket, revealing the brown freckles on her tan skin, that hint of her half-Native American great-grandmother sneaking in.

"They just don't get it."

She tosses the book on the windowsill and sits down, staring at the room. The room is so white, white ceiling, white walls, white floor, white hospital bed, white sheets, and the color makes the room feel empty, even when it is so full of stuff. The machines are off-white, but they blend in with the rest.

Beyond the window, at least the outside provides color. . . kind of. The weather is grey, grey clouds, and outside just looks cold. There are small droplets on the window.

She looks at the cars-themed coloring book, and she mutters, "You've got to be kidding me." She wants to add an expletive or two. "He's going to heal." She nods, tells herself that her son must heal. He will heal. He will graduate. He will. And I'm sure the voice of the devil wriggles up her neck and into her ear, "How do you know? How can you be so certain? What if he doesn't end up achieving anything? What if he doesn't go to college? What if he ends up working a minimum wage job at Kroger? What if all of his former plans and former dreams crumble under the impossible weight of his disability?"

No, no, no, no.

The serpent slithers into her eardrum, "But, what if he can't even do that?"

And with both hands, she rips the coloring book down the middle, tearing a big gap into the flimsy red cover, a sharp line down the middle, showing a smiling Corvette, his face cut in two.

Slump, her back hits the window. She can't cry; she's too tired, but she's breathing, her chest going quickly up and down, her blue fleece over a white T-shirt, rising and falling, "Stupid, so stupid."

For a moment, she needs to sit there. She holds the coloring book with a jagged tear down the middle, and she drops it. "Why can't I just believe?" she thinks. She knows her son will get better, and she tells him often, "I know you will get better. I always believe you will get better."

But isn't it always that way with belief? You believe, but nothing's 100 percent. You always have this little part at the back of your mind that says, "Yeah, but do you?" It's not even that the part in your head that doubts is loud; the problem is that it never goes away; the door of doubt is always open. And you can push, heave, breathe in steady, labored breaths, sweat drip-drip-dripping from your forehead as your knuckles go white from exertion, but the doors stay stalwart, refusing to budge. "Really? You sure about that? Is that so?"

And by the grace of God, she is able to fight it, shout back, "Yes!" But that doesn't make it easy. Especially for me.

"God. Heal him. Lord, just heal him. Father, make him better. Make him remember, Lord. Strengthen his body. Make him walk. God, and. . ."

Her head is lowered, grey spot, thinning hair at the top. Black rimmed glasses falling to her nose, she must put her hand up to make sure they don't hit the hospital floor. Granny is leaning on her walker, heaving heavy breaths, wearing black pants and a black sweater. Then, her Southern accent dripping with sweetness.

"Debbie."

Mom turns to see the large woman hunched over her walker, the wheels slowly squeaking along. She has a wavy collection of grey strands, some that go off in their own directions; Though, most point down. Her face slides into a chin and around neck, but before that chin, there is a smile, a big smile, always laughing, ready to try and whisper an inappropriate joke, ready to tell her grandkids how much she loves them and how proud of them she is. Today, she doesn't have that smile on.

"Debbie, how's he doing? Roland told me he's more awake. Did you say that?" And when she sees me, in my bed, hair growing in under the puke-colored foam of my helmet, she immediately brightens, "Will, how are you?"

I look at her, steady my gaze; I've had an exhausting day of therapy: trying to work on my short-term memory in speech, trying to make my left fingers more dexterous through grabbing and agility exercises in occupational therapy, trying to stand in physical therapy, working on playing Ben Fold's "Brick" in music therapy, and trying to convince Ashley that I do not want to play any sports in recreational therapy. My eyes are weary, but I see the large woman I remember, "Granny."

I smile at her, and I'm focused on her, and she is all I see, nothing in my periphery. That is until a large, tan man with a gut under a flannel shirt steps forward, a voice with a cheery gruffness, "Will. Good to see you." My Uncle Roland puts out his big hand for a handshake. I nod and shake, "Hey."

Roland waits for more, but I can only give him a smile, my brain searching for words like a swimmer in the ocean searching for the dim light of the surface.

He steps his brown work boots forward, "Well, are you doing all right?"

People will you ask this question, and what are you supposed to say? Am I supposed to be honest? Do you really want me to tell you why I'm not? Do you want me to say I zoned out a little bit, while you were asking this, so I don't really know how to respond to this question? I want to look at my dad; I want to say, "Can't you do the conversational lifting?" But I only nod and say, "Yeah."

Mom moves in, "He's doing great. He's working on standing on his own, getting his left hand stronger," she says, aggressively hitting my left arm, which has, unbeknownst to me, crept up to my chest. Pulling my arm down, Mom continues, "He's doing great in music therapy."

A twinkle in her eye, Granny, sits up, "I do love when you play piano, Will. Did I ever—"

Roland moves to her, a leathery hand on her shoulder, "That's great, Will. Do they have you doing any writing?"

As a man who went to art school against the word of his mother and has faced constant slights about this decision, he

34

always tries to support my creative side. I shake my head, "No, not yet."

The awkward pause I would become familiar with after my accident fills the room. I don't have anything to add but the blank space of my mind, so tired; my mind always functions like the ball in Pong, but now, imagine the Pong ball is on morphine.

"Well, did I ever tell you. . ." And Granny is off on one of her stories she's told a million times; I don't remember it, one of the good side effects of the brain injury. I can hear these stories a million more times and not remember them. Dad rolls his eyes. He can't help it, must be a reflex at this point. Mom tries to get her back on track, "Mom. Mom."

"Well, I hope you get better. Somebody told me that you might not get better, but I know you will. I hope you can walk again. I'll be praying you will."

We exchange hugs, I love yous, my pale cheeks against the soft dough of her face. People are ushered out; Roland gives me a, "Don't forget to get back to writing!"

And I just want to nap. My eyes are starting to see the black fuzz of drifting back to sleep when I am interrupted.

"Is now a good time?"

I hear the sound of a man in his thirties or forties. The distinct nasally sounds of someone I know. I know I've heard this voice, but my mind is circling for who it could be.

"Let me see," I hear my mom say into the door, and then, she strides back, coming up to my bed, the blue of her fleece shining like a big blueberry stripe in these fluorescents and the blurriness of my tired vision.

"Will, do you want to see some visitors? The debate team is here to see you. Do you want to see them or go to sleep?"

Debate team? "Yeah."

"Yeah what?"

"Yeah, bring them in."

Who's on the debate team? Peter, I remember Peter. Peter was my debate partner and the guy who was part of the phone call at the start of this mess. Who else is on the team?

Then, they walk in; Mr. Irwin strides in, tall, lanky, pale, glasses, and his usual goofy, overbite smile replaced with somber seriousness. Followed by him are the Nguyen twins, Tanya and Kathy, half the size of Irwin, skinny, the same short haircut and similar black tops and jeans. I don't understand it. These are twins who look the same, same haircut, similar outfits, have no outward distinguishing feature, and they get mad when people confuse one for the other. If you're going to dress the same down to the haircut, at least, for the rest of us, wear name badges. Then, there's Biplab, tall, decent gut, 16 years old. He's full of energy—dorky dad energy. I don't mean he's creepy or anything. I mean, he likes a good pun, and I know he likes Jeff Dunham. I just know it, the comedian for dad-level humor. Mona and Alisha stand behind Bip.

Now, it's strange to see Peter. I haven't seen him since I woke up, and he's got a more reserved demeanor than the energetic guy I know as my best friend. Straight brown hair, usually greasy, a forever five o'clock shadow; he would say he shaved every morning, but this guy grows facial hair as fast as the rest of us shed skin cells. He's got on his usual dark blue sweatshirt, no logo, and blue jeans. Hands in his pockets, it's clear he's uncomfortable; does he think he did this? Does he feel responsible? I think Mom told me he was on the phone with me that night; he was the last person I talked to. I guess he must have told my parents at some point, which must have been one of the hardest things he's ever done. I know he must have looked at me, half-dazed, half-exhausted and felt his stomach churn. Every time he visits me, he probably wants to run. And, that does not make him a bad person; Peter Ianakiev is a great guy.

If I were him, though, I couldn't help but put the blame on myself because that's what we do as people. We think we're in control, so when bad things happen, we look for someone to blame—usually ourselves; especially when things don't go our way, it's easy to point fingers. Peter must've struggled to see his friend fall so far from glory and wrestle with himself not to think he pushed him.

But God, seeing me with my eyes half open, smiling but not cracking a joke or offering an opinion, just lying there, he can only offer, in his usual, Bulgarian accent, "Hey mate, how's it going?"

Even after all the Ensure, my light blue long-sleeve shirt almost swallows me as I push with my right arm to sit up in bed, "Good, good, hoping to get walking."

I look past him at Mr. Granville, a man as tall as Irwin but much older, with a gut, thinning hair, and those brown spots on his forehead that men in their fifties start to get.

"Hey champ, you're looking good," he says with his gold, typical middle-class, middle-aged glasses on the bridge of his nose.

I want so badly to be able to talk to them; I want so badly to be my old self; I want to be able to exist in this moment actively; I want it so badly I could cry, but I can't. I can only really nod, offer a few words, smile, and try to enjoy the visitors. Tanya and Kathy are standing next to each other as always.

They hold up a poster board, reading, "Get Better Debate Champ!" I read the poster and smile; I think I can remember that, before my accident, Peter and I were somehow winning a number of debate tournaments, despite it being our first year on the team.

"Hey, so, we thought you would like this. I hope it helps." Kathy says, holding up her side of the poster board.

"Thanks guys. . . I. . . really. . . appreciate it." I smile, my hair starting to really come in under my helmet. I reach up my hand to scratch it. I can't take it; for some reason, this foam makes my head feel like tiny little ants are crawling over my scalp. It always itches. With my mom out of the room, I can slip my hand under the foam, trying to avoid the part of my head missing the skull, and I find the part at the back of my head that is so unnervingly itchy, and go to town, "Ahh."

Irwin claps his hands and holds them, as people do when nervous and looks at me and asks expectantly, "So, when did they say you'll be outta here?"

I pause, taking my hand out of my helmet and running it down the back of my neck. God, I can't wait, Mr. Irwin. You want to take me out today? C'mon, Peter can make a distraction, and, as long as you can get a wheelchair, I'm good to go. Let's rock it.

But I feel the need to be real, "I think by Christmas. I need to get to walking, but I think. . . I think they said. . . they said by the end of the year?" I'm used to ending things with a question mark. With my short-term memory, I'm used to being wrong, so it's easier to not take any hard stances, just in case I get mixed up. End everything in a maybe, and no one can tell you got it wrong. It's a funny thing that when you gain new limitations, you learn how to manage disappointment.

Granville claps his hands in celebration, "That's great, Will! When did they say you'll come back to school?"

I scrunch my cheeks, thinking, looking deep in the recesses of my memory, and it's the same usual boat on the empty dark water, desperately, hopelessly searching for land, "I don't know. I figure not too long."

Irwin pipes up, coming next to Granville, "I was talking with Rumble, and he said that it looks like sometime next year, possibly end of January at the earliest. I think it depends on when you go to outpatient and, of course, how you're doing.

We want to have you at school, but you know, you gotta get better first."

I smile. The idea of being back at school is everything I want. It's funny. Before my accident, I spent so much of my mental energy on the thought of leaving school: doing math tutoring to get my SAT score up, participating in debate team, Model UN, theater, and National Honor Society to make sure my extracurriculars were appealing, looking and hoping for a college where I would succeed. It's funny. When you make college the focus of high school, teenagers like me find it hard not to cast all of our hopes and dreams on those four years. Good college equals good life, and bad college equals. . .? Well, let's not even think about that. I spent my freshman, sophomore, junior, and the little bit of my senior year I was awake for, thinking about leaving high school, and now, I can't wait to go back. At school, it's better. Yes, the elusive better.

There are stories traded from them to me: debate wins, stories about teachers, Biplab doing and saying silly things, and I am happy to hear them, but when old friends come like this, it's also hard because it's a reminder of who I used to be, who I no longer am, and who I wish I could be. What's hard, too, is that my memory's clouded, so the me of the past is even more idolized because I can't quite see myself for who I was. I don't really remember what it was like to live life like I used to—think, or feel, or experience existence as who I was. It's a strange thing to think about, I know, but what if you could always wonder: was how I experienced life the same way I used to feel I experienced it?

It is easy to think that, before I was injured, before I was broken when I was so much better, the life I lived was lived better. All these visitors, all these people coming every day talk about who I was, talk about moments I lived. My AP English class came, bringing a poster with the dumbest thing I think I've ever said on it, "The human condition of man."

One day in AP lit, I said very obnoxiously, "I think this story is about the human condition of man." Now, in my defense, I had two things in my head: the human condition and the state of man, and I said both at once. It was really stupid, and that day, when I said it, we all laughed about it when Mrs. Williams, this tall, skinny woman, with long blonde hair, and the confidence of a federal prosecutor with the heels to match, cracked, "You're right, Will. Man is human."

All these visitors are nice, sure; they are kind to come and come so frequently with poster boards with well wishes in marker, which are preferred to Hallmark cards from CVS, but for someone with a brain injury, visitors are also hard. I am starting to heal, starting to offer some sarcasm, but I am still mostly a passenger, and I'm longing for better, and visitors are a reminder that I'm not there yet. Mom tells me I'm getting better, tells me I'm going to get so much better, and I want to, but it's also hard because it fuels my desire and struggle for better. I know they are visiting me out of duty, which is not a bad thing, but I know they feel like, "Okay, got to go see Will," like I'm their grandparent in a nursing home. Not that duty is bad, but you want to think that people are talking to you because they want to, not because they have to, that your friends want to be friends with you.

And this duty is hard because they are here for the friend they used to have, to support the older version of him, not necessarily to see this newer version. And I know this. I might not be able to remember what happened during the day; I may not remember everyone's name; I may struggle to follow others' sarcasm now; I may forget to rinse the shampoo out of the left side of my hair, but I know they are here because they feel they have to be. I don't know what the solution to this is. Obviously,

they have to show up; they have to come see me, but because I
know they don't necessarily want to be with me, it also hurts
that they are here. Soon, after receiving a series of awkward
hugs due to my being seated on my hospital bed, I am alone in
my room for the briefest of moments. Now, no one leaves me
alone for more than a few seconds, though, and Mom's brown
bob bounces in, recently colored, "Have fun with your
friends?"

I sit on the edge of my bed, my black Avett Brothers shirt
wrinkled and barely sticking to my skinny form. I nod, "Good
to see them."

"Well, you've got one more visitor on the way."

"Who is it?"

Mom comes in and sits on the bed, "Anna's gonna be here
soon."

"Good."

Her eyes always look wet these days. I think she's sad
because she knows I'm hurting. She's always been a good
momma bear, and I think it hurts her to see her boy in pain, to
see him lonely, to know he's not where he should be.

"Will."

"Yeah?"

"Do you ever get sad?"

I think she's asked me this before. At first, I was taken
aback. Such a weird direct question, but I say, "No," because I
don't know how to tell her. I don't know the words to put to my
emotions yet. Now, not only am I fresh out of coma with a trau-
matic brain injury—sure, yeah, that's going to slow my access to
words—but also, I'm an internal processor, and I haven't had
any time to process. I don't really know what I'm feeling. Every
day is what every day is. I'm trying to make it from alarm to
alarm. I just want to get better. I can't focus on what I'm feeling
or how I'm responding to this situation.

41

"No, I'm okay."

I can't tell her about the dark places my mind goes. I don't want to do that to her, and I don't think I have the words or the formed thoughts to tell her.

"Okay."

She waits for a moment more, like she's waiting for me to break; though, I know it would hurt her. That's the other reason. I already feel like a burden; I don't want to put on another.

"Well, Anna's almost here."

"Wait, when?"

"Anna. She's almost here."

"Okay."

There is a softness in this moment. I love my mom. I tell her so much more now. It sucks that it takes a brain injury, ruptured spleen, collapsed lung, and a coma to realize the wonderful value of my parents, but hey, some people never figure it out. . . and you could be dead, Will. Be happy. Be grateful. Though, when you have to remind yourself of this, it is far less effective. Soon, Anna comes in, a little bit more weight on her, but she's still so skinny she gets comments from middle-aged women about how they'd kill to be that skinny, or "Just wait 'til you're older." And, funny thing is, she wants to murder them.

"Hey, milkshakes?"

She gives my mom chocolate and me strawberry from Chick-Fil-a, the wellspring of life for any suburbanite.

"Where's Bob?"

"He's on the phone. He should be back up."

I give that first obnoxious sounding sip of slurping a milkshake. Ahh, sweet diabetes. Not that I have it, but if I drink more of these milkshakes, I might be close.

Mom smiles, "Let me go get Bob. I'll be back soon."

Anna kicks off her shoes, as she slides next to me, "Okay."

And Mom is off, and Anna and I are sitting on the bed as she puts her hand in mine.

I look to her, "Can I lie down?" Sitting on the edge of the bed is killing my lower back, which is always hurting these days.

"Okay."

I lie down, and she lies next to me, curling up her soft, cold body next to mine, her head on my chest, one hand across my stomach.

I look up, "Where'd Mom go?"

"She went to find your dad."

"Okay."

It's silent as we lie in bed; she rubs her leg against mine, kisses my cheek, and I smile. Rain hits the window, a soft sound of thunder. Florescent lights battle back the dark grey of the storm outside as I feel her cheek next to mine. I appreciate the touch, but mostly, I love that we're close, enjoying the moment, and we're not talking. A quiet moment of alone together. It's not about her being my girlfriend. It's that someone is enjoying a moment with me, and I'm not forced to talk, forced to remember; I don't have to feel awkward or confused or like I'm being tested. I'm simply allowed to exist with someone else and enjoy them existing beside me. I wish this was every interaction. I wish I could enjoy every moment without being reminded of my brain injury, but I feel like there's always a moment of awkward silence created by something I've said. It's my mom asking me, "Okay, what did you do today?" Sara asking me, "What was that string of words I asked you to remember?" And it's how with every single, solitary interaction with a group of visitors, there's always something I get wrong, something I forget, something weird I say. I wish I could just be. I wish all my days were moments of existing and forgetting that I have a brain injury. That's not an option. There's so much work to be done, so much I must do. I need to get my left arm stronger, need to strengthen my memory, need to get back to playing piano, and most importantly, I need to walk. But for now, I enjoy the silence, the warmth of someone else next to me, the joy of being able to say nothing at all.

5

WALKING

The beautiful thing about Shepherd Center is these great spots outside where you can sit and enjoy the morning. November in Georgia is a weird beast as far as temperatures go. Four seasons in a day as they say, but now, this morning, it's crisp. It's the kind of air that bites, but I'm bundled up beyond belief with a jacket, gloves, and scarf. It's the kind of day that looks grey: sky grey and white, air both windy and full of moisture. It's nice to be outside, eating a Nutri-grain bar and drinking an Ensure. Mom is checking over my schedule, folded paper in hand. She is looking better, still tired, but she looks less sad. I like this. I hate to see my parents in a place of weakness. She folds up the schedule and puts it in my brown jacket's breast pocket. She stands next to my chair, indicating she's ready to go, "Physical therapy is first."

I nod, my helmet sliding a little, "Good."

Bending to tighten the strap, she asks, "Why good?"

"That's the one that's actually helpful."

"The others are not?"

"I don't know. I guess OT is good; speech feels like a bit of a waste."

"You don't need to work your memory?"

I pause. I mean, yeah. Of course, my memory is garbage right now. I can't even remember what happened yesterday; I don't even know who came by, don't even know what happened right before this conversation. Though, I do feel in a better spot than others. Gerald can't even talk, just makes noises and gives the therapists dirty looks. I feel like I'm in the brain injury gifted program, even though I am clearly impacted. I guess it's true what they say: we're all always looking to feel better than someone else.

"I can work on memory, but I don't know that I need to do that here."

She gives a half smile, "You're almost there. Discharge is expected before Christmas. Do you know what day it is today?"

"Uh. . ."

"Will, come on."

"One of them?"

She smiles; she wants to hit me, sure (not really, just to clarify, my mother has only *wanted* to hit her kids), but she smiles because she sees me a little bit more. There's the smart-ass she raised.

"Okay, think. What was yesterday?"

I hate this. I hate being quizzed on stuff I don't know. Before my accident, I felt stupid when I didn't know something at school, when somebody asked me a question I didn't know the answer to, but now, here, sinking in this wheelchair, I collapse in hatred. Why are you doing this to me? I don't know what day it is. Stop asking me. Though I know she's only trying to push me to recover, all I hear is a reminder of my failings at this moment.

"So, did you have therapy yesterday?"

46

"No?"

She nods, so, "What do you think?"

Shoot. Two options. . . Better choose right, "Saturday?"

"Good. You got it."

A smile as there is an internal sigh of relief from me, hoping this is the last quiz of the day. My white sneakers are more scuffed on the right foot than the other.

A gentle reminder, "Use your arms."

I can't help but snarl as I put my arms to the wheels and push, making my wheelchair go in a diagonal to the left, down the paved path back to the hospital.

"More from your left side," she orders as we make our way back to the hospital, passing the trees with no leaves, empty branches wet with the drops of an evening storm, leaves in a brown and gold heap in the mulch below.

We make it through the hospital doors, and we are in therapy gym—not a real gym, but a room with white walls, two bathrooms, and a collection of workout equipment and mats set up on what look like wide wooden tables. They are close to the ground, so you can easily get from a wheelchair onto them. There are containers of balls, a stack of THERABANDs and pool noodles, a StairMaster, treadmills, exercise bikes, and a variety of other implements of torture for use on all of Shep herd Center's physical therapy victims. I know this place well; this is where I have spent many a day doing leg presses, trying to stand on my own, flipping to my stomach on the mat, and every time, I ask, "When am I going to walk?"

"When you're ready," Ashley always replies, nodding her blonde ponytail, tied back tight enough to keep her smile in place.

"When you're ready," is an answer I hate. Everything with recovery is an indistinct note of future, the darker side of better. There's no way to know what ready is, but you keep holding out for it, as it gets harder and harder to keep your grasp, your fingers slipping, the stones of resolve tumbling to the ravine below. I've stopped hoping that this will be the day when I walk. I believe I will walk again, but then, the other side of my mind imagines me in a wheelchair forever, a constant battle between belief and unbelief. I look out at the gym, patients on the other mats, straining and working; we're all trying to get better. A therapy tech named Gustavo, an overweight guy in a tight blue Shepherd shirt one size too small, wheels me over to the mat. I notice something in front of the mat, and I start to hope. I'm scared to get excited, but I hope anyway. It's a folded walker leaning against the blue of the mat.

Ashley walks over, waving goodbye to her last patient, "You ready?"

"Ready for what?"

She can't help but smile, her teeth revealing genuine care, "To walk, silly."

My face shines the light of a million suns as I nod aggressively, "Yes."

After a pull on my gait belt, she stands me up and puts my hands on the walker, "You feel steady?"

I look down on the grey rubber handles and squeeze, "Yeah."

Ashley shakes my gait belt from the back, "Well, go ahead."

This is everything I've dreamed of since I got here to Shepherd, to get out of that stupid chair, the black, movable prison. I'm so tired of having to ask to go to the bathroom. I'm so sick of peeing in my pants because the therapists tell me they just took me to the bathroom a few minutes ago. I want to be able to run and say ever so politely, pushing my way past them, "I know. You don't understand. I really have to go," as I quickly scurry off to the nearest toilet.

First step.

"Now, push the walker."

Push. Step.

"You got it!" I smile.

Ashley looks up, "Gustavo?"

"I told them."

And I look, and I see Mom and Dad, smiling and cheering, "Go Will!"

I can't contain it. I'm smiling and laughing as I slowly but so excitedly scoot my walker forward and move my legs under me. Ashley pulls on my gait belt, so I stop.

She leans into me, "You're doing great, Will. Let's go and make a lap around the gym. You think you can do that?"

"Yeah."

And Mom takes a picture, and I see how happy they are, and I must look crazy I'm so happy. I'm walking! With a walker, yes, but I'm walking! I'm on my own two feet! Ha, ha, ha, yes! Have you ever been this happy? You're not laughing because something's funny; you're laughing because you're so happy, and this is the best way to express the fireworks going off in your soul. I am laughing in this moment, and I am full to bursting. My soul crackles and sparks explosions of green, blue, pink, and yellow. I am trying to go fast, but my legs haven't done this in almost two months.

"Will, great!"

I turn to see Lisa, who's short, small, and in her fifties with thin brown hair and the classic personality of a sweet Southern woman; she raises her arms for me from her wheelchair. Caitlin, my OT, claps, smiles. Thomas raises his fist in support, and I feel so tall. I feel so amazing.

"Okay, okay, slow down," a tug on my gait belt, "You did great, Will."

I did great. I walked on my own. . . sort of. I did have a walker and, sure, a physical therapist holding onto my gait belt, but I stood on my own two feet. It's a hard thing to describe how amazing walking for the first time after being in a wheelchair feels. I have not had an experience prior that quite compares. To be free of that chair, that contraption I have grown to hate, the thing that represents my weakness and insufficiencies, was like soaring through the skies. I stood on my own two feet, and people cheered. People were happy for me. I felt like a celebrity for the briefest of moments.

My mom snaps pictures, even as I sit down, and Ashley takes the walker. I can't be sure, but I think Mom's eyes are wet. She wasn't sure that this was going to happen. She believed it would; Ashley told her it was the plan, but still, it's something that's hard to believe until you see it.

Dad knows how she's feeling, so he takes her hand in his, squeezes it.

"He did it."

She smiles, "He did."

Then, the saddest transition: the transition back to the wheelchair. I just enjoyed the briefest taste of freedom and, immediately, went back to confinement, back to needing help to go anywhere. Sure, I might be able to pedal with my feet, but I can't get out on my own. I can't go to the bathroom; I can't go get food; I am back to being dependent. But I did it. I walked.

I go through another day of strengthening my left hand and doing some vision tests to work on strengthening my left eye; I do some memory games in speech therapy that, while a chal lenge, also feel beneath me, a weird paradox. I know that I'm better than this, and at this moment, I believe I will soon be better than this. At least in music therapy, Thomas asks what I pieces I want to play. He reminds me of my high school counselor. He's always relaxed and has the smooth personality of both a dad and radio DJ. Then, there's lunch, and there's a time of lifting some weights, and next, there's a snack (an Ensure), but soon, I'm back with Mom and Dad in the garden. Mom and I are reading through *Much Ado About Nothing*. I read Benedict and Dogberry, and when we get to a break I say, "Does today mean I can go home soon?"

Mom looks down, "I think they said soon. Sometime next month."

"Next month?"

"Yeah."

I don't really know what this means. Sure, I know a month is roughly thirty days, and I know next month is a long time, but when you're in the hospital, time is an indefinite thing. What I mean is *tomorrow, next week, next month*—these are just words. They don't really have any meaning; she might as well say you are leaving next Mozambique, or your therapists were thinking you will graduate in a cucumber or two. *Cucumber* makes about as much sense as *next month*. Each day is only something to get through. I only care about one day: the day I get out, the day when I'm closer to better.

"Okay. Is that close?" I ask, looking both hopeful and confused.

"Thursday is Thanksgiving, so we can start thinking about it in two weeks."

It's the vague answer I've come to expect. Everyone wants to wait to see how you heal before they can predict how you'll do.

"I walked."

Pursing her lips, she nods, "I saw honey, remember? Your dad and I were right there."

Stillness, breeze, the faint shouts of profanity from one of the patients.

"I just want to get better."

Mom taps my knee, "I know, sweetie."

"I want to walk."

51

A stillness.

"I want to go home."

"I know, honey. You will go home soon."

The breeze kicks the leaves up, making it look like we're really outside of these hospital grounds, and I want that moment to come. I've never been particularly good at living in the moment, but now, in this moment, I am decidedly terrible at it. I want to press fast-forward, juice up the flux capacitor, and speed through Shepherd, the remainder of high school, maybe, even speed through college. I want to get to the point where I have a wife, kids, and a job, and everyone can think of me as just another respectable adult, when no one will think of me as that disabled kid, and my injury is beyond me. Now, though, I'll settle for the fact that Thanksgiving is on Thursday, and it's almost time for me to leave this place.

Chad yells, "Fuck!"

Then, I hear someone hitting his shoulder and his mother say, "Chad." I feel like I can even hear his sarcastic smile as he says, "Sowwy." Even though I agree with your first point, Chad, I will allow myself to a bit of hope. Maybe, just maybe, I will recover, and one day, tomorrow might be better than today. I need to get through these next few days. I think I can. I think I can. I think I can. Better feels closer.

6

LAST DAYS OF SHEPHERD

I t happened again, and I hate it. As I sit in the squishy boxers and a wheelchair seat soaked with pee, I feel this is a setback. Will they even let me leave if I'm peeing myself? Why can't I hold it? Why do I always have to pee so much? Why, when I have to pee, does it feel like an emergency? After getting changed, I sit in my chair and watch the door. Maybe, Dr. Kaelin can help me out. It's time for my weekly checkup. A decently tall man with black hair and charming smile, he looks like if he wasn't a doctor, he'd probably be a basketball coach.

He enters with a rap-tap on the door, "What's going on, bud? How you doing? Almost time for you to leave!"

Mom sits down in the chair near the desk, "I can't believe you're working this week. I thought you'd be on vacation."

Dr. Kaelin points his pen, smiles through the chubbiness of his middle-aged face, "Normally, I would be, but there's a lot work that needs to get done this week, so I promised my wife I'd fly up tomorrow morning to meet her and the kids in Louisville."

A smile. My mom likes Dr. Kaelin, even though she knows it will always be a short visit with him.

"But never mind my family, let's talk about yours, more specifically, this guy right here. Big day is coming up soon, yeah?"

I shift my weight in my chair and turn my head, "Big day?"

"You're going to be leaving us!" Kaelin exclaims with exuberance, raising his fists in the air as a point of celebration.

"Oh yeah. I'm excited."

"I bet you are! That's great to hear. Sad, you can't go have Thanksgiving out of here, but at least, it looks like you'll be spending Christmas at home."

I sit up, "Yeah, I really can't wait."

He leans in, and I can see the product in his hair, "How's the Ritalin working?"

"Working good."

It's clear he's already thinking about his next appointment, "Is there anything else?"

I shake my head. I'm ready to be done as well.

He scribbles something down on his pad, and then, "I think Ritalin is really the best option right now. Twice a day. You may be able to take it down to once a day eventually, but for him," he says, looking at my mom, "I think twice a day is probably best."

"Yeah."

A turn, "And, I hear you're still having problems with the frequent urination?"

I look down, remembering what happened in physical therapy, "Yeah. I have to pee a lot."

Another scribble on his pad, a move to the door, "Well, I think Aricept might be a good bet."

Mom pipes up, almost out of her chair, "Now, I don't necessarily want him on anything else."

A little laugh as Dr. Kaelin has become accustomed to my anxious mother, "I understand your concern. I don't think this is something he'll be on for long. Not only will it help his memory and focus, it should really help with the frequent urination, the sensation of having to go all the time. Isn't that what you're experiencing?"

"Yeah. All the time."

"I think this will really help. Is there anything else you need?"

Mom takes out a pen and pad, "How do you spell it?"

A finger to his lip, thinking, "A-r-i-c-e-p-t."

Scribbling, Mom doesn't even look up, "What does discharge look like?"

"That'll happen in two weeks, hopefully, and did you make the adjustments we talked about?"

"Still waiting on the shower stool."

He's almost out the door, ready to move on, "But other than that?"

She's not done, "Yeah, Bob put up the railing."

"Good. So, two weeks at home, and then, we'll look at doing Pathways."

Thinking almost out loud, she offers, "That's not far—"

He's almost got his body pointed to leave, "Not far at all. You know Toco Hills? Up the street?"

"Oh yeah."

He points at me, still smiling, "They'll want him there for a while."

"Want me there?" I ask, a worried look in my eye as I take a deep breath.

A laugh and a point, "Don't worry, it's outpatient. You'll be there for a few hours; then, you can go back home."

Deep breath of relief. I think I was starting to feel my stomach tighten, "Okay, good."

"Good? All right, well, we'll get you ready for discharge in about two weeks. You guys have a good Thanksgiving!"

Mom smiles, "You too!"

And he's off, partly because he's got a slew of other patients and partly because he knows she might have more things to ask.

Mom lets a little breath out and smiles, "Well, he stayed longer than usual."

I smile, "Yeah." I like when Dr. Kaelin talks about discharge. He's got power. He's a doctor; plus, he's always so busy and caught between appointments, which helps me think of him as more of a big deal. When he says that I'm leaving, I actually believe I am.

"Ooh." My lower back feels like I've been through a couple rounds with Mike Tyson[1], and unless my nurse is abusing me in my sleep, it's a result of my injury. I put a hand back there like people do when they're in pain, but why? It's not as if my touch is going to make it stop hurting.

Mom moves her face closer, "What's wrong? Your back?"

Quick nod.

"We should've talked to Kaelin about that," she says, a look of sadness in her eyes. She is harder on herself than anyone else is on her.

Scrunching my nose, I say pathetically, "It hurts."

"Lower back again?"

"Mhmm."

"I'm sorry, buddy. You should talk to Ashley about it."

"Okay."

Another moment. Hello, silence, my old friend. My head turned to one side, "When is Thanksgiving?"

"Thursday. Remember?"

This word has become a natural part of our conversations. She will ask this "remember" question repeatedly, probably seven or eight times in the course of a fifteen-minute timespan.

There is a light as I think back to blurry Thanksgivings of days past, of our house or Aunt Linda's place full of family, of half remembered days, "Wait, do I get to go home?"

She exhales, taking off her glasses, "No buddy, remember, you're getting discharged in a couple weeks. We're doing Thanksgiving here."

I try to hide my disappointment, "Okay."

Standing, she moves to me, "But it'll be good. Everyone will come here."

"Everyone?"

"You know, Granny, Uncle Johnny, Aunt Linda, Haley, Daniel."

A smile, "Oh, good."

It's good that they are coming to my room for Thanksgiving because it will be nice to see them, but I also hate it; I hate feeling like a burden, and I know I am. I know that I am a burden to my parents, to my family, to my friends, and I want to go back to adding to the world, versus feeling like I'm taking. To be clear, none of this feeling comes from my family, especially not my parents, but it's hard when you know everyone is doing something because they love you rather than because they're enjoying it. Soon, I will be better. I'll be walking in a week in or two. I used the walker. I'm sure I'll be using a walker before I leave; then, I'll get used to that over the holidays, and within a week or two at Pathways, I'll be on to a cane and then, nothing. In my mind, I see my recovery on steroids: like those intense, vein-popping, looking-like-I belong in some squad of superheroes, doping to heal. Who knows? I might even get back to driving this summer. I'm going to get better so quickly. I'm not like some patients here. Some of them need speech therapy because they can't even talk, and some of them will never walk again, and some of them, like Chad, weren't that smart before their accident. I know I sound like a jerk, but he calls people "shawty," so it's not like he was on track to be a Nobel Prize-winning physicist.

I am a mad man, travelling back and forth from dreams destroyed to dreams soon to be realized and back again. Walt Whitman once said, "Do I contradict myself? Very well then. I contradict myself. I contain multitudes." What an annoying thing to say in an argument. Even still, his larger point is accurate. We all contain these multitudes. I can think that I'm not that bad and that I will never recover while also believing in a total recovery a second after ruminating in self-hatred. It's even harder because I don't want to tell people how I feel. Doctors take the desire to share right out of you. They make you want to keep your struggles inside. That expression, "When you live life like a hammer, everything looks like a nail," is very true for therapists and doctors. You tell them about a little struggle, like having water run right through you, and they will put you on a drug for frequent urination. You might forget one piece of information, and they will all see it as a sign of a serious condition. So, why would I want to open my mouth about my emotional struggles to them? They'll probably send me to another hospital, or at least pump me full of antidepressants—who knows?! Maybe even give me an electroshock treatment.

Everything inside; every struggle can stay with me. Sure, Mom and Dad can know about the struggles they can see; they can know about my peeing my pants at therapy. They can know when I forget things; they can know how much I desperately want to walk, but I need them to feel I'm doing okay. I know they want to see me well, and I guess I want to make them happy by telling them I'm happy. You can only really have a dark thing grow within you if you don't let others realize what's going on. The darkness grows roots and slithers deeper down into your body, multiplying more and more if you pretend like you're doing good. It's why one of the real problems with Modern America is the pandemic of "Fine." No one is ever sad, depressed, upset, or having a bad day; everyone's just "fine." I tell people I'm fine; no, I tell them I'm good. I guess because, sometimes, I am good. Sometimes, I am happy; sometimes, I realize how lucky I am. So, why should I not be good? Everyone tells me I'm a miracle. I guess that's the hard part; sometimes, I feel like it's not enough that my life was saved because I felt more of a sense of a purpose or point to my life before my injury. I can't quite see who I will be clearly; I see him through a mirror dimly, and I can't quite imagine he will make more than a scratch on the metal of life. Maybe, I'm greedy. I never wanted to make a dent. I wanted to break the whole thing. I know I sound like a supervillain, but a dent feels like being a manager at Denny's and letting teachers and nurses eat for free. I wanted more. Dents are for those with low expectations. I want to crash right through. Now, I guess it feels like life smashed right through me.

Wednesday, there's no therapy. Shepherd realizes no one wants to be sweating, aching, and screaming for mercy the day before Thanksgiving, which is probably a fair assessment. Mom and I finished *Much Ado About Nothing,* and she immediately mentioned that she needs to get something else for us to read, so we start on *Twelfth Night.* Then, after the nurses come and take my vitals, Mom and Dad get ready to leave, even though she doesn't want to. If it was acceptable to throw a sleeping bag on the floor,—and if Dad did not discourage it—she would've been by my bed every night. But they're gone, and I've already forgotten tomorrow is Thanksgiving. The day is wiped clean; if I strain, I can recover grains of memory, but most of it has vanished away to nothingness. Then, I close my eyes, and I dream. Ever since my accident, I dream intensely vivid, active, and clear dreams the moment I'm asleep, and, then, they're gone a few moments after I wake up.

The next morning, there is breakfast from the nurse, vitals, and then, a knock at the door presents Mom and Dad, dressed in clothes I remember them wearing before my accident: belts, buttons, and shirts without wrinkles. After setting some food on the desk, they sit down with that over fifty "Humph."

Dad with his checkered button-down makes him look like the dad of my memory, "Morning, Will."

I'm not sporting anything close to his polished look in a grey long sleeve T-shirt and black exercise pants, "Morning, Dad."

"Happy Thanksgiving," Mom picks up the white remote attached to the bed and raises the bed. The *berrrr* sound lets out as the bed lifts. It's weird to see my parents looking like this, no sweatpants, showered. I almost don't recognize them.

"How far are they?" Dad says, adjusting the food, looking in the Kroger bag for the plates.

The distinct chirp of Aunt Linda, "Hello! We made it!" She enters in a pink sweater and khakis; I don't know why, but every time I think of Aunt Linda, I always see her in pastels. You know those people? You think of them as Precious Moments figurines people? I mean, that's just based off her style, not necessarily her personality.

"Where can I set this down?"

I can hear Uncle Johnny, but I can't see him until Linda parts to reveal the dentist in his sixties, using both arms to bring in a cooked turkey and set it down on the counter with a heave. Johnny, who has a belly, not a big one, but a belly, with a nice polo, tucked into his jeans, a blackberry hooked to his belt, looks like a man who owns a house in the nice part of North Georgia. It's funny, because he's my uncle, and I know him for taking me fishing and for us getting into it about politics, yelling at each other how right we are over someone else's birthday cake. I remember him for cleaning my teeth and giving me a bag with a new toothbrush, some floss, and a sticker, but if I were to be objective, Uncle Johnny looks like a Southern man who has a very organized gun cabinet next to his bookshelf, which I think, honestly, he probably does.

"What about Granny?"

"Roland, I don't think this is the right hall," she says, as we hear the slow squeak of her walker.

"Momma, trust me, this is it." His voice is at the volume that, if anyone on the hall was taking a Thanksgiving nap, they're not anymore.

"Roland, I don't think this—"

"Momma!"

Okay. Now they're definitely up. Then, the two are in the door, Roland first as he motions Granny over. He's wearing a shirt without stains on it, and Granny's in a black sweater with what looks like silver glitter sewn in.

"We're here!" Roland laughs, his usual red cheeks rising to reveal his yellowish smile, "Ready to eat some good food."

"Do we have enough chairs?" My dad is up and looking across the room, the way dads do when they want to feel useful, which is a moment to be seized by any father. "Let me go to waiting room."

"No worries, Bob. Linda and I brought some chairs."

"Let me help you."

And they're off, and soon, Andrew shows up; Haley, Daniel, Abigail, Trent, Lacey, and the nurses poke their head in, asking for a plate, and to be honest, this is one of those moments I am embellishing, because I don't really remember all the details. I might be mixed up with who was there, but you know what I do remember? I remember feeling loved. I remember feeling safe. I remember that warmth of family, that feeling of obligation, sure, because they wouldn't be family if we didn't have to see them, right? But that love of family is knowing you can say the dumbest thing in the world; you can create the most awkward silence; you can tell a joke that lands so incredibly flat crickets can be heard from miles away, and they'll still be there. They'll still want to be there. They pass the plates around, and I am so grateful to get my year's supply of salt: turkey, ham, mac and cheese, green beans—heck, I think the salad may have even had salt in it, but my oh my, there is nothing like a Southern Thanksgiving, and there is nothing more glorious than my family. Even without me in my current state, they might be a few brain cells short (especially in the area of impulse control), and they might look like an odd collection, but they love so well. This day, this moment, I feel loved for who I am, who I've become since the accident; I feel like they really wouldn't choose to be anywhere else. Afterwards, all the trash is cleaned up, the gravy is dumped back into the Tupperware; paper plates are covered with plastic wrap and divvied up between the family equitably; hugs are exchanged, even though I know that I will see them again real soon. Two weeks. Two weeks.

Though, I also don't feel like I thought I would. Leaving Shepherd, I thought I could point to some mark of recovery as hope, "Okay, I am healing," but now, I have to try and grab, like grasping for sand in ocean water, at the intangible "better." Soon, I fall in physical therapy. In occupational therapy, I find it impossible to find an item in a search; I am unable to play a piece in music therapy, and these moments sting. I hate myself as much as when I peed on a mat in the therapy gym. I hate my struggle over who I could have been. What if I amount to nothing? My brain spins around to the toys they gave me at the start, the word searches with cartoon animals, the crayons, the markers—Will I get a job bagging groceries for the rest of my life? Am I a disappointment? I shake my head and try to fight that notion, but it hangs around my neck, choking my air. I have no proof to battle it.

But then, the day comes, the day that challenges that, the day I leave. Breakfast, a walk in the garden, and then, onto therapy—physical, occupational, rec, music, speech—and I'm hugging Chad, Chris, Lisa. Lisa, sweet Lisa, about the age of my mom (maybe, that's why I can appreciate her sweetness) hugs me, "You're going to be great, Will. I'll see you at Pathways."

"See you there."

Mom, tears in her eyes, behind my wheelchair, "Thank you, Lisa. You've always been so kind."

Her genuine Southern smile, "Of course, you are good people."

And, there's a moment when I can't say what I want to say. I don't know what the words are, but they all taste like gratitude, and I want to give the feeling I have to Lisa, to my therapists, and my parents. I don't have the words; It's just a feeling, but it's bubbling over. Gratitude. I'm going home in the morning, and I can't wait to start the next phase, but I'm ending my time at Shepherd blessed. I'm one step closer to better.

7
THE SKULL FLAP

From Shepherd Center to North Fulton, I am excited but with a little feeling that's hard to describe. You ever had an experience that was different than you thought? I guess it feels like disappointment, but it's not quite the same. I'm excited to receive this step towards better, but I thought when I left Shepherd, I would feel good enough to leave. In some ways, yes, I feel that I've made enough progress. I'm more aware than when I entered, but I don't feel like I think I used to. I don't know what it is, but I don't really feel anything close to better. If someone asked me, "Why did they let you leave?" I guess I would reply, "I served my time." But. . . I'm still lost in most conversations, still can't walk, still peeing my pants sometimes, still can't really use my left arm that much, and I think it bears repeating I'm still in a wheelchair. There are no words but a scream; I feel so helpless, so lost, so incapable because everybody greets me with a high-pitched squeal of emotional distance, "Hey there, sweetie," and I want to yell at them, and, at the same time, I want to curl up in a ball and cry, and it's not something you can really know unless you've experienced this level of helplessness yourself.

They each open a side of our forest green Dodge Caravan, scuffs along the edges, 10 years old, the perfect car for a '90s family; Dad helps me out of the seat while Mom takes my wheelchair out. The morning is just beginning, the sky bursting forth in purple, orange, and red as the sun begins the day. The air bites and stings as my dad rushes to get me in the chair, and then, he runs back to the driver's side to go park as Mom takes the back of my wheelchair. I guess surgery is one of the only excuses for me not to have to wheel myself. Before I know it, sliding doors open, and I'm back in a hospital. The back of my head is screaming, "Oh no!" My frontal lobe, though still healing, is telling me, "Calm, calm; it's going to be okay."

I don't really remember this place; I don't remember these doors; these faces at the front are the faces of strangers, and the white floors, the fluorescent lights, the pictures on the walls—all of it is new to me, even though I should know it well. I spent so long here. Mom and Dad smile and greet the woman at the front desk, an older lady in a cardigan, and I try to take it in. I want to remember it. I want to remember this place, remember this moment. My brain fights me, challenges me, pushes back, "No, you can't; you won't," but I know I won't be back. At least, I believe in my soul I won't be coming back here ever again. The waiting room is ready for the season with poinsettias, yellow Christmas lights, and a bowl full of candy canes. Oh right. I almost forgot it was almost Christmas.

"Will!" Shani excitedly yells, "You do not remember me. No, no, it's okay, but I? I remember you, and," she stops to hug Mom and Dad, "I remember you. How are you guys?"

"Shani. Good to see you."

"How was Shepherd? How are you, Will?" She bends

down, her hands on her pink scrubs, a reindeer sticker on her right breast pocket, "You are a lucky young man."

"Thank you."

I don't know what else to say when people tell me this. People call me lucky, a miracle, that God has a plan for my life, and it always makes me feel awkward; it has the sound of a compliment, but I have nothing to do with it. I was simply there to receive my recovery. I guess the only other thing I could reply to, "You're a miracle" with is, "Damn straight." Though, something tells me my Presbyterian pastor father would not quite appreciate that. At the very least, it would make me feel better to transfer the awkwardness I feel from being expected to reply to the person who made the statement.

They wheel me back to the surgical suite, and Shani and Rochelle help me change into a hospital gown, and after taking my vitals, they wheel me down the hall. I see an older woman smile and wave, and I give a half-hearted hand up as we make our way down the hall, sparkling white floor with the spots of grey—you know the linoleum hospital floor I'm talking about. The doors swing open, and with some assistance, I'm on the operating table, and a middle-aged man with black hair, turquoise scrubs and a mask on says, "Will, I'm going to count down from 100, okay?"

Okay. Do I have a choice in this matter? Is something going to happen, or are you just telling me what you're going to do? I'm going to lie here, converting oxygen into carbon dioxide, and then. . . anesthesia is weird. Sleep is planned; you get in your bed, pull the covers up, and you choose to close the door to active consciousness. Anesthesia takes your choice away; there's no fighting it. Try to hold your eyes open, fingers shaking as you push your eyelids up, but you will fail, and. . . black. Nothing. Do you dream? I think you do. I don't really know. Maybe, you do. When you wake up, there's not a feeling that you were sleeping. For me at least, there's a moment of acclamation, of figuring out where the heck I am, and what exactly is going on.

This time, there is a slight, bleary-eyed waking.

"Aghhhhh," I'm moaning as I writhe in my hospital bed, gown falling open at the back, as I twist my body. My skull is coming out of my head; it has become sentient, and it is forcing its way out, done with this crippled kid's failing teenage body. It's pulsing, and I feel my head screaming out in pain. I hear my pulse.

"Don't touch your drain," a faint voice, commanding, and the older nurse smiles, "Are you in pain?"

What kind of question is that? No, no, I'm just over here casually screaming. Of course, I don't say that. . . I promise I'm usually nicer than this. I yell, "Yes!"

"On a scale from one to ten, how would you rate your pain?"

What kind of question is this? "Ten!"

She goes to the door, and I close my eyes. This is the end.

I'm dying. I'm dying. Shit. This hurts so bad. I must be dying.

She comes back, a foggy, distorted picture of an older lady, "Dr. Weaver said to give you morphine."

Great. Great. Whatever. Just put it in my head. Now, please! Stab the needle in my cerebral cortex; it might get their faster, and my skull is pushing, pulsing, pushing, pulsing, and I am ready to go, ready to depart this life; make this pain go away. And the morphine works; the morphine starts to calm my body, starts to take every feeling away; the pain drips out of my skull into the drain at the back of my head. Then, the itching starts. All at once, I feel like my body is covered in hundreds of tiny little ants, moving quickly across my body, "It itches. It itches! It itches!"

A blonde nurse, young, early thirties, comes over, and she says sweetly (which is annoying at a time like this), "What's wrong?"

"My whole body itches!"

"Oh God. Are you allergic?"

Mom is in my room, "He had so much the last time."

"He must be allergic now."

And there is nothing in the world that matters right now. I don't care about this blonde nurse who checks my stomach for red streaks; I don't care about this hospital; I want this to stop. I want this itch to go away. It is all over my body, and I want a hot shower to burn this feeling off my skin. The nurse sees the streaks and hooks up something in my IV. Itch, itch, itch, itch, itch.

Mom peers at the streaks, bright red across my stomach like a splotchy sunburn, "He must have had too much."

She feels like she should've known as I squirm and wriggle, trying my best in my limited motion to get the feeling of crawling off me. Mom has her right hand on me, "I'm sorry, sweetie. I'm sorry. Will, it's going to go away."

"It itches so bad!"

Mom looks at the nurse who flashes her blue eyes in a reassuring gesture of sympathy. She checks my IV, "It'll take effect any minute now."

And then, as if in a rush, I feel normal. A cool feeling of calm and freshness washes down my back, and my skin is free, "Feels better."

Dad sits in the chair, leans forward, looking at me, and I try and smile. I don't know if I smile well. I feel so lost, so out of it, and I do the only thing I know to do, the thing I did last time I was in this pain, "I love you."

He stands up, "I love you too, bud."

I look at Mom; I don't know what's happening. I can't even

think back to the skull flap, can't remember the puke-colored helmet, can't remember touching my fingers to the stitches, can't remember Mom pulling my hand away, I look to Mom, eyes wet, body steady, "I love you, Mom." A hand on my shoulder, "I love you too, Will."

I am glad that, when I am lost in pain, recovering from surgery, and otherwise adrift from any such anchor of reality, my gut response is to tell the people in my life that I love them. God please, let this be my response when I have full consciousness. When I feel my boat's rope is firmly wrapped around the dock, and I no longer feel the choppy waves of distant shores and no longer try to steady my shaking vessel, God please let me look to "I love you." In some ways, the early days of recovery were easier than life before my brain injury. Yeah, they were hard; not being able to walk caused me pain, but I depended on my family; I needed them. I experienced their love directly, and I wasn't thinking about much outside of them and dreams of the future.

Now, in this hospital room, Dad sits back in his chair; Mom stands by the bed, and I'm drifting, eyes closing, and then, as if stepping on the thin patch of ice on an Alaskan lake, sleep overtakes me quickly and deeply, swallowing me whole. I don't know where I go when I dream. I don't know if I have nightmares about the accident, good dreams about before, whether I remember any part of my accident in the back closet or the crawl space of my subconscious. Do I hear the twisting metal? Can I feel myself choking on blood? Do I remember what Peter and I were talking about? I have trouble staying asleep, so they gave me Ambien, telling me sleep problems are common for individuals with brain injuries. But what they didn't tell me is that Ambien gives you the weirdest, most vivid dreams that stay with you until right after you wake up. I always wake up groggy, not rested.

I tell Mom they aren't nightmares, but I don't like being on Ambien.

So, when I wake up to what appears to be one of the male nurses in his forties in a Santa outfit, I start to wonder what state of consciousness I'm actually in.

"Ho, ho, ho!" he says, in what can only be described as a small-town community theater impression of Santa Claus.

"Hey," I say groggily, nodding at him, still very out of it from the Darvocet I am now on, and I must give off a look of an uninterested teenager enough that he speeds up his holiday cheer, "Well now, we want you to get better. Ho, ho, ho."

"Uh. . . thanks." Man, I'm so glad I am out of it, because if I was my old self, I would have felt obliged to be friendly and engage him in a twenty-minute conversation, even though, all the while, I would be hoping he would kindly disappear. He hands my parents each a candy cane, "Hope your head feels better! Ho, ho, ho," he offers, shaking my dad's hand, "Merry Christmas!"

A beat, the door closes; my mom adjusts in her seat; Dad slouches back best he can in his hospital chair, and another beat, I lie back in my bed.

"That was weird," Dad says with a laugh.

Mom joins in the laughter, "Very weird."

Dad looks at me; my head is shaved again; only, this time, there is a line of stitches going up the back of my head, and under those stitches, there are three screws. However, with these new cranial additions, one big thing is missing: my helmet. Now that I've got my skull flap back in, my brain is not just protected by flesh and hair, so the helmet is in the trash, or at least, I hope it is. Knowing my mom, it's probably in the garage somewhere.

I look halfway to Mom, "How long have I been here?"

"It's almost Christmas."

"It is?"

"Mhmm. In about a week."

I sit in this for a second. How is it Christmas? What does that make today? Am I going to have Christmas at home? They all hit at once, like a word jumble, mixed and meshed.

"Do I get to go home?"

"Soon." Mom touches my arm.

I smile, "I love you, Mom."

"I love you too."

Then, as if a switch is turned on, pain rushes back into my head, and the bone around my brain is pushing in, like it's collapsing, and it's caving in on my mind, and I can't do anything but lie there, "Ahhhhh! Ahhh!"

Mom reaches and grabs the call button to a quick answer, "Is everything all right?"

"He's in pain. He needs more medicine."

An almost robotic, "What's his pain on a scale from one to ten?" sounds on the other line.

"Ten!"

Mom grabs my hand which clasps hers, "He says it's a ten."

"Okay, we'll be right down."

On a scale of one to I'm going to die, ten feels insufficient to describe how much I need some damn medicine. I think one time I said eleven, and they smiled and said, "But really?"

I have no memory of this much pain, and it's a steady drumming on my skull, newly completed, and I can't even enjoy that I'm not wearing my helmet.

Shani comes in, smiles, "You're saying you're in pain?"

A desperate plea, "Yes."

"Okay. Have you eaten?"

I look to Mom, who replies, "No."

"Okay, so let's get you some food and a Darvocet, okay?"

I look, and I hope I nod, but I honestly don't care. I want

71

my skull to stop wanting to come outside my head. Please, for the love of it all, just calm down head. Skull, stay in your place, and I keep trying to count from 100, 100, 99, 76, 82, 12, ahhhh! 1! 1! 1!

The pain makes the numbers fall out of orbit. And after what feels like the steady progress of millennia, she comes back with some turkey and gravy. And screw it, the tray on the table above my bed is yellow, and the turkey looks like a chunk out of a can, and the gravy looks like fresh diarrhea, but I count down from 100, waiting for Mom to raise the bed, which she does and then takes the fork and puts a big chunk of turkey in my mouth, and I start chewing.

"A few more bites," and my mom cuts up two more chunks, and I chew, mostly swallow, and look to Shani, thinking, "Please. Please say okay."

"Okay," and she opens the bottle, puts the pill in my mouth, gives me some water, and I swallow, and the pounding keeps going.

"It didn't work," I look at her, frantic, my eyes pleading and begging for her to do something, anything, to take the pain out of my head, and I wish she could, but she only gives me a soft smile, "Don't worry. It'll work."

I lie back. I hope she's not lying as I watch her say some things to my parents that I can't hear and walk out the door. Then, it slowly starts to fade; the pulse slows to a steady beat, then, a soft tap, and then, I'm asleep. I don't know where I go, but I know where I'm going. I'm going home soon. It's almost Christmas, and I'm going home. This year is almost over.

There's a song from one of my favorite bands, The Mountain Goats, called [1]"This Year." I almost made it, and I would've sung this song before my accident. I was on six hours of sleep a night, stressed about college, my AP classes, and the future I thought I could control. Caffeine and sugar flooded as easily through my veins as red blood cells. I have almost made it through this year; sure, this year did kill me, but it didn't kill me for good, and this year, this year coming up is one I look forward to because I believe, deep in my heart, that I will get better. I want to get home to start to get better. This has been one of the hardest years of my life, and strange as it sounds, I don't think it will be the hardest. God got me through, and I can, at least on this day, with my huge scar down my head and my body shrinking behind my gown, start to think about looking forward to the next one. And it's nice, that hope, that glimmer, that shiny coin I keep at the front of my brain. Hope feels nice. I want to hold tight and never lose the belief that tomorrow will continue to be better than today. Please God, keep me in this place of longing for tomorrow, and then, maybe, at some point in the future, I will have that same hope for today.

8

GOING HOME

My head is screaming, pounding, banging on the roof, the floor, smashing all the windows of my skull, and I'm pressing the nurse button, and they say, "We'll be right over."

But what does that mean? Your "right over" and "my right over" are two different things, and what I really need is right now. I reach for the button again.

"They'll be right over, buddy."

My dad is in the chair, and I'm not sure when my parents got here, or if they have been here the whole time. And I notice that he's wearing a green sweater and his leather jacket, and he looks good. It's weird to see your parents bar for their appearance lowered, so that when you see them decently dressed, you think, "Oh wow, who are you?"

Legs crossed, sipping his Starbucks, he asks, "You in bad pain?"

I nod, but isn't it obvious? I'm not jamming the nurse's button to have a nice morning chat. Don't get wrong, they're nice people and all, but this, this frantic look? This is the face of someone in pain. There is a knock at the door, and it is the friendly, older nurse, all smiles, in red scrubs with what appears to be an intense attempt at holiday cheer. She's got a Rudolph breast pin, and if I didn't need her to stop the pain, I would've rolled my eyes but, please, for the love of God. She's holding a tray in one hand and a glass of water in the other, and she starts in her Southern morning sparkle.

"I've got some breakfast, eggs, fruit bowl, a yogurt, and some sausage. And of course, some Darvocet, but you need to eat some first."

Dad pulls up the table; she places the food and water, and Dad gives me three big bites of sausage, and it hurts so much I'm dizzy, and I take the water and the Darvocet, lie back as I hear the polite Southern voice, "Make sure he eats the rest of that."

I struggle to keep my head up, feel like my neck bones are becoming gelatinous, and I hear the *burr* as my dad raises the bed 'til I'm almost ninety degrees to the floor, and Mom comes through the door as Dad has a clump of hospital eggs on the fork, "He can feed himself."

I turn my head to see her there, and she's got her big red purse over her shoulder because, at a certain point in their life, don't all moms have a big red purse over their shoulders? You know the mom purse I'm talking about, and she's got her arms crossed, and she's back on it.

With a huff, Dad turns to her, "Debbie, he just had his head cut open."

She sits down in one of the chairs next to the bed.

"C'mon, give him the fork."

A laugh from my dad, the other hand running down his speckled goatee.

"Okay, okay. Will, just remember who was nice to you."

A laugh, but then, she leans forward and hits Dad's arm.

"Hey, not fair."

Fork in hand, I look at the food, and I wonder just how much I really want to eat it; how much do I want to strain to put this hospital slop in my face hole. Well, it's worth a shot. With the coordination of a drunkard, I grab the fork and work to bring the fork to my face, but I drop a big hunk of egg on my chest, cold and rubbery.

"Hmm." Dad says with a look to Mom, who retorts.

"He brought it to his mouth."

Dad helps me with a few more bites and gives me the Darvocet. My head hurts so much I want to go back to sleep, want to have anything but this pain, but Dad keeps giving me breakfast, and before I know it, the pain begins to drip away, and I feel my eyes closing, and I'm not fighting it; I want to know consciousness without pain.

"You're going to go home today, bud."

Home? Home? I don't even remember home. I haven't seen home since October, and it's almost Christmas, and I'm going home?

I reach to scratch my shaved head, "What?"

"We're taking you home today."

The light outside almost looks blue through the window; you know how the mornings are in the winter? No snow in Georgia, but it's almost like the cold outside makes the world have a hint of light blue through the glass. Dad smiles down at me, and I can see he's got some tears in eyes. He's not crying, but there's the shimmer of moisture.

"You ready?"

I nod. I've been ready for so long, but I don't have the words. The nurses come in, take my vitals, remove my drain—a sting, a quick pressure at the back of my head, and it is quickly bandaged up. The Darvocet is not entirely effective as a throbbing starts in the back of my head, a steady hum, a low pain, but

I wince, nonetheless. I look like a recent prisoner of war with my shaved head, bandaged, skinny pale, scarred-down-the-middle body, and half a left ear. I look beaten and broken, but now, in this swaddling hospital gown, I gift a faint hint of a smile. Dad stands me up as Mom brings in my chair, and the nurses all beam. Dr. Weaver, the man who saved my life months earlier and just put a fourth of my skull back in place, appears by my bed, turquoise scrubs, an exuberant smile as the mustache of his goatee arches in a smile, "You're going home today."

A faint, faraway look from me, "Yeah."

Pumping his arms in the air, he adds, "That's great! So good! Let me see that neck."

"What?"

He points to my neck, like a carpenter showing off a table, "Not a trace of a scar."

Mom smiles, touching my arm, "That's right. Will, you remember those people at Shepherd with those marks on their necks?"

"Yeah."

Dad points his finger at Dr. Weaver in confirmation, "Yeah, we saw a number of bad ones."

Dr. Weaver has the excitement of a used car salesman as if he was trying to get my neck off the lot before closing, "Not this kid. He had a trach for three weeks, and now, he has no hint of a scar!"

I'm not really following, but I know I need to say something to respond to the energy Weaver is bringing, so I settle on, "That's good."

"Great to see you recovering. The pain will go away," then to my mom, "Clean the wound after 24 hours, redress it, and we'll see you guys back in about two weeks."

She wants to hug him; she wants to thank him for giving

her boy back to her for making sure her sweet son did not taste the bite of the death; she wants to give him one of those hugs where you wrap your arms so tight it hurts the other person's chest, one of those hugs that would make Dr. Weaver have to push her off, the biggest hug of gratitude. There's no time for that. Weaver's better at hiding it than Kaelin, but he's a busy man, more heads to stitch back together, more lives to save. And as if clicking his heels, he is gone, a handshake to both Mom and Dad, and the miracle man is off.

"You ready?" Dad says, hands behind my wheelchair.

I don't know why everyone asks me this. Yes! Please, I'm ready to go home; I'm ready for life to go back to normal. No, I want to stay here in this room of this trauma center. Of course, I'm ready!

"Let him push," Mom says, looking down at me.

I'm kind of pissed that she's making me push my own wheelchair after I just got screws in my head. I'm aggravated each time she makes me do something for myself when someone else offers to help me. Though, she's not doing it to hurt me; she's doing the hard thing to make me better. It's not easy to see your boy push himself in circles in his wheelchair, to see him spill his food all over his chest, to see him fight, kick, and struggle to remember, but she pushes me, pushes me to get better. I'm mad, but I know I shouldn't be. Help me out a bit, okay?

I'm pushing myself, but I'm so tired, so out of it, and I'm not pushing really; my arms need a break after a few thrusts of my feeble limbs, and Dad quickly steps in, "He can start when we get home."

And it's so much better to be pushed than to push, and soon, the sliding doors of the hospital open wide unto the December morning. The blue-grey sky, the bright orb of daylight already climbing most of the way up the sky but hidden by the clouds that seem to offer no chance of precipitation, the white wisps of the day all remind you it's winter. The parking lot looks emptier, like more people are choosing to avoid getting in car accidents right before Christmas. I'm sure there are probably more; statistics are sick like that. Dad hands Mom the keys, and after a quick transfer of me from my wheelchair and everything is stowed away, we are in and heading home, stopped of course by the metro-Atlanta traffic, and after my dad gives a couple, "Jeeze Louise!" quips to some idiots who don't know how to drive, we are back in the driveway of the house.

It's weird to arrive at somewhere that is familiar, well-known but not fresh. It's like going back to your old high school; you know it; you remember the teachers, remember the bench at the bus lane where you and your friends used to hang out, remember which portable you took political science in, but you don't quite know it anymore. If you went back, you'd have to relearn it. This is what it feels like to come back home. I know this place, and I know that I know; I just need to relearn it.

"Dad's been busy with the renovations," Mom says as we get ready to get out of the car.

"Renovations?" The house looks exactly the same. . . I think.

Dad takes the key out of the ignition and starts to get my wheelchair set up outside my door and then get me, "She means moving your bed downstairs and installing a handrail for the stairs on the other side."

"Oh, downstairs?" I'm picturing this new life.

"Your bed is in the dining room," Mom says, getting out. Home sweet home. We go into the kitchen, filled with the Christmas accoutrements, Advent candles on the black kitchen table, angels scattered on the countertops, and in the den, a big,

WILLIAM CARTER & (12/29/2022)

fat Christmas tree, the kind my mom likes, the kind she and Dad always fight over, "No Bob, we can find one fatter."

He would ask her, "Isn't this one fat enough?"

And she would always reply, "Fatter!"

And he would let out a sigh and offer an annoyed, "Okay," and we would continue our search until we found a tree that could be considered morbidly obese. You know that scene in [1]*Christmas Vacation* when Chevy Chase opens the branches, and they knock out the windows? Yeah, Mom thinks of that as a starter tree. But there, in our living room, the tree is in its magnificent obese beauty, wrapped in a collection of white and multicolored lights, weighed down by ornaments going back to the early '80s. Underneath this mammoth is a slew of presents, all wrapped, and stockings hang from the brick fireplace, each with names embroidered across the top: Mom's, Dad's, Andrew's, Anna's, and mine. A green one hangs next to the family's for our dog Shelby, who quickly welcomes me with a loud bark. She's a black lab mix, a runt and so loving. She's followed by Jack, my brother's beagle mix, who jumps at Dad.

"Down, Shelby, down," Dad commands, as Shelby plops her paws and head on my lap.

"Will, you got to tell her to get down," Mom offers.

"Hey girl, miss me?" I pat her head as her tail moves with a fair amount of g-force. Jack pushes her out of the way as he makes his way to my lap.

"Jack! Down!" Mom orders him.

I don't think she likes him. He's sweet, but he definitely thinks (even though he doesn't have the balls for it) he's the alpha male of the house.

"Hey Jack," I say as Mom pushes the wheelchair to get him out of the way.

It's like I pictured it in my mind, bright wood floors with scuff marks galore, den with Dad's red recliner, the red and green stripped couch, big wooden coffee table, and pictures galore. Mom loves pictures.

I wish I could capture this moment, wish I could freeze it in my brain, but I know it will soon be gone. Most things are. I'll try and repeat something in my mind, try my best to try and freeze an image in my brain, but sure as anything, it will vanish moments later.

Mom can't hide it; her face is all a glimmer, "Want to see your new room?"

"Yeah, let's do it."

And she pushes me over the red kitchen runner, past the white wooden cabinets, past the stove with its oven hood, past the big fridge, rounding the corner into the dining room and then the connected room, with an old wooden, scratched piano, and, now, my bed, white sheets, blue comforter, [2]Mickey Mouse printed several times over with red stripes between him and his blue background, and everything smells like home. You know that smell? You don't notice it while you live there, but leave for any extended period of time, and when you come back, you find the reassuring aroma of safety. Everyone's home smells different. Remember going to some friends' houses growing up? And you'd think their home smells weird. But your house never did? Well, that smell of your home always takes the tension out of your shoulders and the stress out your back.

However, my lower back always hurts, and I want to lie down and take a nap, ready to curl up in my own bed, in a house without nurses, in a room without therapists, in a place that doesn't remind me of my disability.

I look out the windows at the end of the piano room into the street. It's always been a quiet street, mostly old people whose kids who have moved to far away states like Ohio and Maine, and they sit alone at home, watching [3]*Jeopardy* or [4]*The*

Price is Right. It was a weird place for a young kid to grow up, but it's always been home, and sure, I had always wanted kids on this street, but now, recently returned from the hospital, I am glad the pavement outside my house is not teeming with the screams of children.

It's quiet, and I wish I could remember what day it is, how far away Christmas is. I don't want to ask my mom because I know I should remember. I know she's told me, and I know she's going to ask me to remember, and I know I'm going to try really hard, but I'm not going to remember even after she tells me again. I know I'm not going to remember, and I'm going to hate myself for not remembering. Or she's going to tell me, and then, a couple minutes later, I'm going to ask her again, and there's going to be five seconds of awkward silence, which I'm going to know I caused, and then, she might look at Dad, or she might look at me with sad eyes, and I know I'm going to know I should remember it. I should know. I should remember. I want to remember. I want to be better.

"You tired?" she looks at me sadly as I gaze at the small, plastic Christmas tree that used to always be in my room which is now under the window on an end table.

"Buddy?"

"What?" I look at those reassuring brown eyes of hers, the ones that look exactly like mine, and she gazes down sweetly.

"I asked if you were tired."

My bed looks so inviting, so welcoming. "Yeah, I am."

She locks the wheelchair, and lifting on the gait belt, she helps me stand, and we pivot to the bed as I slump down on it.

She helps me scoot up to the pillow and puts the Mickey Mouse comforter over me, making sure I'm nice and tucked in, the way she used to when I was kid home sick from school, and I guess I am. "I love you, Mom."

"I love you too, Will."

I close my eyes. This feels like this will be the first true rest I've been able to get in a long time. No one is coming to check my vitals; no one is coming to make sure I'm changed; no one from the room next door is screaming profanities; it feels surreal. I dreamed of this day for so long, the day when I would be out of Shepherd Center and home, and it doesn't feel as good as I'd thought. I thought I would feel an inch or two closer to better, but I don't. I don't really feel any closer to what I want. I'm still in a wheelchair, still coming up blank on what happened today, still having flashes of faces but no static images, and I do not know what day it is today. I'm so weary, so ready for rest.

"God, forgive me Lord. . . I don't. . . I don't have faith. . . Forgive me God. . . Jesus, I need belief. Give me belief. . . I need you. . . I need you to heal me, Father. I need you to heal my brain, God. Please. . . Please heal my brain. I want to remember, God. God, I just want to remember. I want to be able to know what happened today. . . God. . . I want to walk. Hear me, Father. I want to walk. God, help me. Help me walk. Give me legs that will walk. Give me legs that will walk and a mind that will remember. . . I love you, Lord. . . Amen."

I know he hears me. I am wavering whether I believe I will be answered. As I close my eyes for a nap and drift to only God knows where, I both believe I will walk again and pray God gives me the faith to believe I will walk again.

9
CHRISTMAS EVE

On Christmas Eve, I wake up before everyone, which has become common since the hospital. Ever since the accident, my body gets me up before six, sometimes, at the obscene hours of four or five. I lie in bed and try to fall back asleep, but that feels a little like sitting in a running car, waiting for it to run out of gas. My mind turns and turns, spinning dizzily, flipping, dipping, dropping, rolling, over and over, and as I try to hold an empty space in mind, it keeps filling up, "What if you never do walk again?"

"What if you can't graduate this year?"

"What if this is as healed as you get?" Then, I decide to wake up, and wait (wait for someone else to get up). Normally, this is the case, as I wait patiently in my bed. I wait for someone else to wake up and take me to the bathroom or make me some breakfast.

Today as I turn from my back to my right side, to my left side, then back to my back, I hear Mom getting up. There's the sound of water filling the thin metal of the hot-water heater, hear the clang of a porcelain plate being placed on the granite, the squeak of the fridge, the grumble of the freezer drawer opening, the whistle of the hot water kettle, the soft chiming of the butter dish opening, the clang of rummaging in the silver-ware drawer, the hard slam of the microwave door, and then, the beep, beep, beep.

I know I shouldn't. I know I should call her in here and ask her to help stand me up with my gait belt and transfer me to my wheelchair, but I'm tired of that. I'm sick of being helpless, sick of depending on others to move, transfer, and transport me, so I try to do it quietly. That way, she doesn't come in and stop me.

I sit up, easy enough, push the blueberry blue Mickey Mouse comforter off to the other side of the bed, turn my legs slowly, ever so slowly, to the edge of the bed, until they're touching the cold, hardwood floors. I grab the side of the mattress, concentrate hard, and then, in a determined, slow strain, I stand on my own. My mouth opens wide with joyous surprise. Next, with more determination, I look down at my right leg, try and remember what it felt like for my body to move, and with all of my accessible mental energy, my right leg moves, and I can't help it; amazed, I let out a laugh, "Ha!"

From the kitchen, I hear Mom's voice, "Will?"

With more determination, I move the left leg, left foot, and ha! Forward!

With my arms out, like I'm trying to balance on a tight rope,

85

I make small, stuttered steps as I hear Mom putting her tea mug back on the table, "Will?"

I feel like Isaac Newton, discovering the theory of gravity—exuberance, jubilee— "Ha, ha!" She rushes in, the legs of her blue snowmen pajama pants brushing quickly against each other, and the serious look on her face is undercut by the matching snowman pajama top as she sees me walking. Well, I'm taking steps, short, stuttered, little steps, but my legs are moving nonetheless.

Her eyes go wide; her back straightens, "Will!"

I open my hands, "Whaddaya think, Mom?"

My hope for her excitement is not met; her eyes tighten, and she says, "Will, get back in bed."

"Why?"

She comes next to me, worried, "You could fall!"

I keep moving as she tries to encourage me back to sitting, but I keep going, meticulously moving each foot, "Look!"

Her glasses on her nose, she's giving the mom look, "Will, I'm not messing around."

I may have a brain injury, but I'm smart enough to know what that look means, "Okay, okay."

I sit down, and she sits next to me. A moment of silence, and I see the fear and anxiety in her face.

"What were you thinking? What if you fell?" She says softly, a hand on my shoulder.

"I guess, I stood up by the bed, and I figured, if I fell, I would. . . I would fall on the bed."

She looks at me, and her eyes meet mine, and I can see there is some dark thing wrapped up in her mind; there's some great terror that she cannot explain. I see her eyes are pained, and her mouth is tight, and I know she's serious. She keeps her voice low, rubs my shoulder as she searches for the words. In the silence, as I worry I did something bad, my stomach starts to coalesce into a knotted string of intestines. I hate being in trouble. I've always hated it.

"Will," she starts, "If you fell, you could really hurt yourself. Right?"

I nod. A moment, "Yeah."

The heat turns on again as it begins to drizzle outside, light droplets tapping on the window.

She exhales, "And if you hit your head, you could really hurt it. . . It would be really bad to erase all the progress you've made. Right?"

I nod and look out the window, while she looks at me. I see a hydrangea leaf that's close to the glass, and it's so green in the rain. Have you ever noticed that? In the rain, all the plants look so much more alive outside the window. Maybe, it's the fact that their life blood is falling from the sky; maybe, it's God's way of distracting us from the heavens turned grey, but the life around us looks so much more alive when it's raining. It's a truly beautiful gift from God, and I'm distracted by this thought, until I hear, "Will?"

A second. Oh right, we were talking, "Yeah?"

She looks at me, not mad, not mean, "You understand then? You understand why I don't want you walking unsupervised?"

I nod, "Mhmm."

"It's not that I'm not proud of you because I am. It's not that I don't think you can do it. I worry about you falling and hurting yourself."

I put a hand on her shoulder, "Don't worry, Mom. I understand."

Her chestnut eyes and soft smile send me sweetness.

"You want some eggs?" she asks, as she starts walking back into the kitchen.

"Sure." Eggs? Okay, sure. I don't mind eggs. I hope she puts cheese in them, and I hope she lets me salt them. It's probably not a good idea because just like my three-hundred-pound diabetic Granny, I like my eggs as salty as the Dead Sea.

I hear the sound of the cast iron skillet hitting the metal of the stove's eye, the whoosh of the gas creating a flame, the soft crack of an egg, sizzle, crack, and sizzle, the quick sound of a whisk bringing the yolks together.

Forget hoping, I need to take action. "Cheese?" I pipe up.

"Sure."

I hear the fridge open and close as she takes out a big block of cheddar and slices off clumps into the eggs. I wait on my bed, feeling the tension in my lower back, the low steady strain, the throb in my head coming back.

"Mom?" I hear her scraping the eggs onto the plate and moving to me. She appears between the rooms, "Yeah, buddy?"

"My head hurts."

She brings the wheelchair to the bed, "You want to get some eggs, and then, I'll give you a Darvocet?"

I move to the edge of the bed, "Okay."

She doesn't even make it look like she's going to push my chair. Once I'm settled in my chair, she gives me a quick look over in a blink and then, moves back to the kitchen. I laugh to myself; I shouldn't expect a push from her. I dig my heels into the floor as I use them to drag my wheels into the kitchen. There, I see little waves of steam coming off my eggs, a glass of ice water next to them, and to the right of that, three pill bottles. The vitamins are in the cabinet, but I don't worry, I know they're coming. Mom is by the food, taking the chair out, so I can scoot in, "Breakfast is served."

"Thanks Mom," I say as I pick up the fork, look at it.

"You feel good?" She asks.

"I think I can try. Just a few bites?"

"Then, you can have a Darvocet."

I pick up the fork, a little wobbly, almost drop it, but I take it slow and steady to the plate, pick up a chunk of eggs, and bring it to my mouth, chew.

"Eggs are a good source of protein," Mom notes as she sits down with her tea.

"Mhm," I offer, mouth still full.

"How does it feel to be home?" Mom asks, holding her white mug to her mouth.

"Good. Good. I'm excited to be home, glad to not be at Shepherd." I quickly shove in a few more bites as the pulsing in my head gets worse, the steady hum of pain from recently having your skull screwed back in.

"Shepherd was good to you," Mom says with a decisive point.

"Yeah, but I like not having to go to physical therapy," I quickly take the bottle of Darvocet, struggle a bit with the cap, which does not want to budge.

"Make sure you push down," she directs as I push and.. nothing.

"Are you pushing on the cap?"

I'm pushing, and nothing is working, and I hold it out. She wants me to do it, but she can tell by my eyes I am in real pain, so she pushes and twists, "Push like that," and gives me a red oblong that I quickly take. "Now you open the others," she directs, as I try hard to push on my Keppra bottle, and it slides open, and I take one of these yellow-brown tablets and swallow. That's the important one, the one that makes sure I don't have a seizure, the one I have to make sure I don't forget. The Ritalin bottle, though, that one is not moving. I push down, try to spin, and nothing.

89

"Make sure to push down."

I feel a bubble of anger, "I am pushing."

She gives me sweet eyes, "Push down, and then turn."

I try again, again, and again. Nothing. "I can't."

"You've got it." She says, patting me on the back, which only makes me angrier because it makes me feel like a seven-year-old in little league.

"Can you open it?" And I shove it at her, pissed she's making me fail because I hate trying and failing. Finally, she takes it and tries to open it, holding it down with her left hand and pushing and twisting with her right. She grits her teeth, raises one eyebrow, the vein in her head visible, then a sigh, "Okay, that one is hard."

"See?"

I'm annoyed because I said it was hard, but everyone has to double-check me. I can't be right without verification. No one thinks I know what I'm talking about anymore. After a big grunt, the bottle opens, and she gives me one of the white circles, and she also gives me ginseng and fish oil tablets. And, once again, this is why she calls herself Dr. Debbie, not sincerely. Don't worry, she's not practicing without a license. But she does have an opinion about most medical things, and she has a heavy supply of over-the-counter drugs and vitamins that might help an injured brain.

After I take my regimen, she continues from before, "Don't worry about therapy, you'll go to Pathways soon."

Looking in my memory, I come up blank, "Pathways?"

"Remember? Dr. Kaelin told you about it? It's like Shepherd Center, except you get to come home." She takes my plate to the sink.

"Oh no, all day?" I'm thinking back to the pain of therapy: how exhausted I was, how I hated getting told what to do, asked for my feelings but feeling like they were dismissed.

"I think it only goes 'til four? I'll have to check on that." She washes my plate.

"So more—"

"More physical terrorists as your dad says."

"Oh joy."

I don't know how to feel. I'm excited to think they might be able to help me walk again, help make my short-term memory better, help me get my left fingers stronger, so I feel comfortable using my left hand, but I don't want the feeling of being in therapy. God, can't you just make me better? You snapped your fingers, and a dead guy came back to life; can't you do the same for my brain and heal it? C'mon, I'll pray every day, and when I get a job, I'll make sure to give you twenty percent. What do you say?

I want to get better, so I try to focus my mind on that. At least, Pathways will help me get better.

"You want to watch a movie?" Mom asks, as she comes back to the table.

"Sure."

And this is the thing I wanted coming home, the comforts I remember from my childhood. I want so badly to be an independent teenager, to feel ready to leave the nest, but now that I'm home, back on this lumpy, sunken red, green, and tan striped couch, I just want to have the feelings I'm used to. Remember your childhood? I believed in magic, was dominated by imagination, and felt nothing but optimism for tomorrow. My life was going to turn out because why wouldn't it? I guess that optimism led me to becoming the cocky son of a gun I had been before my accident. Cocky, not as in mean to anyone, but I definitely felt this sense of promise. Partly, that came from a privileged childhood of comfort, and I want that same warm, gooey feeling of no worry I used to have, the same feeling of being swallowed by the couch, in a blanket, drinking hot chocolate while I watch *A Christmas Story*.

Right now, I'm so close to having that feeling—enjoying the moment, not thinking about the next one, just watching this movie with Mom and Dad during a rainy Christmas Eve. Soon, we will have to get dressed and pile into the car. We will go to P.F. Chang's, and my brother and I will make dark, inappropriate jokes with each other; I will see people I haven't seen in a long time, and I'm sure they will all ask, "Remember me?"

And I will nod, but I will have no clue who they are, and I'll be angry that they thought it was a fair question to ask a seven- teen-year-old kid who has a brain injury if he remembers you. Do you ask a blind person what they think of your haircut? Or do you ask your deaf friend to judge your singing?

I kind of wish I could say what I want to say with these people. I wish I could put the awkwardness on them. "You remember me?" I could conjure up a reply—now, only if there were other people listening— "Oh yeah, you're the one who pushed me down the stairs." Their half smile would turn to a look of utter confusion, and there would be a couple of good seconds of awkward silence. I would never want to get anyone in actual trouble, but it would be fun to watch them squirm. Sorry, not sorry.

Asking a person with a brain injury if he or she remembers you is asking for that person to feel insecure. But we are at church. There are so many people talking to me, and there are so many people hoping I can make them laugh, or I feel that's what they are hoping, and I'm so anxious that I'm going to disappoint, or I'm going to be awkward. While I used to like attention, having everyone focus on me now, I'm thinking they're simply waiting until I screw up.

So, it's good to be at church, and it's bad to be at church. I know I'm not focused on God in this moment, but I don't know how to do so when my insecurities are wearing me like a suit. Soon, though, we're able to go into the service, and Randy Pope, a man in his sixties who is surprisingly fit, preaches a sermon, but I'm not really listening. I'm thinking back on the prior interactions, examining and dissecting them.

Soon though, candles are passed around, and it's time for "Silent Night," and Mom hands me a candle. When the time comes, she helps me light my candle from the flame of hers, and we're singing. I tilt my candle absentmindedly, and I drip wax on my other hand, and ooh, it burns. I lift the candle up. And, this feels nice. This song, this moment. This reminds me of an easier time, and as I sing "Silent Night," I yearn for that easier life, and I hope I can get there soon.

After the service, we go back home and each open one present, sitting around the room, taking turns as Vince Guaraldi's [1]*A Charlie Brown Christmas* album plays over the stereo. I get a striped blue, brown, and grey sweater, and sure, why not, it'll do. It looks nice enough. I didn't get anyone anything, and it's okay. No one asked for anything. And as we sit here as a family and listen to music and talk about tomorrow, I sense that, maybe, the easier life is within reach. In this moment, sitting in my chair, looking at the presents under the tree, the red and white stockings on the brick fireplace, and Dad in his red chair, almost ready to go to bed, I feel like this looks like it used to. I'm not as active, but this has the look and feel of life before, and I hope—and I'm trying to hope—that life can return there again.

10
TUTORING

My junior year, I took AP environmental science, and so, I had to take physics my senior year. Not being the best with math, I knew AP physics would steal at least half of my eternal soul, and since I didn't know which half, I decided to take regular physics. It was a breeze; before my accident, I was crushing it. I came to class, not really having studied, and I would answer questions, make jokes, and I felt on top of the world. Most of the students were a year younger, and I knew I was the star student. I know it makes me sound cocky, and yes, I was, but I need you to see who I was before to understand how hard what I'm supposed to be doing today is for me now.

My teacher, Mrs. Foss, is an obese woman, in her fifties, with long black hair and short chubby arms with stubby little fingers. She's got the softest little whisper of a voice that she will try to turn into a yell, her knuckles up against the soft sides of her stomach, but to be honest, none of her students really take her seriously.

Me, though? I was trying to go to Wake Forest, so I was a great student. Did I crack a joke here and there? Sure, but I was always friendly with her, always asked her how she was doing, talked with her after class, having a "These kids, huh?" approach to my fellow students. God, I want to slap myself just thinking about it. I definitely wanted to be the favorite student though, even if I didn't care about her class at all.

So, a few days after Christmas, I follow my routine: my breakfast, my pills, my shower, and change into today's exercise pants and T-shirt. Dad helps me down the stairs, going in front of me, making sure I don't topple. He helps me sit in my chair, gripping my gait belt, as I fall with a plop in my black-cushioned seat. Now, I'm at the kitchen table, looking at the red circles where the black paint is starting to wear away when I see a gold Honda minivan from the early '90s speed into our driveway and come to an audible halt. Mrs. Foss, gets out, her hair matted with sweat as a lone black strand breaks away from the others, choosing to fight gravity and shoot upwards. She rushes in a waddle to the passenger side and grabs an armful of folders and a pink grocery bag. She closes the door, locks it, and rushes as fast as her short, stubby legs will carry her to the front door, ringing the doorbell, and my mom opens the white wooden door to my physics teacher, who starts off in short, bursts of air, "I'm. . . so sorry. . . I texted you. . . I was running. . . running late."

Mom smiles, having changed into jeans and a purple sweater, happy Mrs. Foss is helping, "No worries at all."

I'm in my wheelchair at the table, just waiting, excited but also, a little stressed. I'm both ready and not ready to get back to school. I mean, I'm ready to go back, finish, and graduate in May, but I don't want to try and fail. I don't want to put in the effort and look stupid. Now, I get why some kids give up; it's just easier.

"It's, you know how it is. . . woo, let me catch my. . . catch my breath."

I can hear her, frazzled as I remember her, her tan sneakers squeaking on the white tile of our front entry.

"A long drive for you?" Mom asks.

"No, not at all. Just got focused on planning, and I, you know? Whoa, look at the time."

Mom laughs, being her extroverted self, "Don't worry at all, I completely understand. I'm the same way."

"Where's Will?"

"Sitting at the kitchen table."

And, Mom ushers her in, blue pants, her white top with pink lines, all stretchy and easy to handle, and she smiles her big smile, "Will, it is good to see you!"

I smile, "Hey, Mrs. Foss."

She leans down to my wheelchair to give me the awkward hug I'm used to receiving, "How are you, sweetie?"

"Doing good." I don't have access to anything else, and I guess, generally speaking, I am doing good. I'm alive; I'm home; I've got everything I need. So, yeah, sure, I guess that qualifies under good, right? I'm good. . . I guess. That's probably a more honest answer—you know, "I'm good I guess," but I can't give that answer. I can't say that because people will get uncomfortable.

Mrs. Foss smiles like I told her I am doing gloriously.

"That's great, Will! That's great! So glad you're doing good!"

She's a sweet lady. Man, I wish I had genuinely appreciated her when she was my teacher. I mean, I thought she was nice, and like I said, I was always nice to her, but I viewed her class as an obstacle, something to get through, a placeholder in my schedule that I needed to fulfill in order to graduate.

She steadies herself and sits at the table, taking one of her books, a heavy, turquoise-green hardback textbook, and a composition notebook out of her pink bag and with a heave and a thud, and puts them on the table. The next thing she says with a smile, and she says it honestly, genuinely, like this is a question which has an equal chance of being a yes or a no, "Do you remember Newton's laws?"

"Newton?" I'm racking my brain, looking everywhere frantically. I should know this. She said it like I should know it.

I look over, hoping for a clue, but I only see the Christmas tree, full of presents, and the light from the sun shining through the window behind the tree, making it look almost from another world, you know the soft yellow glow I'm talking about? Like it's a tree ghost?

Mrs. Foss smiles, hoping I will remember, "You know Isaac Newton, had the apple fall on his head?"

My mouth goes wide with a yawn as my hand scratches what looks like a very short buzz cut, "Gravity?"

Those big cheeks of hers shoot up, as her teeth shine in a smile, and her fingers point at me, "You got it! He discovered gravity. Now, he had these laws of motion. Do you remember any of those?"

I shake my head, "No."

That silence again, a good three seconds, as Mrs. Foss is realizing where I'm at, how impacted I am. Earlier, when my mom asked her if she would be willing to do some physics tutoring, Mom explained how I was doing, and I'm guessing Mrs. Foss hoped that, since she was able to come by, I would be a little bit more with it. She thought I was doing much better. I can sense disappointment the same way dogs smell cookies. Sure, she must've heard from the principals I was in a bad state when they saw me earlier, but that had been a while back. Now, realizing I remember nothing from physics, she must understand how much I'm impacted, and she breathes out, looks at me. I can see the sympathy in those brown eyes, "So, let's talk about force. What is force?"

A nod, "Force."

"Yeah. What is a force?"

"Like strength?"

Then comes the so-drawn-out nature of answering a question that is not quite the answer sought after, "Yeaaahhh, sure, but. . . uhh. . . let me see."

Fishing in her pockets, she pulls out a pencil and holds it steady, "Okay, what can you do with this pencil?"

A second or two. Is this a trick question? "Write with it?"

She holds the pencil out in front of me, looking at me with that look of waiting, "If you want it, how can you get it from me?"

The silence is palpable as I shift tension between my cheeks, lips pursed, "Just grab it?"

She points it at me, her elbows on the black of the kitchen table, "If you grab it, what are you doing? Which direction?"

"To me," I say, pointing to myself.

She points the pencil at me "What is that called?"

"Bringing it to me?"

She never loses the sweetness in her voice, even in the "No, that is it called when you," and she makes the gesture of bringing her hand back, "What is that?"

Spelunking in the caverns of my mind, I search for something, anything, "Uhh. . ."

Mrs. Foss has her elbows on the table and her hands pointed at me, like she's trying to make a big sell, "Think, if I have a sheet and I nail it to the wall, and you want it down, what do you do?"

"Uhh, pull it down?" I say, biting my lip.

A slap on my arm from her pale hand as encouragement, "Yes! So, you can pull the pencil toward you. How else can you move it?"

I scratch the back of my head, trying to avoid the stitches. It itches so bad, "Grab the bottom?"

"That's still pulling. Let's say you want to move it to me. What do you do?" She says shifting her weight, making her old lady sneakers squeak.

"I hit the top towards you." I answer, still thinking about the itch. Not only is it the healing from having my head cut open again, but I'm starting to get hair, slowly and surely.

"Another word for hit."

"Punch?"

A hand to her mouth as she thinks how to say this, "No. Let's see. What do you do when you're in kindergarten, kids always get each other to the ground by. . . what?"

"Pushing?"

Two stubby fingers point at me, "Yes! Exactly! So, combine them! How can you move the pencil?"

"Pushing?"

A smile across her face, "Yes! And what was the first one?"

I bite my lip, "Pulling?"

"Put them together." She slaps her hands together to a small thud.

I'm not sure, and I don't want to be wrong. "Pushing, pulling?"

"Pushing and pulling."

"Okay."

She sits back, puts her hands atop her stomach, "That's force. Force is an interaction between two objects that's either a push or a pull."

"So, pulling and pushing is force?"

She doesn't sigh, doesn't close the book. She doesn't say, "Remember?" She never makes me feel stupid; though, I feel stupid; it's not because of her. She wants to encourage and egg me on.

"Yes, but what must be involved?"

I move my fist to my mouth in a thinking motion, putting my teeth on the back of my index finger, "What?"

She holds up the pencil with her hand, tilting it toward me, "What is pushing or pulling?"

"Me?"

Her voice tilts up in an attempt at leading me to the answer, "Sometimes, but if I have a car accident, what is being pushed or pulled?"

"The cars."

When she moves excitedly, her white shirt with the bright, pink horizontal stripes, swishes with her.

"Yes, so it doesn't have to involve a person. It's two objects. It might a person. A person can exert force or have force exerted on them, but a tree falling is exerting a force on the ground when it lands."

I'm trying so hard; she can see this as I stare at the pencil, "Okay, let me see. A force. . . is a. . . can you say it again?"

She reaches down in her bag and takes out another pencil and holds it next to the first one.

"So, think of it as an interaction between two objects. Two objects can either interact or what? What else can they do?"

A silence, a pause, I have both hands on my head, trying, hoping, believing I can get it, "If they don't interact, I mean. . . I guess. . . they. . . hmm."

I hate it. I hate it. I hate it. I used to be so good at this class. This class was a breeze, and now, how am I struggling so much? Mrs. Foss isn't seeing that. She keeps her soft, steady tone, like she's soothing an infant back to sleep, "If they don't do something, they do..."

"Nothing?"

"Bingo!" she yells excitedly, banging the table, and then, she continues, her hands up and acting out her physics lesson, "So, if they are doing something, they are interacting. Again, think of this pencil. You can pull it or push; you can have a force on it."

I want to put my head on the table and go to sleep, but I think I know this, "A push or pull." Her eyes show her care, as she tries to get me there, "Between?"

Oh God, uh let's see here, "Objects?"

"How many?"

Another three second pause as I search and search, "Two." A big pat on my back, "You got it!"

She's beaming at me, her chubby cheeks arched in a big grin, her strands of black hair mostly lain down now. I hope this is it. I can't take it anymore. I feel so stupid, so dumb, so ready to be done. Please, God, let this agony end.

Mrs. Foss looks at her watch, "Okay, so I think we have time for this."

I wish I could say that the next thirty minutes were enjoyable; I wish I could say I started to get it, and my abilities in physics improved, and it ended with a tearful hug as Mrs. Foss cried into my shoulder, "You've got it, Will. You're back." Wouldn't that be nice?

No, no, I do not think it will end even close to back to how it was before, nowhere near, and this becomes even clearer when we try to practice applying what we're talking about to Newton's Second Law of Motion: force equals mass times acceleration. It becomes obvious that I have struggles with division. DIVISION. This was what, second or third grade for me? I took algebra and geometry in middle school, and sure, math did not come as easy to me as it did in elementary school, as easy as it did for some of my advanced peers, but I did it. I got As or, maybe, Bs. I don't remember. It was middle school, and as long as no teacher was calling my parents, and I was getting credit for a class, what was the difference between an A and a B? It wasn't the same in high school because, at least for me, high school is when grades felt like life or death. I must get an A. If I don't get an A in this one class, I won't get into a good college, and then, it's time to start looking for the bridge I'm going to sleep under.

I knew what it was to struggle in school, sure. My junior year, I took AP computer science. My teacher was taking an online course in programming while she was teaching us how to program, and, well, I'll leave that up to you about how that went.

But this was on-level physics; people pass this class who don't even get into college. How could I ever get back to my former self if I couldn't do well with this? If I can't divide, how in the heck can I get anywhere close to where I used to be? I mean, dang son, don't you need to know how to divide and multiply to navigate daily life? Waiters are going to remember me, either for my stinginess or my generosity.

Mom trots quickly down the stairs with the thump-thump-thump of her rubber soles. She turns into the kitchen with her morning, chipper energy, "How did it go?"

I look down as Mrs. Foss smiles for me, "We made some good progress. Covered the major vocabulary. We had some trouble with the equations, but I think we can get those down."

I love her for sugarcoating it for Mom. I love her for leaving out my staring at a simple problem of division for a full ten seconds without saying anything. Do you realize how long ten seconds is? Do you have any idea how painful ten seconds of silence is? The next time you're having a conversation with your romantic partner or close friend, just be silent for a solid ten seconds. It is agonizing. Most of all, I love her for smiling and making my mom feel like there's no problem. Though, I'm sure Mom knows that a little trouble means more like real trouble. It's not something I would say I can articulate. It's a feeling; maybe, it's my insecurities creeping in, so I think everyone thinks of me as stupid as I feel, or maybe, it's that sixth sense for disappointment. You can call me a medium for disappointment. I'm like a psychic for sighs.

So, after a lunch of eggs (of course), Mom makes me use this hand strengthener on my left hand. You know the kind? It's a yellow plastic thing with a black-rubber grip and then plastic buttons with springs, so you can isolate pushing down each finger? It's supposed to strengthen my left hand, and I don't know if it works or not. All I know is, there is no rest for the weary, even if you have fresh screws in your skull. If there's a moment of downtime, Debbie Carter will find something for you to do. Right now, I am so very annoyed by her. And, yes, like, okay, I get it. Her pushing me at Shepherd is part of what helped me get this far, but I'm tired. I just had my head cut open and put back together with screws—that kind of tired— but no rest for the weary, I guess. I try to send this message of my exhaustion to Mom by showing her my drooping eyeballs, my sinking face; though, she sits at the chair next to mine on the square table and matter-of-factly responds, "Well, now, for English, Mrs. Williams said we need to read some *Twelfth Night*."

I blink twice, "Do we have to?"

With that, she folds her arms, crosses her legs, and offers, "I mean, if you don't want to graduate, and you want to live at home with your dad and me. How does that sound?"

I squirm a little. She does not know this is my secret fear, not my belief—like, yes, I believe I will get better and go to college, but there it is again, that secret fear that questions everything, picks apart every hope, eats away at the supporting beams of my optimism, devours the floorboards, chomping out holes in the foundation as dust spins in the air.

"Okay," I sigh. I know there's no use fighting.

"So," she says, flipping to the first page in a blue, white, and black No Fear Shakespeare edition of the play.

"Thank God," I think. I don't want to have my English abilities questioned; that was something I was good at before the accident. I don't want that taken away as well. Physics sucks, but I can take that, you know? Math was never my strongest subject, so it's better to see diminishing abilities there, but English? I was the star English student. Please don't let that go as well. That's like telling [1]Rob Gronkowski he can't play football. He won't have anything to do with his life. Gronkowski can't be like a fourth-grade teacher or something. He's Gronk.

After she skips through the introduction, we take up parts in the cast. I try and have fun with it. I hate that I keep going back to the modern translation. I should be able to grasp it. I mean, I'd done Shakespeare before and done well. I did a monologue for Malvolio once in my theater one class.

At least, though, it's still nice to get my energy up for something. We're not even finished with act 1 when the house phone rings.

"Hold on. One sec. Why don't you read ahead and tell me what happens," she says, and then, answers the phone with a, "Hello. Don?" And takes the call in the living room.

Even though she's trying to keep a hushed voice, I can still hear her saying, "Don, I don't know why the insurance won't pay."

Oh God, what is it now? No, no. I hate that I'm expensive, that I've cost Mom and Dad so much money. I lower my head, close my eyes, and in my head, I'm on my knees, "God, make the insurance pay for whatever it is. Please God, help it get worked out. Don't let me make Mom and Dad's lives worse." I almost hang up, almost say, "Amen," but my heart's pulling, beating for me to submit my requests before the throne, "And, God?" I swallow, pause. Am I being selfish? Is he going to answer? Does he care about this? "Help me get better. Amen."

It's the weebly, wobbly journey of belief that I'm on, a very honest one. I realize that doubts are part of believing. The back-and-forth of hope and despair, of an answer to no answer, is just part of what it is to have faith.

When you look at everyone else, you feel like you're doing it wrong, like a relationship with God and belief in him is a straight line, and if your line is zigzagging from start to finish, you're not really a Christian. Or maybe, I perceive that from the polished believers, the ones listening to Christian radio and sporting bible verses tattooed on their shoulders. Maybe, it's my insecurity, but the feeling that you don't have it all together is the thing that makes you question, in a little space at the back of your mind, if you've even had a real encounter with God. Or are you just fooling yourself? Funny thing about it is that the tiny, little question is it is the proof of a real relationship. It wouldn't be faith if it was a simple belief. If you encountered God, and it was like you got a photo with a celebrity, and if somebody was like, "There's no way you met [2]George Clooney," you could easily say, "Oh, really? Here's the picture."

That's not faith. Faith is believing in something you cannot see, and that whisper in the back of your mind sewing doubts is what makes faith necessary. And me? That whisper is kicking, stomping, having a tantrum, trying to pull me away, whenever I'm praying.

But at least, in the story I remember, I died. I lost my heart-beat, and, maybe, God wants me to believe that story because, right now, I'm struggling. I'm reading Shakespeare on my own, and I can't remember what I just read the page before. Even with my Ritalin, my mind is a Ping-Pong ball, and I straighten the pages by pulling on the book as though I might rip it in half and focus really hard, my black plastic glasses falling to the bridge of my nose as all glasses are wont to do. "Focus, just focus," I breathe to myself, but before I know it, my thoughts are on to the next thing, and it's not always anxieties and insecurities. Often, it's random things, like, "I wonder when I will get to go to outpatient, will it be nice? Who will be there? Where's it at? Is it at the hospital? I hope it's not at the hospital, because I don't ever want to go back there," and on and on.

In the span of an hour, I have tackled eight pages, and I'm not sure what's happened, and I want to know; God, I wish I could remember. I need to get back to it, but. . . I need to get back and try again. I need to go back, and I open it up, and I try again, and I get mixed up, and I'm tired, and I'm ready to lie down, and I want to go to bed. I can do that at least.

"Mom!?" I call to her from the kitchen table. I'm done, so simply done.

"Yes!?" She answers from the dining room, where she is on her computer. I can tell that from hearing her hunt and peck on her keyboard.

"Can I take a nap?" I try to say in the most pathetic way possible.

She's focused on whatever it is she's doing. Researching how to fight insurance? Planning for when she goes back to work?

I smile at her sweet reply, "Of course, honey. Come on in here."

So, I take my feet and scooch my chair from the carpet to the hardwood, and I hear her say, not even turning her head to me, "Use your arms."

A sigh, an eye roll, but I put my hands to the black metal rim on the outside of the wheel and push, my right hand doing more work than my left, so I stop, push just with my left hand, a little bit from the right. I try for more from my left and then, a little bit from the right, and it is a sight to see, me zigzagging through the kitchen to the dining room.

Mom is sitting at the end of the table near the back

window, working on something on her computer. I would be lying if I said I cared what it was or about anything other than going straight to bed. The day is shot; my mind is shot, and I want nothing more than to lie down.

"You ready for a nap?" Mom says, turning from her computer.

I know I probably should read more Shakespeare. I know I shouldn't give up, but I just want to do the thing where I don't have to think, where no one questions my doing it, the thing I can do by my lonesome, the thing that can stop all of these negative thoughts.

Mom locks my wheelchair, grabs the buckle of the puke-colored belt, now with a speckling of brown and red food stains. She'll wash it soon, but now, she helps me stand and, with three steps, helps me land safely in a quick thud on the bed. I'm the worst at sitting quietly, always with an announcing thump, as my skinny body lands with the help of gravity.

As I turn on my back, she asks me, "What happened in act 1?"

I smile as I turn to look at her looking over me, "British things."

A blank look, "Will."

I grab the comforter and pull it over me, "Can I tell you after the nap?"

"Do you remember?" She asks with her hands on her hips.

I turn to the side, away from her, facing the wall, "No."

I know she's sad for me, and I like that she cares, but I hate to feel pity. I hate it so much. I don't say that, but I stare at the yellow wall and at the nightstand with the small glass lamp about the size of a spray bottle, with a little glass lamp shade on it, with clear white plastic beads on it. I want to nap for a long time. I want to nap until dinner, so I can eat dinner and get ready for bed and not have to do anything the rest of the day.

She's still looking down at me as she says, "Okay. We'll talk about it after."

And she turns to walk back to her computer. I hear her unplug it, take the computer and the charger, and sit down at the kitchen table, and the typing continues.

I roll over to one side, and my mind is spinning, "What if I can't figure it out? What if I don't understand *Twelfth Night*? Will I be able to get the work done for it? What if I fail the major assessment on it? What if I fail the class? What if I don't graduate? What if I have to graduate in 2009? What if I don't graduate high school at all? What if I don't get better? I have to get better. I'm going to get better. I am going to recover. I am going to get back. What if I don't? And, since my accident, this is why it is hard to fall asleep.

I wish I could have one of those pain pills. I know I should not take them to fall asleep, and my mom is so worried about me having an unhealthy relationship with pain medicine that she cut off me off quickly. But I don't want to get out of bed. If I get out of bed, I have to do work, and if I do work, I have to feel stupid, and, well, I don't want to feel stupid. I want to lie here and close my eyes, close my eyes and try to believe, try to have faith, try to trust God, try to have hope that tomorrow will better than today.

I know. I know. I know one bad day of tutoring, one bad day of schoolwork does not mean my life is over, but what about one stroke? One brain injury? I used to be on top of the damn world, and now, I am most certainly under it, and what do I do with that?

This week, I will go to Shepherd Pathways. They will help me walk. Then, two weeks after that, I think, or is it the same week? Or a week after? At some point soon, I will go back to school. At some point, I will feel better. At some point, I will get better. Focus on Pathways. That's the hope.

11

PATHWAYS

After a weekend of searching on my laptop for summaries of *Twelfth Night*, utilizing the original text in my No Fear Shakespeare and rediscovering SparkNotes, I am actually able to tackle two of the worksheets for *Twelfth Night*. That night as I lie in my bed, I have my silver iPod Mini, and I'm listening to a Christmas mix I made, and [1]Dan Wilson's "What a Year for a New Year" comes on with the major piano keys hitting slowly, and I close my eyes as the drums kick in slow and steady.

And I smile halfway. Yes, Dan, you have no idea how much I am ready for a new year, how much I want to have everything back. I can't accept this new normal, this new me. It's hard to accept yourself as someone you don't desire, a person you cannot stand to be.

No, I will not accept. I will get back to school, and I will go to Pathways, and they will help me heal, and I will graduate high school, and I will go to college, and then, I will be successful. Maybe. And after I wake up and have a bagel and sausage (and reassure my mother I do not need eggs today), and after I take my regimen of pills and vitamins, and after Dad takes me upstairs to get showered and dressed, and after I get taken back downstairs and put back in this wheelchair, and after my mom looks on her computer to figure out where Shepherd Pathways is, after all of this—I am put in the car, and my wheelchair is folded and put in the trunk, and we are on our way there. I cannot wait. I am so ready to be there and ready to be walking. I am going to tell them how I walked in December, and if there's like an advanced therapy group at Shepherd Pathways, they should probably put me with them because I can already walk.

"Are you excited?" My mom asks, as we merge onto a crowded highway.

"I am." I say, looking down, and after a pause, I add, "I can't wait to walk."

"I know." She says as she checks her mirrors and tries to get over. It's weird, it's only 10 a.m., and still, there are so many cars on the highway.

"We should've left earlier," she says, as she successfully makes it over. She glances at me briefly, her black plastic rimmed sunglasses on.

"Yeah." I'm trying to figure out how far we're going down the road.

We pull into the parking lot. With a brick exterior and a glass entrance, it almost looks like a school, except for the sliding doors of course, and then, if you look to the left side, you can see windows curving around the edge, so that part looks like a fancy midtown office building. Either way, the grounds are kept up, and even though it's January, and the lawn care in Georgia is mostly done by Mother Nature, the bushes in the front look green, while the little bit of grass is yellowish brown.

Soon, Mom is wheeling me through the sliding glass doors through the front door, and we are inside. It feels big, with a brown faux-tile floor and a big brown front desk with a white top that you might see at a hotel or a doctor's office, and a sweet, small woman with a splattering of greys in her hair, old and skinny enough that you can see the veins in her neck, looks up and smiles, "Hello there, welcome to Pathways."

I'm looking around and taking it all in, looking at the grey walls, the high ceilings, and the fluorescent lights and thinking this looks more like an office park than a medical facility.

"Will Carter here for his first day," Mom says, pushing me forward.

"Sure thing! Welcome, Will," the woman at the desk says with a sparkle of genuine enthusiasm and kindness.

"Thank you. Excited to be here." I say, trying to match her smile.

"I'll let Greg know you're here," she says, as she dials the phone and calls Greg, and we take the usual clipboard of papers to fill out.

Mom gives them to me as I use my feet to bring myself to the couch where Mom chooses to sit. She sighs a, "Will."

I give her the same smile I gave the receptionist, "Don't worry, Mom. I'll be out of this wheelchair soon."

She then gestures with her left arm for me to take my left arm down. My left arm has curled up, my hand to my chest, without me realizing it. It does that. It's the weirdest thing. I can't, of course, just take it down. I can't comply with her reminder by doing what she's asked. I curl it up intentionally into an almost chicken wing. "Which arm are you talking about?"

With an eye roll, she picks up a magazine, "Let me know if you need help with those forms."

"Sure," and I go back to them. Of course, I need help with all my numbers: weight, height, all of that. And then, my signature, after so many forms, looks like an echocardiogram, a loop, a squiggle up, down, a squiggle up, a squiggle down, a squiggle up, and done. I have signed so many forms that my signature, which at one time I would painstakingly try and make look as much like Will Carter as possible, now looks like a W, and then, it would appear I died shortly after writing the W, the line going off after a squiggle or two.

"Hey, Will."

It is the same Greg from the Shepherd Center, blue Shepherd polo, khakis, and the same total dad energy. He ushers us back, through yellow wooden door, down the faux-hardwood floors and off-white walls with wooden trim to the faux-hardwood therapy gym, with four windows in the back and three therapy mats against the wall, with the same blue padding, the same brown, wooden legs, and there are two grey plastic tables with four grey plastic chairs under each. I know exactly what this is, as I see the same workout equipment against the wall perpendicular, and I know I'm not going to enjoy this place either.

There's a whole room, separated by two pillars, with more mats, more equipment, and windows on that wall as well. The light comes through these windows, and the Georgia afternoon sun really lights the place up; they could do well to turn off these fluorescents.

"This is the therapy gym."

I see an overweight, not terribly but noticeably, woman in her fifties with curly brown hair come over, wearing exercises pants and a pink Shepherd shirt, smiling wide, "And is this him, Greg?"

Greg gives the laugh that every dad in their forties and fifties can give, "Who is him?"

Rubbing her hands together, Siri looks side to side, "Our next victim—I mean, uh, patient."

That laugh, and then, a pat on my back, "This is Will

Carter. Will, this is Siri; she's going to be your physical therapist."

Siri sticks a hand out, "Nice to meet you, Will!"

I shake it, noticing the black brace on it, canvas and Velcro. The canvas is rough to the touch, and I try and figure out, as I do with most therapists, whether I like her or not. I can see her pants have a green stripe down either side, and this coupled with the red streaks in her hair give her the kooky-aunt vibe. I figure she might be all right.

"Nice to meet you."

She dismisses this, "You can do better than that."

"What?"

She pumps two fists in front of her, "Give it more energy."

A hand to my mouth, "What do you mean?"

Pointing at me, she commands me, "You can say, 'Nice to meet you,' like you mean it."

I agree, "Yeah."

She sticks out her hand, "So try again."

"Nice to meet you!" I yell, as I shake her hand.

"That'll do."

Greg nods and bites his lip as he knows, and she knows, that they have nothing more to talk about, "Siri, you've got this. I'll continue to take Mom around."

Mom looks at me, gives me those it's-my-first-day-of-school eyes, "All right, I'll see you in three hours."

My eyebrows furrow, "Three hours?"

She sighs, nods; she knows she's told this to me, and I've forgotten, but I can't believe I'm going to be here for three hours.

"Well, Mom, we will see you soon." Siri says, ushering Mom out, with which she complies, looking at me, before she does so, "See you at three. Love you."

"Love you, Mom."

Siri wastes no time as she finds a rolling stool, brings it to her with her foot, and sits down on it, her elbows on her knees, her torso hunched over. I can see there are five other patients in the room: an older lady working with a smiling blonde therapist, a young guy laying on the mat with a middle-aged woman with brown hair sitting on the mat next to him, an older man in the wheelchair at the arm press with a younger man next to him, and we all pretend like we're not in the room with each other; no one eavesdrops on the others' conversations, and we all focus on what we're doing. Siri isn't looking at anyone else; she's looking at me, and her eyes look heavy in her pudgy face.

"What do you want to do?" she says, serious, direct. She has this vibe like a substitute teacher who doesn't want to be played with.

"Take a nap." I retort quite honestly.

Her hands on her hips, "Ha, ha, mister funny man, but seriously, what are your goals?"

"I want to walk."

She holds up her index finger and looks like she's counting, "Okay, we can do that. What else?"

"Use stairs by myself."

Her face is straight, no real indication of her feelings as she adds her middle finger up with her index, "Okay, that one will come before walking. What else?"

I scratch my buzzed hair, "Uhhh. . . I don't know."

She steps forward, "What about standing?"

"Yeah, that would be great."

And she holds up her ring finger and shows me the three, "Okay, let's do that."

"Okay."

She transitions me to the mat, and oh, how I remember this plushy rectangle so well.

"Now steady your feet," she says as she holds onto my gait belt in front of me.

I put my feet where they need to be, like she said, concentrating, hoping to get it right.

"And push down with your hands, as you put your weight into your feet."

I work to push, and I stand, and I'm doing it, I'm almost upright, and I. . . I start to topple over, but she catches me and sits me back down. I look at her face. Have you ever met someone who looks like they've lived a life full of stories, of tears, disappointment, and darkness, just by the lines and the heaviness of their face? Sure, there is some fat in those cheeks, but I'm not talking about age here, more about pain, about struggle, about long nights and early mornings, about loss and hardship. Siri has that face. Maybe, maybe that explains the gruff exterior, and maybe that explains the "I don't have time for your BS" substitute teacher vibe. She seems sweet and like she cares, but she also makes me feel like she would fight me if I challenged her.

"What happened?" she asks, as she sits down next to me.

"What?" I don't like these vague questions. What happened? When? Today? Well, when I woke up, I had to poop really bad. What do you mean what happened?

"With the fall, why did you have trouble?"

I have to think on this, remember back, think back to just now which is usually a struggle, but I offer, "I guess I just, like, I put all of my weight forward, and it made me fall."

She nods and stands, demonstrating, and I'm looking at her white sneakers, the only part of the outfit that doesn't seem to fit. White sneakers say responsible older lady, not kooky aunt, but she takes two fingers and points them to her eyes and then to her feet in a "watch this" motion, "Okay, let's try again, but this time, put your weight on the heel. You see that? If I put my weight on my toes," which she does, and she starts to lean forward, "you see I'm starting to go forward. . ."

"Yeah."

She shifts her weight back to her heels, "And here, I'm stable."

A nod. I want to be able to do that.

"Okay, you try," and she stands back up, takes the belt, and I focus on my heels. C'mon, Will, you've got this. You've got this. Back of the foot. And, I stand, and I've got my weight on my heels, and I'm doing it. I'm standing on my own, sort of—I mean, sure, Siri's got my gait belt, but that's more for safety—I'm standing, and I'm not leaning on anybody; no one is holding me up. I'm standing!

She's smiling, "Now, do you think you can take a step?"

I look at her, unsure, "You mean it?"

"Just try one."

I nod, as I say, "A step," clarifying.

A double fist pump from Siri, "Yeah!"

"Walking?"

"Isn't that what you want?"

"Yeah."

"Well come on, you've got this! It's not like you're walking on the moon. Just one step."

"There's a great comedy bit. . ."

And I'll spare you, but there is a great joke by the comedian [2]Brian Regan about how he wants to be one of the astronauts who walked on the moon, so he can one-up anyone in any conversation, and I do it verbatim. Don't ask me why. I have no idea, but my brain might struggle to remember people's names, might stumble with recalling the details of the day, might even falter with the recovery of information mentioned to me only minutes before, but stand-up comedy bits? Those come to me through a pneumatic tube, and with a whoosh, it comes to the front of my brain verbatim.

She gives a legitimate, gut level laugh, "Okay, that's good. What's his name?"

"Brian Regan," I say with a smile, happy to be making a connection.

"Brian Regan. I will have to remember that."

A moment, as new patients start coming through the doorway to the gym.

Siri looks to the clock, "Shit—I mean, crap. Is it time?"

A tall, darker skinned man in a black Nike tank top and basketball shorts looks around, and in a West African accent asks Siri, "I have physical therapy now. Are you Siri?"

She smiles in a forced sweetness, "Yes, just finishing up. I'll be right with you," and she turns to me in a softer voice says, "I'm sorry I lost track of time. We'll do more of that, maybe even some stairs, next time."

"It's okay."

"Ready?"

I nod as I stand, and she helps to guide me to my wheel-chair, which I land in with a thud.

Siri looks around the gym, "Do you know who your next person is?"

And Caitlin, the skinny, smiling, sandy blonde from inpatient, waves as she comes in, carrying her water bottle and a folder. She's somehow smiling, while looking apologetic, a skill only acquired in the South, "That's me. Sorry, Siri."

And she takes the back of my wheelchair and pushes me put of the gym into the hallway with the white walls and wood paneling, and we are in a room that feels more like a doctor's office than anything else, only space enough for a mat, a table and chairs, a counter, and a sink.

It's pale and dull, and I see there is a bin with the same eye exercise tools from before: a string with beads on it, glasses with a red lens in one eye and a green lens in the other, clear cards with black letters and numbers on them. I see a blank wall, and above, I see a projector. Are we watching movies in occupational therapy? Please say yes.

"Long time no see," Caitlin says with sweetness, a little bit of a drawl sneaking in there.

No matter how hard some Atlantans try, they can't quite rid themselves of their Southern roots.

"I know," I say with a smile, my forehead glistening in the light, my acne really starting to flourish as the dots on my face are even more evident in the bright light. Additionally, I really don't know what happened, but after my accident, my acne became more intense.

"You better remember me," Caitlin says, shaking her finger at me as she smiles her extraordinarily white smile at me.

She's short and sweet, but I've seen her be firm and direct when she had to be. A little shorter than me, just about as skinny, she doesn't have quite the physical presence of Siri. "You wouldn't happen to work at Shepherd Center, would you?"

"Will."

"Don't worry, I remember you, Caitlin."

The hard part about being sarcastic and having a brain injury is people don't know when to take you seriously; when you pretend to be stupid, people aren't sure if you're actually intellectually deficient. It kills me.

She gives me a pat on the back, sits down in one of the grey plastic chairs; in front of her on the table is a manila folder with green and purple sticky notes on the front. She opens it up and looks at some of the papers in the front.

I am so tired of being defined by papers, boxed in by little tests given to me, whose scores determine exactly how well I am healing. I guess it's the best gauge of objective recovery, but it also feels so limiting. To put who I am, essentially, into a scaled score misses that part of me that is beyond these tests. I feel, at least, that I have healed more than these tests seem to indicate.

Crossing her legs, she asks, "What do you think you need to work on?"

"A heckuva lot," I smile.

She gives a pretend playful punch in the arm, "But, seriously."

My glasses slide down my nose, as I have my head cocked forward, "This is OT. . . uh. . . let me think." I have to push those plastic frames back up. I look at the white linoleum with specks of grey in it.

Caitlin sits forward, engaged, her hands on her jeans, one moves up to offer a suggestion, "What about your vision?"

I cock my head, raise a finger to my temple, "My left eye."

"Good."

Another silence. OT was more useful to me than speech therapy, but it was nowhere near physical therapy, so I really have to think. "My left hand."

"Very good."

"God. . . uh. . ."

"What do you think vision and hand dexterity would help out with?"

"What?"

"What do you think your hand-eye coordination can help out with?"

I'm searching. Also, I know I've said this, but please, people, stop playing games with disabled people. They hate you for it. Now, don't get me wrong. I don't dislike Caitlin; I'm incredibly annoyed with her in this moment. Just tell me. Don't make me feel stupid. Just tell me.

"Something you want to do?"

I'm thinking, searching, running my right-hand fingers along the smoothness of my exercise pants. Caitlin is pretending to be doing something and using both hands to do it. "Driving?" I think as it clearly looks like she's miming a steering wheel.

"Now, I'm not saying right at the start, but it is definitely something we can work on here."

My face is glowing; driving is freedom. Driving means I don't need to ask my parents for a ride; it means I can go when and where I want, and I would feel much more like a young adult, rather than the dependent child I am.

Caitlin notices my smile and puts up her hands as her face gets serious, her small pink lips moving into a straight line, "Now, it's only a simulator, and you sure as heck would have to do any car driving at the actual Shepherd Center, but it's a start."

"Sounds great." I'm kind of disappointed it doesn't involve an actual car, but I'm still excited, nonetheless.

"Good."

She wants us to be on the same page; I can tell that. She doesn't want me to think I can get too much out of the outpatient experience. She's opening her mouth when I offer, "You don't think I can use your car?"

A smile, a headshake, and an eye roll. The trifecta of appreciating sarcasm but not wanting to admit it.

"Now, I figure let's start with vision."

She takes a remote out of her pocket, turns on the projector, walks over and flips the light switch, has me take off my glasses, and for the next fifteen minutes, she gives me an eye exam. This includes her giving me what look like plastic spoons before they get indents, just circles on plastic sticks, and I cover my left eye; not a problem, I get to the second to last row. She asks me to cover my right eye, and. . . I can get the second row from the top.

"Can you read the next line?" she asks so kindly.

"X. . . no. . . K. . ." I hate any and all tests.

"No worries at all. We know where we're starting from," she says as she goes to flip the lights back on, and I put my glasses back on, feeling defeated.

My vision's never been great, but it's never been that bad. Then, she does a periphery test where she sees how soon I notice her fingers in my field of vision.

"I'm going to bring my index finger out by the side of your head. I need you to look forward and tell me when you see it in your field of vision, not the whole finger, just when you see a hint of it."

Look forward. Do not look to the side. Stay focused. This is just a test. It's okay.

She starts on the right side, and this is not too bad.

"Now."

"Good."

"Now."

"Now."

"Great job, Will," she says, as she takes a pause.

I know it's going to get harder. Everything having to do with the left side of my body is worse.

"I'm going to try the left side now. Don't worry if you don't see it. Just try your best."

Try your best, but there is an outcome we're desiring. I guess that last part is always implied, but it's still annoying because it makes it sound like effort will produce the desired result. Just try your best, and everything's going to be okay.

As a teacher at my high school used to say, "Try your best. No one can ask for more, nor should they expect less." I never actually had a class with him, but my friends did, and they said he used to say that before every test. Just do your best. What if my best gets me a 53?

And her finger gets almost in front of my left eye, when I say, "Now."

A sigh. I know. It's bad. I definitely should have got it, but I didn't see it. I wanted to see it. I wanted so badly to have seen it, but. . . I just didn't. It's so hard to explain having abilities taken from you and then clawing and failing to get them back.

Caitlin's soft voice is almost a whisper, "It's okay. Let's try again. I know you have some vision loss in this eye but try your best to let me know when you see my finger."

Another seven seconds pass before I say, "Now."

"We'll continue this. Don't worry."

Again, another helpful phrase. Kind of like, "be careful," a phrase that offers no assurance. Don't worry? Okay, that's all my anxiety needed, a little assurance. Of course, I want to get better because I want to get out. I want to be done. I look at the clock, but of course, I'm not as stealthy as I would like to be, and Caitlin notices; her blue eyes look at mine, and I know she knows I'm ready for this to be over.

"Not yet, buddy. We've still got fifteen more minutes," she says as she crouches, opens the grey cabinet, and takes out a red box which looks like a board game.

She lays it on the table, and I see a cartoon of Cavity Sam (a naked man, minus the genitalia of course, with a surprised look on his face, probably because he's naked in a room full of strangers), as we prepare to play ³Operation.

"Have you ever played this game before?" She asks, as she sits in the chair next to me.

"Yeah. A long, long time ago," I say, and I don't know how to tell her I've always been bad at it, even before my accident.

"Well, we're going to play today. The only catch is we're going to use our left hands. Deal?"

"Deal."

And my left hand is shaky. When I strain it, I look like I'm detoxing from heroin, but I pick up the tweezers, and I strain, going for the funny bone, and buzz, buzz, buzz.

"Dang." I lament, dropping my utensil.

Caitlin takes it up and successfully removes the funny bone with a, "Take that."

Did she just want to play Operation, so she could trash talk a brain-injured kid in a wheelchair? And my left hand is shaking up a storm as I go to pick up the tweezers, and I get them, but again, I fail to get his ribs, and I fail to get the next thing, and I want to be done. I'm so ready, and I know Caitlin is sweet, so I'm trying my best not to project this through my body language or an eye roll or anything.

"When do you go back to school again?" She asks, lowering her head to meet my overly focused grimace as I work to help save a cartoon man who has more going on than I can fix—what with his Three-Stooges haircut, clown nose, and missing genitalia.

"Next week. I think."

"That's great! Are you excited?"

"Yeah, I just want to graduate."

"That's good."

I get the wrench, "Huzzah!" I declare with exuberance as I take it out, and it falls to the table with a little clink.

"Still counts," I say as Caitlin nods.

And then, people start crowding by the door, and it's like school; you know it's time for a class change by the number of people in the hall.

"Well, this was good. Let me get you over to speech."

And it's an easy push across the hall, and this room is almost identical, two tables, grey chairs, cabinets, a sink, and the same shiny floor, and boxes in the corner. The table is clean except for two black binders. There's a painting of a duck flying in front of a blue background on the wall opposite the cabinets. The table is right under this painting, and I still don't understand the décor choice. Is this duck supposed to be me? Flying to freedom? Please God grant me flight. I don't want to work on speech.

"Remember me?" I see Sara's face pop in, brown hair, pale skin, and almost the same Shepherd shirt and jeans combo as Caitlin, except the jeans are a little darker.

"Do I know you?" I ask. I try to stay as deadpan as possible.

She steps back, "Will. It's me, Sara."

"I know. I know. Joking." I say, breaking with a smile.

"Hey now, no jokes allowed," Sara says, as she sits down at the table, and Caitlin leaves with a, "See you tomorrow!"

I'm never quite sure what to do with Sara. We never really clicked, and I don't know if we will.

"Just so you know, halfway through, we'll be joined by Horus."

"Okay."

And it feels like I'm in school. I've never much enjoyed speech therapy. Maybe, it's because I feel like I know I need physical therapy. I'm in a wheelchair. With occupational therapy, I know my left fingers shake when I try to button a shirt. I know that I struggle to tie my own shoes. I know my left eye periphery needs to improve if I'm ever going to drive again. I have clear obvious markers of aspects of my body that I need to improve, but speech? I never had trouble talking before the accident (my family is more than happy to tell you that), and I don't have trouble talking after. Some people lose the ability to form words after a stroke. There was that guy Gerald at inpatient. He would shake his head no, and he would make these weird gasping-like noises, like he knew what he was trying to say, but it was in a language he invented, so nobody could understand him. So, I never had much of a fondness for speech therapy. Gerald? He needs speech therapy. I need to let my brain heal, and then, my short-term memory will come back.

She scratches her nose, as she tries to start our session off right.

"You ready for school?"

"I think so." I nod, one hand scratches the brown shade sprouting across my skull.

She leans in as she opens the binder and flips to a blank page, pen in hand. "What do you think you need to work on?"

"I guess the big thing is memory."

She writes this down and looks at me with her chestnut eyes. I guess being in her early thirties, she feels she needs to have this authoritative tone to stay in charge. I look for the clock, white with big black numbers, and what? Forty more minutes?

"Memory. Yes, I would say that's good. What else do you think you need to work on?"

She sits with her pad in front of her and her legs crossed like she's my psychologist or something.

"Uhh. . . I don't know. That's my biggest struggle." I'm drawing a blank here. Really. Look, I'm trying to play ball, but mostly, I want to walk and drive. As much as I hate who I am mentally now, hate that I struggle to remember the events of the day, struggle with my physics homework, say many awkward things that bring conversation to complete halt just because I'm trying to participate, I don't think there's much speech can do for me. It's going to get better with time, right? Isn't that how healing happens? She looks at me intently as if I'm going to start suddenly spouting off ten additional things I should want to work on. I stare back at her. Blink. Blink. Blink.

"Okay. Memory. Yes, but how is your reading?" she says as

she opens her binder and flips to a page a third of the way into it.

I mean, I've done a tiny bit of reading, "Good. I guess."

"Well, let's test it," and she flips the page to a passage, slides it over to me.

God, why? School doesn't start until next week, and I am still doing all these tests. Why? Plus, the result is never, "Wow, Will! You're doing great!" It's always, "Will, you suck, and here is why." So, yeah, perfect, let's do another test. That's exactly what I want.

Of course, I say none of that but, instead offer, "Okay."

And it's a story about a boy who has lost his dog, and it's pretty straightforward, pretty clear. He's upset about it; he's looking for his dog, and then, he finds out it's dead. I think. I'm not sure. I'll have to go back, but my mind is getting distracted; halfway through, I start looking at the questions on the next page, as a tall dark-skinned man in a wheelchair appears in the doorway, "Hello, Sara?" he asks.

There is a hint of an accent, but it's only a pinch of one. He is older, sixties, maybe even seventies, with lines across his face and splashes of grey in his hair; he looks like he has lived a hard life, and I am so interested to talk to him.

"You must be Horus. Come on in."

And he wheels himself in quite gracefully, not the slow sputtered motion of me trying to use my wheelchair, but powerful thrusts from his arms that glide the chair quickly over.

"Horus this is Will. Will, Horus."

We shake hands and smile. He has a firm grasp and big, weathered hands. He wears a black shirt, no signs of who made it, and black exercises pants—all black and simple. It's the most distinguished look I've seen from a patient here.

He offers a "A pleasure to meet you, Will," his words flowing with a smooth lilt of a Jamaican accent.

I nod, "Nice to meet you."

He doesn't slouch, but he sits up straight, and he looks like if it weren't for his wheelchair, he would be commanding this room. But we have no time to talk as Sara gets him started on a test as well, and I'm working hard. I know I'm supposed to be done soon, and I want to finish, so I try really hard to focus, mentally slapping myself in the face, and I go to the questions. Question one, "What can you infer about John from his buying of Oscar?" What? What can you infer about John? It's a dog. He bought a dog. I can infer that he would like to own a dog.

Sadly, that is not one of the choices, and I've got five minutes and fourteen more questions to go, so I see, "Desire for friendship," and I circle that one. I blaze through the rest, because I want to get done in time.

"All finished?" Sara asks, as she comes over.

"Yeah," I say softly, not as cocksure as I was before.

"Great, we'll go over the answers tomorrow."

Oh good. Thank God. I don't have to know if I did poorly or not until tomorrow. I really don't know if I could take it. I was good at reading. See, I'd never been good at sports, never been a party guy, yes, I played piano in a band, but we weren't going anywhere, and I never really had any ability in acting; I liked it, but I also knew I wasn't really that good. But I was literate, or at least, I used to be. It was my one saving grace, so please, don't tell me it's down the drain, Sara. I have nothing else.

She stands behind my wheelchair, "Ready?"

And she pushes me down the hall as everyone else pushes themselves, limps, or walks with me towards a big room, just carpet, and a projector, little desk up front, and all the patients crowd the floor.

"What is this?" I ask Sara.

"Dismissal," she says as if that explains it fully. And I guess it does. I am ready to go home.

The patients and therapists crowd in, and I see Lisa and Horus at the other end, wheelchair by wheelchair talking, and I notice Chris, smiling in his chair, and I take note of a whole bunch of new faces I have yet to meet, but there's no time for friends. I want them to call my name, so I can go home.

Siri is up front, "Car riders, listen up. Okay, Chris, Chad, Lisa, and. . ."

Oh God, please tell me Debbie is not late; please God, let Mom come on time. Don't make me have to stay here and try and make small talk. I would hate that so much.

"Megan and Will."

And we are all shed out the door into the lobby, and I see her at the door, beckoning me, holding my coat, smiling big, trying to get me to a place of excitement because she can see across my face that I am done. I am ready for a nap. I get so tired. Even with two doses of Ritalin, by three o'clock, I am exhausted.

"Ready for a milkshake?" she asks, as she comes behind my wheelchair, and I lift up my arms as she puts my jacket on and, then, pushes me to the exit.

One of the patients holds the door for her as she takes me out into the sunshine, the sweet January sunshine, and sure, it is winter, and there is a bit of a bite of cold, but it's also January in Georgia, so you know, I'm fine in a light jacket. Even though it was almost fifty this morning before we left, Mom asked me, "Are you sure you won't get cold?" She brought a bigger jacket just in case.

After she helps me transition from the chair to the seat behind the driver's seat in our Dodge Caravan and gets back in the driver's side, I know we're going to go through the whole Pathways situation. I know, and I love her, and I know she's trying to do what's best for me, but I don't know that I want to tell her I'm kind of disappointed. I don't know what I thought today would be, but I thought I would feel more like I was progressing, that I would be able to tell Siri, "Hey, you know when I was home, I was able to walk with no support, and I didn't fall or anything."

I want to tell her this, but I know she's so excited I'm at Pathways; she's so overjoyed that she got me in here, that I'm on track to get better, and I don't want to let her down, and I don't want to make her feel bad, so I smile and await the questions.

"How was it?"

I nod, "Good. Everyone seems nice."

I'm trying to evade talking about what we did; though, I know she's going to ask.

"What did you do?"

I knew it was coming. "Well, worked on standing. . . uh. . ."

My short-term memory. I hate it; I hate it; I hate it.

"What else?"

Oh God, why can't I remember the day? Why does it have to vanish? Where does it go? Or, am I forming Teflon coated brain cells that just can't stick? "Uh. . ."

"What about in OT?"

OT. . . occupational. . . arms, and oh yeah, "Left hand."

"Working on strength?"

"And the fingers."

"Good."

Oh, thank God. I'm glad she primed that one, so thankful she helped me out because I was drowning in a black void with nothing to grab onto. Thank God.

"What about speech?"

No! The water's rising, and I can't tread water, sinking, sinking, sinking.

She repeats the question, as though I could answer it but just didn't understand it, "What did you do in speech therapy?"

Bubbles popping, I'm under, and I've got nothing to hold onto.

"I don't remember."

"Did you work on school?"

"I think so?"

Everything's going to be a question, because I am coming up with nothing. It is such a challenge it, and I hate it. There is a part of my day, well, to be fair, many parts of my day, that I have no access to. I have no edges to the picture, no clues, no smattering of an idea what I experienced; I know it happened, because I am told that it did.

I mean, I guess I can remember what Sara looks like. I can remember that she's a speech therapist, and I can kind of remember that we talked about school, but. . . that's it. I hate that that's it. Why is that it? Why can't I remember anything? I can't even picture what the room looked like. It's starting to fizzle and burn up, the whole day. Like I said, key bits of knowledge stay: I remember who my therapists are; I remember what Pathways is, but what happened there? That will remain a mystery. My head starts to hurt; I get a little dizzy. This is what happens when I start to feel inadequate and unsure.

"You don't remember?" She asks in a way that, to me, feels like pity. It's soft and sweet and slow, and I know it's Mom hurting for her baby, the way all moms feel when their kids are struggling, but I hate it.

A sigh, "No."

Silence. I wish I had some way to cheer her up, some way to say, "I know I messed up, but look at this," and then, like, stand on my head or something. Obviously, not that. I think it will take much more than a day of outpatient therapy before standing on my head in a moving vehicle is advisable. So, I'm thinking of what I might say or do to cheer her up when we pull into the Chick-Fil-a. Oh good, a milkshake. Mine is strawberry, while Mom's is not a milkshake but, instead, a Diet Coke.

Mom starts to pull away, "You don't remember what you did in speech?"

"I mean."

I feel like I always need to justify, explain, offer the little I have in order to explain why I don't remember the large part I don't; I'm not that bad, even though I hate that I can't get it.

"We talked about school, and she was nice, and then. . . I feel like it was mostly based on that, on school." It's always good to start with feelings, because they are subjective, and no one can question your feelings. You'll notice in interviews politicians love to start sentences with "I feel" because your feelings don't have to obey the facts. Starting a sentence with "I feel" is like I'm going to say something you cannot question, and whatever I say is true to me because, you know, I feel it.

"But you don't remember what you did relating to school?" She sees right through my plans. I shake my head. And we are back on the highway, and it's beginning to get crowded, just beginning to clog up, but it's not quite there. It's not five o'clock. Five o'clock in Atlanta is also considered a parking lot.

"Are you excited about school?"

I completely forgot about that. Wait, what day is it? "Yeah."

"Tomorrow, Dad will take you to school and Pathways."

Oh right, tomorrow is school! I completely forgot. I am beyond excited. Getting back to normal is everything I crave. "Awesome."

"Awesome that your dad is taking you?"

"No, just. . . school. Though, yeah Mom. Awesome that Dad is taking me."

She smiles. Sarcasm is the Carter love language. "Hey."

And after we make it home, and we eat dinner and watch a

little bit of *The Office*, I'm in my bed, when my Razr buzzes; I flip it open to read, "Can't wait to see you tomorrow. Call me if you get a chance. Love you!"

I'm a bad boyfriend because I don't want to call her; I want to go to bed. So, I text her that I need to sleep and I love her, and then, I lie back down to sleep. Though, sleep is not joining me, choosing instead to remain very far away. See, I am a buzz with first-day-of-school jitters. What is it going to be like? What will I say? Who will I see? Will I be awkward? Please don't let the teachers call on me. Please don't let me be singled out. Are they going to announce my return over the intercom? "And now, it's time for the morning announcements. First off, we'd like to welcome Will Carter back to school. He's the guy in the wheelchair you'll see around the halls here. Just don't get in too long of a conversation with him; it might make you uncomfortable, and oh by the way, unless you were a close friend of his, he probably doesn't remember your name, so if you want to make him feel awkward and terrible, ask him if he knows who you are. Let's all see if he has the mental ability to pass his classes."

God, please no.

God? Help me get better. Lord, help me walk, help me remember. . . Help me heal. . . I'm so tired of being stupid. . . God, help me feel smart again. Lord. . . please. . . please God. . . I want to be smart again. . . or. . . just not stupid. . . please God. Love you, Lord. Amen.

12
FIRST DAY OF SCHOOL

The first day of school is one of those days of great anxiety where all your nerves are on the edge. Of course, I'm not thinking about that. I'm thinking about how I hate this, how I hate peeing the bed still. I look down at the dark spot under me, "Why?" My boxers, my pajamas, the sheets are all wet, cold. See, I had a dream I was peeing. Have you ever had one of those? I thought it was just in the dream, but clearly, it was real life.

I pick up my phone from next to me: 5:00 a.m. Not too bad, better than waking up at four. I have always been an early riser compared to my peers, waking up around seven, but five? Why? Thankfully, I'm soon joined in rising early by the sounds of scratching as Shelby and Jack paw at my parents' door, Shelby whining all the while. Dad grumbles to the door and trudges down the steps onto the tile through the den to the kitchen to the garage, where he opens two cans of dog food to the most excited pair of dogs you ever did see.

After he comes back in and flips on the kitchen light, I call, "Dad?"

"Oh, sorry," he says, as he flips the light back off.

"No, I'm up."

He flips it back on and shuffles to my bed in his grey shirt and exercise shorts as though he might have worn this to bed to wake up and go to the gym, but no; he'll get changed and go to Starbucks soon. As he stands at my bed, I want to offer an explanation. I want to say that I meant to hold it, that I was going to wake up; I wanted to tell him about the dream, about how I'm not responsible, that I couldn't have done anything to stop it, but he just looks and mutters, "Oh. One sec."

Then, he goes upstairs to get a change of clothes as I sit in my pee-soaked sheets, and I hate this. He wasn't shocked at all, as though he was expecting it, and no, I wouldn't want him to be surprised; I wouldn't want to let him down like that, but this feels like he started at a point of let down, and I don't know what I want his response to have been instead. I don't know how he should react, and I just hate it. I hate that I'm seventeen years old and I pissed the bed. And, I hate that no one is surprised I pissed the bed while I'm seventeen years old. This is how I'm starting my last semester of high school, and I hate that this is the way I'm going into the day. "God, make it a good day."

I want to believe today will be better. I do, and I don't, that same ole seesaw again. Dad comes back with a change of clothes, moves me to my wheelchair and then the kitchen table. He takes the sheets off and puts them in the garage with the dirty clothes.

After a cinnamon bagel breakfast and my regimen of pills, he takes me upstairs to shower, and I know I can't look my best. After my shower, Dad takes me to my room to get my outfit. Per usual, I rock some exercise pants and a black band shirt. I'll go with my Sufjan Stevens one, a blue car with the phrase [1]"Ride the Hatch," and yes, I have no idea what it means. I did not know what it meant before my accident, and I don't know now. I went to a concert, and I needed to document it with a shirt; this was part of my "cool," as I might perceive it.

Once we get to school, Dad looks at me and offers, "Do you want to pray?"

"Yes."

We bow our heads, and I let him lead.

"God Father, we come before you, Lord, as your humble servants, but we also come as princes to the Most High. God, we ask that you would give Will a good day at school today. Father, we ask that you help him do well, focus well, and retain the information he receives. We pray, Lord, you will fill him with your spirit Lord, so that all his interactions today will bring glory to you. In your name, we pray, amen."

"Thank you, Dad."

"Of course."

It's a foggy morning with the mist settling outside as the sky begins to break free, yellow bursting into blue of the morning, a glittering of reds as the embers of the dawn's explosion sprinkle the sky. As we get me into my wheelchair with my backpack on the back, I can see students starting to filter into the school. I don't think I'm ready to see anyone yet. It's not that I'm shy or anything. It's that I'm not prepared for that conversation yet, the, "Oh hey, yeah, I'm alive. Oh yeah, I'm in a wheelchair, and oh yeah, I'm totally different." You know that conversation? You ever had that conversation? Probably not. But I bet you have had something happen to you: illness, divorce, job loss, losing a parent, losing a child, having a parent that's an addict; the list goes on; I bet you have had something happen to you, and you know that when people see you, that's all they see. You have all these gifts, abilities, positive personality traits, but you know that you are a monolith of suffering, defined entirely by the one event you wish did not happen. And you have these brief encounters of small talk, of "how's the weather?" conversations, but all the while, the other person is jumping to talk about the trouble they have defined you by. They want to ask you how the recovery's going, want to ask if your son really did kill himself, want to ask how it feels to have brain damage. However, of course, the courtesies of modern conversation do not allow for this, so all they can put up as a mask of their true intentions is, "I can't believe it's January," which, of course, is the most meaningless phrase ever. Don't get me wrong; I've said it countless times, but it's saying, "I am amazed at the progress of time." Don't say this to a person recently living with a brain injury. Time is a relative concept. To be fair, don't say this to anyone in tragedy; life is floating by, but what day is it? Who knows. What time is it? Now.

I don't want to make small talk. I used to be good at it; I used to be a master at talking about nothing, but now? I'll say something awkward because I don't know what to say. I'll create a silence, and I'll hate myself, and the other person will feel bad for me, and that will make me hate myself even more.

But let's do this. There is a point soon where I won't want to flee from this body and this broken brain; a day is coming when I will like the person in the mirror, a day when I'm healed. A day is coming when I can get back to my life of before, when I can drive down 92 with Anna in the passenger seat, and I can be confident, laughing, and I can feel that people like to be around me again (that I don't have to find the joke in every moment to validate myself to the person I'm talking to).

And as my dad pushes the button to open the doors and wheel me into the entrance of the school, I see the atrium I know so well, the atrium where I spent plenty an afternoon waiting on my dad or walking through it with friends on our way to rehearsal. I see the brown brick with the grey tile; I see the photos on the wall of great moments in Roswell High

School history. Of course, there is the desk of Sharon, the woman in her late fifties in charge of making sure everyone coming or going through these doors is a person who should be here.

A distinct older woman's Southern voice, "Is that Will Carter?"

"Hello. Bob Carter," Dad says, shaking her hand, "This is Will's first day back."

"Sharon Adcock, nice to meet you Mr. Carter, and I know this young man. I hope he knows me."

"Of course." This is my typical reply to this statement, whether I remember someone or not. I feel that, if someone says this to me, I should definitely remember them, so I just pretend.

And after a nice conversation about my healing and recovery, Sharon picks up her walkie-talkie, "Can someone send Mr. Archambeau down to my desk?"

"Roger. Aaron's on his way," I hear from the other end.

Sharon looks to my dad, her brown, veiny hand coming up from her desk in a confirming gesture, "You'll like him. Aaron's a great guy. He'll be taking Will to his classes."

"That's great," Dad says as he smiles politely at Sharon.

Soon, I see him turn the corner; Aaron is a tall guy, blonde buzz cut, well-built, khaki pants, yellow polo; he's coming down with a smile, so maybe, his assistant basketball coach look doesn't mean I get to hate him. At least, at the very least, he's smiling like he's a nice person. He sticks his hand out to me first, which I'm grateful for, "Hi, Will, right?"

He takes my backpack off the wheelchair and puts it on.

He sees my dad and turns, a little flustered, "I am so sorry. I completely spaced. Aaron Archambeau. Nice to meet you."

"Nice to meet you, Aaron. I'm Bob, Will's dad."

"Very good to meet you. My job is to get this guy," he says, patting my shoulder (not so sure about this guy anymore), "from class to class."

"That's great to hear. I guess I'll leave you to it then," Dad smiles, shaking his hand again, and looks to me, "See you outside the physics room at 11:30."

"Okay."

And with that, Dad does what I know must be hard for him; he leaves me completely alone at school, almost on my own. Thankfully, there are teachers and Aaron to watch out for me, but he can't control my interactions; he can't save me from an awkward silence; he can't pick me up if I should somehow fall over, and for any dad, this is hard. The first day of school when kids go off to kindergarten puts a dad's stomach in knots, and dropping your son off after he has suffered a brain injury is probably even harder.

"You ready?" Aaron asks as he comes up behind my wheelchair.

Mrs. Adcock looks at him with a straight face, "You'll want to go to D Hall, to the Tag Office. Ms. Colvin and Ms. Spradlin will be in there," then to me, a sparkling smile, "So good to see you, Will. So glad you're back."

Spradlin and Colvin. I know both of these people, and I actually remember both of these women, and as we make our way down the white linoleum that looks actually a little yellowish from all the teenage sneakers, I see Spradlin, a woman in her late fifties, long black hair, and as big a smile as I could imagine right now. She's got some edge to her, but that's why I always liked her. She liked me, and I knew there were many people she did not like, so being on her good side made me feel special.

"Will Carter!" Spradlin screams, as she runs up to give me a hug. Awkward in the wheelchair but welcomed.

"Will!" Colvin comes up to hug me too, smaller with a head of blonde hair to match her sunny disposition.

Mrs. Rice, always looking like a New York housewife, enough perfume to choke a room and earrings that could land her on the floor in the event of a gentle breeze, comes to give me a hug, even though I don't know her that well. We've had some interaction, so I'll allow it. Mr. Shackleford gives me a handshake.

"I'll be back to take you to lit." Aaron says, as he leaves with a fist bump.

After the announcements and pledge of allegiance, which I kind of like that I get to do in my wheelchair, Spradlin sits in a desk next to my chair, slapping her arms on the faux wood, "So, how are you? How are ya feelin'? Did your mom tell you about our conversation with Spurka?"

"No, what happened?"

A smile opens wide across Spradlin's lips; I know she's been dying to tell me this, whatever it is, "I met with Spurka about you coming back, and I told him, 'Will is going to graduate. I don't care what we have to do. We're going to make it happen.'"

My smile grows, "Awesome."

She adjusts herself in the desk, crossing one leg of her black pants, "You have economics, physics, PE, and lit. That's it. That's it, and you're done. You don't need your Euro, your stats, and I know you loved theater, but you don't have time for that. So, look, you're going to take econ online; you'll finish PE via the book, physics, of course, you're still with Foss, and lit, you're now taking with Colvin. I know you love Mrs. Williams, but you'll be at therapy in the afternoon, so Colvin will have to do."

"Hey now, Will's gonna love my class," Colvin pipes up in her cheery, nasally voice.

"Of course!" I smile.

I got to know Ms. Colvin when I was doing a directed study course on modern Africa last year. So, I wasn't lying when I said, "Of course." I mean, I'm actually kind of excited to see how that goes.

Colvin's all smile; her skin color doesn't match her personality. What I mean to say is that, for somebody so cheery, smiley, and always wanting to laugh, she is far too pale.

"You're gonna love it, Will. That's Anna's class," she chirps from next to Spradlin.

"I'm sure I will."

A smile forms. I'm beginning to believe this might actually happen. I might graduate. Spradlin's the kind of woman who gets what she wants, and thankfully, she wants me to graduate high school, so I think, by that logic, I'm going to finish. I hope I don't let her down.

"All right, let's get you logged in," Spradlin commands as she walks over to the computer I'm by, her right hand with three rings on it guiding the mouse to start setting me up. She then proceeds to show me how to log in to my economics course, while directing Mr. Shackleford, a short heavyset cheerful teacher, to get me an economics textbook from the bookcase, hardback, the way all school textbooks are, stains and tears across all the pages.

"Luckily we got one of these hanging around," Shackleford chuckles as he hands me the book.

"Thanks," Spradlin says as she sets up my account.

"Okay. You've got fifteen modules. Easy breezy. Once you finish your econ for the day, get your PE, your lit, or your physics. You got a lot to do, but you can do it, okay?"

Even though she's got a rough exterior, even though she's pissed off the people she works with because she shares her opinion freely and speaks her mind without regret, she cares so much. At first glance, she might look so sure of herself that she'd chew you up and spit you out, but that's all until you actually get to know Cindy Spradlin. I think she likes the rough exterior, but I also think what she likes even more are the students who look past that to see the sweet, caring, loving heart within. I think that's why she always liked me. Once I got to know that side of her, I really liked her. I felt so special to have her on my team.

I open the website for the course, and. . . oh. . . no. . . fifteen modules feels like a lot. . . multiple quizzes, little assignments embedded within, and a major unit test? Thump, thump, thump; my heart is starting to go against me as my head gets light, and I feel woozy. I can't do it. How can I do it? I've got so much to do. So much to do on my own. Don't they know I have a brain injury? Oh God, what if I can't do it? What if I can't do all of this? What if it's too much? People tell me I'm a miracle, but what if I let them down? What if the miracle in my life was coming back from the dead, and what if the miracle fizzled out after that? All the miracle juice went to the saving not to the fixing, you know? So, the seventeen-year-old boy is not dead, but he's broken. What if I never get better? What if I stay broken?

A hand on my shoulder, and I can feel the hard metal of the rings, the soft touch, Spradlin's voice in my ear, "You okay?"

"Yeah. Yeah."

"All right. Just whatever you can get done today."

Whatever I can get done today. Focus, Will. You can do this. I look at the screen so long it all blends together, colors crashing into each other as my eyes move to give up. I shake my head. Focus. God, grant me the ability to focus. I open the module, and I open my textbook, and it's like a guided quiz. You read a passage, and you take a short one to three question quiz over what you just read, and I don't need the book. They have the reading on the screen, economics systems. Cool. I've got this, and then. . . quiz. . . crap.

"Which of the following is not a feature of mercantilism?" Crap. Oooh. . . let's see:

1. Private property
2. The use of markets for basic organization of economic activity
3. Government exercising much of the control over production, exchange, and consumption
4. Private individuals having total authority over production, exchange, and consumption

Oh no. . . no. . . agh, what? I. . . I have no idea. I don't want to screw this up. I look down at my book. I see there is a section on mercantilism right in front of me. I look around. Ms. Colvin is focused on her computer; Spradlin is on her cell phone. Mrs. Rice is helping another student. I mean, it would be bad to have to fail this class. I hate it. I hate it, but. . . I see the phrase "government exercising much of the control over production," so I click the one with those words, and wrong? What? Wait, hold on. I look back, "Which is NOT a feature of mercantilism." Guess I failed this quiz.

Man, I finish the rest of the unit, get a 77 on the unit test.

At least I'll pass. My grades might be crap this semester, but a 77 is passing. Man, a 77? I knew football players with singular brain cells who had As in econ, and I'm looking at a C? Well, I guess one healthy brain cell is better than a million damaged ones.

I click back to the main page, and I accidentally click on the unit I just looked at. Wait, what's this? I click on the unit test. It takes me back to an empty, fresh test. A fresh empty test. . . wait? I scan over the questions. These are the same questions as before. Wait. . . so. . . what if I? I feel a hand on my shoulder, a quick recoil.

"Scared you, did I?" Aaron smiles.

"Oh gosh, is it that time already?" I look at the clock and, yeah, ten minutes before the bell's set to ring.

"'Fraid so," Aaron says as he swings my backpack over his shoulder.

"See you tomorrow!" I get from Mrs. Rice. A wave from Shackleford.

"See you tomorrow, sweetie," Spradlin smiles and waves from her desk.

And, we're off. Sweetie? It's Sprad. I'll allow it.

"But class isn't over for another ten minutes," I look up at Aaron as he escorts me into the halls, rows of locker and ugly white walls.

"Remember? We got to get you early, so that you're not in the halls with anyone." He says as he charts a course up D hall to the doors to the parking lot.

"Oh."

A pause, as I try and think of a good reply. Aaron hits the button as the doors open, and we brace for the January air, light as Georgian January air really is.

"Is it because I'm so good looking?"

A surprised laugh from Aaron, out the belly, "Yeah," shaking his head, "Yeah, buddy, that's it."

"I knew it," I smile.

I like it when I tell a joke, and there's laughter. I like when I take part in normal, everyday conversation, and there's not an awkward silence, or I say something, and people high-pitch, uncomfortable laugh, like they're seventeenth century women participating in polite high-society conversation; you know the laugh I'm talking about. That laugh which is clearly not the genuine laugh that people do because they don't know what to say—the laugh that is uncomfortable but unwilling to acknowledge the awkwardness. Aaron, though, he's really laughing.

"You got jokes," he says, as he takes me onto the asphalt towards the portables.

"You like jokes?"

Aaron stops the wheelchair, "What do you call a fish with no eye?"

"A fish with no eye? I. . . I. . . I don't know."

A smile as he keeps pushing, leaning forward, "A fsh."

"Wait. . . what?" I'm thinking and thinking.

He doesn't make me feel bad; he pushes me up the ramp to the portable, "How do you spell fish?"

"F-I-S-H."

"A fish with no I then?"

"Ohhh. That's good." I laugh.

He opens the door. I've got some jokes for him, but I am met with a, "Will!" as some of the students are in here already.

Aaron leans down, "Where do you want to be, over here by the first desk?"

"Yeah, that will work."

There is a collection of students here I know; well, I know most of them, but I don't like to know all of them, but I try and trade conversation with them; it's pretty easy questions: "What does your schedule look like?", "Are you at home?", "Are you going to graduate?" Sometimes, I have to think; sometimes, my answer doesn't come right away; sometimes, I take three or four seconds to answer, but some of them know what I was like after my accident, so to them, this is an improvement. I hope nobody asks me something I can't remember. I hope Ms. Colvin gets here soon. I can't take being the focus much longer.

"What was it like to wake up from a coma?" this kid, Ben,

asks. He's short and awkward, but I guess I'm the awkward one now.

"I. . . I. . . I don't really. . . can't really remember. . . It's all pretty fuzzy."

Awkward silence. Great.

Lisbeth is about to save it with a question, but the door swings open, and it's Ms. Colvin, frazzled, out of breath, carrying a stack of books, a binder, and her attendance book.

"Oh good. I'm glad Will got to do his introductions. You all remember Will, right?"

A response of "woo" comes from the collective class. I'll take a woo; it's better than a boo. Though, I'm not going to lie, a collective boo from the class would've made the me from before my accident laugh hysterically, sick sense of humor that I have.

"Do you remember this recently hospitalized student?"

"BOO!"

Now, though, that would break me. That would tear through my paper-thin confidence.

"Well, Will will be joining us for the rest of the semester.

Will, do you want to say anything?"

I shake my head. I used to love improve comedy but, now, not so much.

The class starts on this book, *Heart of Darkness,* and quickly breaks into groups. I am completely lost. I see them all find a group and begin working on this book that I've heard of but don't think I've read? I mean, I can't be sure. Try as I might. I can only remember reading *Catch 22* in the English class the semester of my accident, and that was in the summer before the semester even started.

I'm sitting in my wheelchair as groups go ahead and work. Anna comes over kisses me and brings her group down to where I am.

"Okay, yeah, that will work," Ms. Colvin says, and then,

"Oh, Will," and she kneels by my wheelchair, "Okay, so this is *Heart of Darkness*. You didn't read that, did you?"

I shake my head; she's so sweet and kind, so I don't say, "Look lady, I just woke up out of a coma about two months ago, so yeah, I wasn't quite focused on reading."

I smile, "No."

"That's okay; that's okay; we'll get it for you. Try and follow along, but don't worry, we'll get you a copy, and it'll be okay. We'll get it for you, and as far as last semester goes?"

I look into her eyes, her sweet, kind, blue eyes, "Don't worry. What your mom sent me is good; I mean, you know, the work your mom sent me; that's totally fine."

"Good."

Oh, thank God. Thank God. Thank you, Lord. I thought I still had to catch up and complete last semester, and I guess I still kind of have to catch up with PE, but thank God, not English.

I get into the group, and they all start working and talking, and no one asks me a question; no one checks to see if I'm following along; no one seeks to make sure I'm a part of this, and I feel so alone.

"Yeah, page 56? Do you see that metonymy there? I think that counts for figurative language."

"There's a simile right here."

"What is that one called? A syllogism?"

"Let's stick to white sepulchral city as a symbol of all of Europe."

I'm nodding, but I have no idea what's going on. I don't know what these words mean. I mean, I know what figurative language is, but I have no idea what a syllogism is and metonymy? I mean, I know these are words I should know, words I have been taught, but I don't want to ask. I don't want to look stupid. It's easier to nod and pretend I know what's going on. Most people don't question you if you just nod. So, I nod most of the class.

Colvin comes over and crouches at my desk, her fingers gripping the side, the red nails standing out from her pail hands, "How's it going? You feeling all right?"

I nod, "Good."

"Good. . . uh. . . yeah, good." She brings her eyes to mine, "You sure? You feel good about what's going on?"

"Yeah. Feel good."

She stands up, "Great. Glad to hear it."

How can I tell her I am so lost? How can tell her I don't have a clue what's going on? How can I tell her I don't belong here? This is worse than the physics tutoring. The AP class room was my home; Peter and I would strut in like we owned the place. Now, we didn't have the best grades, but what we lacked in straight A's on every test, we made up for in swagger. God, I don't think I would like former self if I met him now. At this moment, I'm afraid to speak up, afraid to be wrong, afraid people will whisper to each other, afraid there will be a silence of more than five seconds after I speak, so I sit there and nod. God, do they know I don't have a clue what a syllogism is? Or, what a sepu. . . whatever that thing was is? Quiet, Will. Say nothing. I know; I know, you want to talk. You always do, but shut your mouth, and everything will be okay. You can figure this out at home. . . maybe.

Aaron comes within ten minutes before class is over, and we start the walk.

"You said you like jokes, right?"

Aaron is smiling and escorting me out into the parking lot off the ramp of the portable.

"I love stand-up."

I feel like Aaron is smiling big behind me, "Stand-up, you say? Who's your guy?"

This is a conversation I can get into, "You know Brian Regan?"

Aaron is up to the school, pushing the button to enter, "I love Brian Regan!"

"He's probably my favorite. Well. . . him, and. . ." searching for the name, scanning the files. I know it. I know it. It's a brain fart, but for me, let's say I'm on mental Taco Bell because my brain experiences constant flatulence.

"Can't think of it?"

We're passing through the halls, and most people are still in class, which is great. I don't need anyone else between me and class. Aaron takes me quickly, not running by any stretch of the imagination but definitely a much faster pace than if I was trying to wheel myself. A moment of silence, which is okay. I appreciate that Aaron doesn't try and cover up the silence with talking, because that would make feel bad, like he was doing me a favor or something.

"Mitch Hedberg."

We're in H Hall, and the bell rings.

"Crap," Aaron says, as he quickly maneuvers me to Mrs. Foss's classroom.

"Do you know him?" I look up.

"Who?" He says, getting me to the classroom door, without running me into anyone. Well done.

"Mitch Hedberg."

A look of shock as Aaron realizes things did not go exactly to plan with transporting me from the portable here. I don't really connect this with not being the right time to talk comedy.

"Do you know Mitch?"

A look of him coming to the conversation again, "No."

I do my best Mitch impression, half-open eyes, swaying hands, quoting one of my favorite jokes.

"I love that guy!" Aaron exclaims as he pushes me into Mrs. Foss's room to a place near her desk, a wave to Mrs. Foss.

"We'll talk about it tomorrow, but God, I love that guy! You enjoy physics. Sorry, I gotta run, class to teach. I'll see you after class."

And he's off. Mrs. Foss is smiling at me, wide and honest. "Good to see you, Will. Long time no see."

She says this with a chuckle, like it's her own private little joke.

"Good to see you," I say, looking up at her. Looking up at her is something I can only really do sitting down.

The room is filling up, and students are coming up to me, "Will, you're back!"

"Will!"

"Glad you're back, buddy!"

Now, most of these students are a year younger than me; many of them are in the social circle of cheerleaders and football players that I care little for, but it's nice to be noticed and cared about, even if it is only because I was in a coma. Pro tip: if you are ever in a place where people are ambivalent toward you, get put in a coma. Now, I'm not saying these people were against me; I made jokes; I was friendly, and I had a fashion sense that announced "please pay attention to me" to everyone who saw me, but I wouldn't say that this group of popular juniors here would cheer me on or want to hang out with me. Though, if people didn't know me before, they know me now. Some of them even show me the wrist bands they have with my name on them. Mrs. Foss holds up hers. I like it as long as they are talking. No questions for me. The bell rings, and Foss swivels her chair to face the class, her soft Southern accent working to command some of the class, "Well, c'mon let's get class started. Ya'll can talk to Will later. Please ya'll. Everyone, sit down. Bryce, Bryce? Bryce, c'mon. Bryce, I need you to put your butt down in a chair please. Thank you. Now, today, we're going to talk about nuclear physics."

Bryce leans back in his hair, running his hand through his sandy blonde mop, "You mean, like blowing stuff up?"

Foss's shoulders fall. Bryce is that kid every teacher would kill for the sake of the class. You know the one. And if you don't know the kind of kid I'm talking about, I'm so sorry. I have some terrible news.

"Bryce, no, not blowing stuff up. We're going to learn about isotopes."

And for the next twenty minutes, with the help of the lights turned off, the light of an overhead projector, a blue EXPO Visa-Vis marker, and a mostly hibernating audience, Mrs. Foss proceeds to lecture about isotopes. I spend the majority of these twenty minutes telling my thoughts, "No, come back. No, don't go there. No, focus. You need to focus." It's no use. I have no idea what she's talking about. I'm trying; I'm trying so hard, but I am so lost. Tired, I'm getting so tired. What happened? The energy is oozing out of my head, and my eyes are getting sore and droopy. Why? Why am I fading?

"Okay, so I want you to work these problems, and we'll go over them, hopefully, by the end of the class."

I look at these problems, and I'm sure, to most of my classmates, they make sense. Nobody shouted anything at Mrs. Foss; nobody complained; nobody accosted her with, "We didn't go over this!"

So, I think I am the only one who is lost. Again, I don't draw attention to it. Foss leans over to me as she gets up from her stool, "Okay, Will, let me go to the bathroom really quickly, but then, I'll be right back to help you."

At least, I ask Kamran, a friend of mine from way back, for a piece of paper.

"Sure, Will," he says as he gives me one.

He's one of those quiet nice types, and back, before all of this, I always tried to befriend the guy who was quietly sitting alone; Kamran had been one of those people when I met him, so he smiles with a "How are you? How are you feeling?"

Kamran, buddy, that's a loaded question, but you're a nice guy, "I'm good. I'm. . . I'm doing all right. Excited to be back at school."

He nods, affirmingly, "And how are you feeling?"

"Tired. I'm very tired."

"I get that. Do you need help with these problems?"

Oh God, what do I say? Obviously, I'm going to be staring at the piece of notebook paper Kamran gave me until Mrs. Foss comes back. On the other hand, Kamran will realize how lost I am. He'll know just how stupid I am. . . I. . . I breathe out. I look at Kamran, waiting expectantly on an answer, and I lower my head, "Yes."

Kamran scoots closer to my wheelchair, "You remember me?"

Oh buddy, you used to be in the category of nice people. Okay, maybe if you help me out with this physics work, you still can be. "Yeah. Kamran. I remember you."

Thank you, God. Thank you that I am not lying. Thank you that I remember his name. Thank you that I did not create an awkward situation. He reaches his muscular arm to bring his notepad over.

"Okay, so you see, question one is about electrons and protons."

I nod. That was not a question, so I don't really know what to say.

"If there are nine electrons, how many protons? This is a simple question."

Okay, maybe for you, but let's not assume anything of your audience. I get distracted by a noise at the back, and I look, only to see Bryce is actually writing down answers to these problems. Seriously? Even Bryce knows what's going on? Even backwards-visor-wearing Bryce?

Kamran's soft voice beckons back, "Will?"

I swivel my head back to Kamran, "What?"

"So, let's see. Nine electrons means there are nine protons. There is the same number for both."

He's slow and deliberate, and, maybe with someone else or maybe in another class, I would think he's talking down to me, but I know his heart "Okay."

"Does that make sense?"

Kamran's built like a runner, but his personality is too humble to be around the other athletes in the class. He's always dressed nice, and he raises his hand completely straight up, you know what I mean? Like not off to the side, not clawing at the sky like an overachiever, but perpendicular with the ground, like from a textbook on hand raising or something.

Okay, I write down what Kamran says. It's not about learning right now; it's about survival. I should learn and ask questions, look stupid but gather knowledge. Screw that. I need to make it to May. I need to pass my classes, hopefully with an A or a B. Who am I kidding? A B.

Kamran smiles, "Good? Now, let's look at how to find the number of neutrons."

"Neutrons. Hmm." I bite my lip. I'm trying hard to not look stupid, but I need context if I'm going to focus, and dear God, I want a nap. My eyes are getting heavy. I shake my face.

Kamran looks at me, "Tired?"

"Very much so."

Kamran looks at the clock I used to stare at for fifty minutes when I was a student in here before my accident, "You only have another fifteen minutes."

"Good."

And we go back to the problems, and Kamran tries so hard to explain everything, and I'm a liar. I nod. I pretend I get what he's saying. I mean, I get some of it. I understand the words he's saying; I just don't get how the math works yet, but I don't tell him that. Mrs. Foss slowly makes her way to her stool and lands with the aid of gravity.

She looks at me, with an almost full sheet of paper, "How's it going? Did you finish the problems?"

"Almost. Kamran's helping me."

Mrs. Foss looks at Kamran, her mouth open in an excitement, "That's great, Kamran! That's great to hear! I think this is a great pairing. Didn't you two work together before?"

"Yes," Kamran nods.

Mrs. Foss glimmers with joy at seeing me working with a classmate and seeing Kamran tutor me in physics, "Well, I think this is great you two are back working together. Was he helpful?"

I nod. I don't want to say any more about it, so I try to stop this conversation with simple head movements.

Bryce puts his phone back in his pocket as he bellows from the back, "Mrs. Foss, are we going to go over this!?"

Caught off guard, she looks up at the clock, three minutes to spare.

"Dang it all. We will go over it tomorrow. You can use the remainder to finish."

Crap. That means I probably have to finish this at home. Kamran and I have five more problems left. And, I don't. . . I don't. . . I don't know. I just don't know. Maybe, I can find the answers online, yeah probably, right? We'll see.

Mrs. Foss looks at me, while the students pack up. Work on problems? For three minutes? You're funny.

Her stool squeaks as she swivels to me, "Did you get what you needed?"

She stares at me, waiting on a reply, truly and honestly. I look at her, trying so hard to be honest. I want to be. I know she cares, and I know she's only trying to help, but I look down, thinking, and she's still waiting, so I say, looking into her eyes, "I think so, but. . . I. . . I think I have to make sure I got it." God, my head is feeling light, blood pooling somewhere else. Why? "Can we. . . maybe. . . can we talk after we go over the problems?"

"That will work great, Will," she confirms as she heaves herself off her stool to go to the hallway.

You know how it is; every teacher must stand in the hallway between classes as though that will really do any good at all. Teenagers have a hard time listening to teachers when they're in the classroom; why should the hallway change that? But oh well, Aaron is blocking the doorway anyway by leaning on it. Maybe, just maybe, students would listen to him; his build says, "I could break you," but his smile says, "I probably won't." Now, I'm not saying he's remarkably ripped or anything; I'm just saying he has guns in those sleeves, and compared to a scrappy fifteen or sixteen-year-old kid? No contest.

Mrs. Foss is taken off guard by seeing him, "Oh, my, why hello!"

Aaron smiles, walking over to shake her hand, "I don't know if you remember seeing me before—"

She points at him, "Remind me of your name."

"Aaron."

"Yes, that's right."

An awkward silence, and Aaron smiles through it all. Man, I wish I could be like him. He's like Teflon to an uncomfortable situation.

He looks at his watch, "Gotta get him in the car and go help teach Algebra. Good to see you again."

"Good to see you, Aaron. Good work today, Will. See you tomorrow."

"See you tomorrow!"

And we're out of there, and we're off, out the door and out onto the sidewalk where Dad's gold Toyota Camry is idling nearby.

After I'm in the car, and my dad is folding up the wheelchair, Aaron looks at me in the encouraging way, the sun shining off his short blonde buzz, "Love Mitch. Had to look him up to remind myself."

"Weren't you teaching?"

He makes a show of looking behind him, and then shushing me, "Don't tell anyone."

This gets a laugh out of me. Then, Aaron does his best Mitch; it's clear he's no actor, but I appreciate the effort.

Now, this gets a real laugh, a real smile out of me, and I point at him, marking him with approval, "You're all right Aaron. You're all right."

He steps back, pats himself on the back, "All right? You know what? I'll take it. I'll take it. See you guys tomorrow!"

In the car, Dad looks at me, before we go, "How was the first day?"

A pause, but you know, he's used to that from me now. "It was good."

We're off driving, and my head is falling forward; it's like I had a blast of energy in the morning, but I'm vanquished now. I remember the important things I learned today, "Aaron likes Mitch Hedberg."

Dad laughs, as we make our way easily out of the parking lot onto the road, "Good. You must love him then."

Love him? I mean, it's not necessary to use hyperbole, but yes, he jumped leaps and bounds in my book by quoting Mitch. Despite being an assistant basketball coach, the polo shirt, and overall definitely-was-a-jock-in-high-school vibe, if he likes Mitch, he's all right in my book, so yeah. "Yeah, he seems cool."

As we debrief the day, Dad wants to know what we talked about in physics and what we're reading in lit, things I can't remember, but he sees this, and we talk about the coming weeks. We drive through Chick-Fil-a, so I can get some lunch, and my dad hands me another Ritalin, and like a shot of adrenaline in the femoral artery, my heart is pumping me back to life as my eyes open. Dad grips the steering wheel as we merge onto 400.

"You know your mom is going back to work."

"Yeah."

"And I can't drive you every afternoon."

Are we breaking up? What's with all the short sentences and pauses? "Yeah?"

"Granddad will take you tomorrow. Aunt Nancy and Aunt Linda will also be taking you sometimes."

"Okay. Cool."

Pathways is a bustling place, and Dad wheels me into the waiting room as the older, woman at the desk looks at me, smiles, "Siri will be out soon."

"All right, Will, sorry I got you here a little early."

In the waiting room, I see Horus, sitting in one of the creaky wooden chairs with the fabric backs, and I see Lisa in her wheelchair, smiling as she always does, old enough to be my mom.

"Hey, Will. How are you?" Lisa asks, her hands on her lap.

"Lisa, I'm doing good. Just finished school. How are you?"

"Doing good. Trusting the Lord Jesus with my every waking hour."

And she says it in that soft Southern way, her words dripping out easily like fresh honey. I don't care what anyone says, but an older Southern woman talking about Jesus is more convincing than anyone else.

"You love Jesus?"

Lisa's smile ripples across her lips, "Every day of my life, I try to love him a fraction of how much he loves me."

Horus smiles, pointing at us, his Jamaican lilt having the same effect as Lisa's Southern drip, making his words feel genuine, "That is what I'm talking about. You are right there Lisa. Right there."

This is glorious; my eyes brighten, my eyebrows go up, "You are Christians?"

"Every day of my life," Lisa laughs.

Horus hits his leg, "You know that's right."

My buzz cut is getting longer as I scratch my growing hairs, "That's so good. I love to talk with other Christians."

Horus points at me, "God is so good brother. God is so good."

Lisa claps her skinny, wrinkled hands, "Yes, he is. Every day, he is so good."

I lean forward in my chair, the sunlight cracking through the blinds to light my face, "I believe it. Where do you go to church? What denomination?"

Horus straightens up, "Denomination? Brother, the one denomination to me is Christian. You love Jesus? That's what it's about."

Lisa is still clapping, "Amen, Horus. Amen. I mean, I was raised Baptist, but no matter what, loving Jesus is what it's about."

It is a beautiful thing, as a friendship is formed among this gang of three. I mean, I liked them before this moment, but I really feel like I am bonding with them now, and it's a feeling I've chased ever since my accident. Every other social interaction, I feel judged. I am aware of how I appear. I think everyone is like this to some extent, conscious of every room's observers' perception of him, even if it is invented?

Since my accident though, I can't relax. I can't step outside of myself to enjoy a moment and be present in it because I am trying so hard not to be awkward, not to say the wrong thing. I try and remember what I'm being told, and I fail at this, but the self-consciousness taught by therapists also is like freezing any inhibition you might have in a block of ice. This moment, though, this moment is glorious. I'm grinning from ear to ear.

Siri comes up to the doorway, her big frame coming into my peripheral vision as she looks at me, waving her arms, "Hey, over here. What are you doing? Come on back."

After saying goodbye to my friends, I make my way into the therapy gym. She bends her body over, leaning one arm on her knee, "You know what we're gonna do today, don't you?"

I look at her, distracted slightly by the purple streaks in her hair, "Uhh. . . something?"

A laugh, she quickly cocks her head back and forth, offers with a genuine excitement, "You ready to walk?"

I look at her for a pause. I don't know if she's serious, and she can tell my thought process by my pause, so she offers, "I'm being for real. C'mon, let's get you on a walker."

And we do, and I'm doing it. It's slow; my steps are stuttered, but I am doing it. I'm not wearing a helmet this time, but I am still grinning from ear to ear as I make my way around the therapy gym. Now, no real crowd to cheer me on; though, Horus does give me a thumbs up, and Siri steps away from my walker to see how I'll do, and with a clap of her hands, "You're doing it! You're doing it!"

"I'm walking!"

Sure, my steps are slow, and yes, it is on a mat, but I'm walking with a walker.

Siri comes up, elbows me lightly, "You want to take it for a spin around the place?"

And we go down the halls, the blue walls never looked quite so blue sitting down, and no, people are not taking pictures or stepping out of their offices, no *Chariots of Fire* theme song, but even still, I am moving around the circle of rooms, moving past the water fountain and bathroom, back up the hall to the gym, all the while thinking, "Don't fall. Don't fall. This is your way to a walker. Just one foot, then the other foot. Don't fall. Don't fall."

And we're back in the gym, and I can't believe it. I did it. I walked.

"Take a seat," Siri says, as she holds the walker still, and I carefully sit down, trying my best not to plop, and I land with a little less help from gravity. I hope she noticed.

"What do you think?" Siri says, sitting cross-legged on the floor.

"About?" I ask as my right hand finds a spot of ketchup from before. I wipe it with a finger and place my hand in my pocket. Smooth.

"About what? C'mon! About walking! You just toured the whole dang building." She gives me that look like, "Am I right?"

"It was pretty great." I look at the walker, all silver, grey rubber handles.

"You want to take this bad boy home?"

A pause. I'm really looking at her. I'm waiting for her to crack a smile, but I can't help myself anymore, "You serious?"

Standing up Siri, shrugs, "Yeah. You did great. I think you can take her home."

It's official. I'm using a walker! And we go to occupational therapy, and Caitlin gives me a big smile and a clap, and we work on my vision, more left-eye weakness. We're trying to get it to see in the periphery, and after a bit of her putting stuff on the side of my left eye where I only really miss one finger that she has to bring so close to my face, I can almost feel it; she stops, "Have you and your mom ever talked about vision therapy?"

Oh no, something else. "What's that?"

She gets up to get me a block of wood with holes, several wooden cylinders filling the holes, "It's an eye clinic, where you focus on vision."

"Oh. Nice."

She sets it down in front of me, "Now, using your left hand —don't roll your eyes at me."

I smile; she knows I'm joking, right? Either way, I put my left hand on the table, and for the rest of our time, I take the wooden pegs out and then put them back into the holes, using my left hand; dang, it's shaking up a storm, but I complete the task. My fingers are tired. Soon, I make my way next door to speech.

Speech therapy is still my least favorite therapy. I don't want to telegraph this to Sara, but I'm sure she knows, right? I'm not good at hiding my emotions, especially now. We go over my answers to the test, and we argue about a few. I posit that I think the questions are worded confusingly, "It's stated in the story. I thought I was supposed to infer it?"

Crossing her arms, Sara gives me the look, the one Mom gives me when she is pissed off, "I didn't write this test, Will, but I think it's a good test. It is not stated in the passage that he is anxious."

"Let's check back in the passage." I know I'm right. I don't know why she wants me to feel stupid. I can feel my face getting flushed, getting hot. My neck itches.

"It's not. I'm not going to argue with you. Now, I think this is about speech. Are you still mad about speech?"

I fidget in my chair, looking down. I don't like these direct questions; they're harder to dodge, so I keep looking down, "I guess with occupational therapy and physical therapy, I don't know, I guess I see. . . I see. . . you know, results?"

Her eye contact is intense I realize, as she is staring at me, "You don't see results here?"

I look up; it's hard to meet her gaze, "I don't know. I guess I don't really know. Like, I know my memory's bad, right?"

"Yeah."

"And I struggle with focus, but I don't know that I see like direct results? Like isn't it part of the healing process?"

She uncrosses her arms, adjusts her ponytail, tight; her brown eyes are intense. She's got confidence and energy enough for a boardroom; I don't really know why she's a speech therapist. She finds my eyes, "Look, you need to improve on some things. You have work to do. You want to graduate high school? You want to go on to college? We need to work on your memory and focus. But you know what? You come back tomorrow with at least five goals, and we'll use our time to work on those goals. Okay?"

I don't want to not like her. I do not enjoy disliking people. I mean, c'mon, I'm Will Carter; I strive to love everyone, but I've never done well with teachers like this, ones who push me, ones who don't let me talk them into my way, and I nod, "Okay."

We finish with some memory exercises, and I don't do well, but I also just want to go home.

In the lobby, Dad is excited to see me come down the hall in the walker, and he stands and claps, "Yeah, buddy! Awesome!"

Siri comes up, hustling her bulky body to the front as Dad is signing me out, "Mr. Carter."

He turns with a smile, "Siri, how are you?"

"Now that Will has the walker, we are taking the wheelchair back. He's good. Keep an eye on him when he's using it. I'm not comfortable with him using it on his own yet, okay?"

I was so close to freedom. Dad confirms the details with her, and I stand with my walker by the door.

In the car, Dad smiles wide, "That's awesome, Will. I bet you're happy you're out of that wheelchair?"

"You have no idea."

And at home, Mom gives me a yell and a clap to see me with a walker, and we have a great dinner of fajitas, and we talk about moving my bed upstairs. I think it's great. Dad says he'll do it when I'm at school tomorrow. I can't wait. Being in my own room will be one step closer to feeling like my old self, one step closer to getting back, getting better.

Today both sucked and was awesome. I hate that physics is so hard; I hate that I am so lost in there. I hate that I have nothing to say in AP lit. I hate that I have to make it through this semester. But then, I love that I have a walker. I love that my dad doesn't have to help me stand up, help me brush my teeth; I love that no one has to transfer me to the toilet anymore. I love that I had a great, positive conversation with Lisa and Horus.

Anna calls me; we talk for a little bit, talk about walking, talk about school. I appreciate her for reaching out; she says she's going to come over tomorrow night. That sounds great. I don't have any other plans. I never have any other plans. I say, "I love you," but of course, I mean I don't really know if I mean it like you're supposed to. She's important to me; I care that she's in my life, so I guess I'm saying that when I say, "I love you."

In my bed that night, I look up, "Thank you, God. Thank you for letting me walk." I know he's smiling down on me. I know he's happy I'm walking, and I know he made it happen. I am in thanksgiving, but I am still needy, "Help me heal. Help me do well in physics, Lord. God, I pray that I can get to a cane. Lord, I pray I will be able to do well in all my classes. God, I pray you will help me graduate. Lord, help me. . . help me get better." Better. Direct results, right? Better is not a direct result; it's a goal that keeps moving; it's a target I can never seem to hit. Walking with a walker is a direct result; graduating will be a direct result. I don't have too many markers left anymore, but I know I want to get better.

I still think I can be me again, the me of before, the me without a brain injury; I still think I can be the cocky kid in camo pants, a Ramones shirt, and highlighter Converse. I still think there is a chance he is waiting to be revealed. I don't like me. I like him. I want to be him. That way, I don't have to ever like the me of now; I just have to get to him. Someday soon, it's coming. I can be rid of me and be him again.

But that day is not today, so I must close my eyes and hope that tomorrow, I can be one step closer to him.

13

THE BIG SURPRISE

The Mercedes pulls up, silver, sleek, small, and probably not the kind of car you would expect for an eighty-five-year-old man to drive, the kind of polished masculinity you see in men of a certain age. Dad is quick to get me out the door, watching from behind, and then catching up as I make my way to Granddad's car.

"Will! Hold on! You forgot your backpack!" Dad calls as he makes his way back inside.

Tall, tan, bald with a small collection of encircling white strands, gold watch, dress pants, sharp black shoes, and a face that can command a boardroom, my granddad's a monolith.

To be honest, I don't know him. I mean, if you were to ask me to tell you about him, I would sound off like a Wikipedia page, "He was an accountant, and then, he worked his up to own and manage a chicken processing company. He's very wealthy. He's had two wives die on him. He lives in Virginia Highlands. He likes to golf," and most importantly, "He gives me a hundred dollars at Christmas and a hundred dollars on my birthday."

I only really see Granddad at Christmas and birthdays. He's usually nice but distant. His wife, Robin, is younger than him and is so nice she's distant. You ever meet those kinds of people? They're so nice that it puts this big vast trench between them and you? Now, when I say nice, I don't mean, like nice. I mean, they are putting on polite and friendly demeanor, but it seems like they're trying so hard to do it that you wonder if they're some kind of sociopath. I'm from the South; there are many of these people here, but I can't think of single, real, genuine conversation I've had with Robin. And, she has one of those laughs which sounds like it comes with a string pull. Those kinds of laughs are so off-putting; I want to say to her, "It's okay if what I said isn't funny to you, and if you don't laugh. In fact, I'd prefer it."

I digress. Granddad is standing by his car like a mighty statue, the way I always seem to place him in my mind, like the last in a long line of patriarchs; I mean, really, even the way he stands indicates authority.

He smiles wide at me, "Hey, Will, how are you doing?"

I'm always happy to see him, and his distance is effective because whenever I'm around him, I want to get his approval, "Granddad, good to see you."

He gives a quick laugh and bends down to a hug and then, turns to Dad.

"So, Bob," a quick handshake between father and son, "I drop him off at school. Do I need to go in with him?"

Dad chuckles to himself, "You need to park, walk him to the front, and Aaron will meet you there, and he will take Will to class. Then, you pick him up on the side of the school near the stadium. Aaron will walk him out, and then, you take him to Pathways—"

"Yeah, yeah, I remember that. Pathways, right near Toco Hills. Pick him up at 4."

Quick, decisive, no time for small talk.

"Okay. Bob. I'll see you around 5."

Dad helps me in the car, shows Granddad how to break down the walker, and he's met with a "Yeah, yeah."

Dad leans his head in, "Remember Will, we're going to see *Much Ado About Nothing* at Roswell. So, your Granddad will drop you off at Panera. Okay?"

"Okay."

It's not like I need to be prepped for disruptions in the schedule. On second thought, okay. Maybe, I can make a mental note and remember to get some caffeine at Panera, because this play will keep me up past eight, the current bedtime for this particular, disabled kid.

In the car, there's a little bit of awkward silence, mindless chatter about school, which, honestly, I don't care to talk about, then, Granddad gets to what I really do care about—well, not as much as before my accident, but I am still, surprisingly up on it given everything—politics.

At a stop light, Granddad quickly switches to what he wants to talk about, "You watching the presidential stuff?"

"Oh yeah." (That might be a stretch, but I have heard and seen a decent bit.)

His grip tightens on the steering wheel. I know he has a pair of driving gloves in his glovebox. That's the kind of guy he is.

"I like that Barack Obama guy."

I am floored. He likes that Barack Obama guy? Robin has Fox News on for all six of the TVs in their house, and he likes Barack Obama? I try to say none of this and reply, "Really?"

"Yeah. Charismatic. Well-spoken. Curious to see how he does."

He's actually hit on my favorite to win. To be honest, in my head, I can't really think of who else is running. God, most of the people who run for president are just a blur of white faces, winkles, and suits. I offer an opinion that makes me feel smart, "I liked him for at least two years now."

His eyes light up, thinking, "What happened?"

I'm searching for the word, diving deep, spelunking furiously for the word, "The uh. . . you know. . . the uh. . ."

"The DNC. You're right. I had forgotten about that."

I smile. We're really talking about something, Granddad and I, and it doesn't look like he's counting the seconds or scanning for someone to talk to. "Yeah, I remember my political science teacher, Mr. Dodd, he said, 'Watch that guy. He's going to be president,' and from then on, I've thought he's a great choice." It's nice to ride with Granddad; his car seems to glide above the rode, that smooth kind of soft drive you can't get from a Camry.

"He's got a bright future ahead of him either way. I think he has real shot at it though. What do you think?"

It's nice. I can't think of the last time Granddad asked for my opinion on things. It's not like he's a jerk or anything, not like he doesn't talk to me either. It's just. . . well. . . he's got the boardroom attitude. He wants to be a part of the conversation. He doesn't want to sit on the sidelines, and I don't know how he did it, but he has everyone seeking his approval, his children, grandchildren, probably even his dog. Though, he's different today; he's smiling, laughing, asking for my input. Strange but I'll take it, and for the next ten minutes, we laugh; we exchange ideas, and when he says, "I want to continue this conversation," I believe him. I breathe in; it's so refreshing for someone to enjoy my presence. It's something I've been chasing in every interaction. I think my parents enjoy me, but it's different; they're my parents; they have to want to be around me, but Granddad? I guess he should have to want to be around me, but he's never been that kind of granddad. I'm looking forward to our next conversation.

The school day is a drudge. Economics is at a place where I'm not just being lazy by taking the book to the quiz; today's quiz was hard, and, even with the book right in front of me, I got a 70 on it. I'll have to take it again tonight if I can remember. I mean, truly, that was the problem with the quiz: I couldn't remember. I read and reread, but all the words were so foreign to me, like *horizontal production integration*. Why can't people use actual, real words? Is that so hard? Experts use these words, so they can feel smart, so they can speak in their own language that people outside of their particular field cannot understand, like doctors and therapists. They use specific vocabulary to make you feel less than and only able to listen to them. You'll say, "My foot moves out," and they'll put a hand on your shoulder while correcting you, "Pronates." And, you feel lesser, and it's the same with economics. Why do you have to call it capital? The definition is one word. *Money*. Just say money.

Screw it. I'll take the quiz again tonight. Remember, Will. Remember to take the quiz again tonight. Don't forget. Write it on your hand. No, no, Sara will look at your hand and, will then scold you for writing it on your hand. Just remember really, really hard.

Lit was me listening to other people talk about *Heart of Darkness* and trying to focus on Ms. Colvin preparing us for *Catcher in the Rye*. All I can think is, didn't somebody believe that book told them to kill someone? Physics, I have a quiz on Friday. Over what? I am sure there is an answer to that question, but, notably, I do not have an inkling of what that answer is. But soon, Aaron takes me out to the Mercedes, and Granddad gets on a tangent about Republicans.

He's got his left hand on the wheel and his right-hand

gesturing, showing his muscular, hairy arms, "And they don't have anybody. Nobody. Not a single one running stands a chance."

And I'm nodding. I'm so tired, and I think I forgot to pack my second Ritalin, so I know; I know the rest of the day is going to suck, but I remember I need to say something to keep Granddad going, "Yeah. You're right."

And, we make it to a stoplight, and Granddad turns to me, his voice low, like he's telling me a secret, "Don't tell Robin this, but I think John McCain is an idiot."

I laugh; I mean, it's funny. John McCain isn't an idiot, but I like that Granddad is telling me things he doesn't want me to tell Robin, creating a bond between us. And we get to Pathways, and to be honest, this sucks too. In physical therapy, we try going up and down stairs. Up, I'm great. No problem at all, but going down? I almost fall. My left foot is piece of crap. It's shaky and needs work, and going down the stairs, Siri makes me use my left hand to grab the rail, another problem, and before you know it, I'm on the floor. Occupational therapy, we try the driving simulator and same story, terrible. My reaction time is just too slow. To be fair, even before my accident, I was always the worst at video games out of my whole friend group. I try and tell Caitlin this, but it's no use. Work on my vision, my reaction time, and we'll try again. Speech? Don't even get me started. So, I ended up writing "take the economics quiz again" on the inside of my left arm, hoping I could keep it down, and she wouldn't notice. But, of course, she did, and she scolds me, "Why not write it down in your agenda? Will, we've talked about this. You need to use your agenda."

This is a fair point, but I think my counterpoint is equally valid, "What if I forget to look at my agenda?"

She shakes her head, disappointed, annoyed, and I know it,

and I can feel my own blood pressure rising because why would that make her mad?

"Will, that is the issue we are trying to work on, and if you can't understand that, we are going to have a problem."

I don't want to have a problem with anyone, and why are you going to have a problem with me? You've got Chad in here calling people, "shawty" and "girl," and we're going to have a problem? But you know what? I keep quiet. I nod. I say "Okay" and am secretly pissed off. That's better because when you actually get upset, they attribute it to your injury, or they want to "have a longer conversation." So, I swallow my thoughts. My left hand is shaking. This happens when I get upset. Please stop. I hope she doesn't notice.

"You need to accept there are things you need to work on. You need to accept that you need to check your agenda and write things in your agenda. Let me see that," and she takes my left arm and tries to decipher the message I've scrawled, "I can't even begin to read this. You see? You write yourself a note on your arm, and by the time you get home, you won't remember what you've written. Write it down in your agenda, and then, you make a mental note to check your agenda every day. I'll tell your mom when we're done today."

I'm looking down. I can't meet her eyes. I can't look at her because I'll say something I'll regret. In the back of my mind, I know she's hard on me because she wants me to get better. At the corner of my brain, I know she has good intentions. At the front of my brain, however, I want to tear her down. It's building and building because I feel like she's making me feel small, less than, and I want her to feel that way too. Thankfully, the back of my brain is telling the front of my brain to suck it up. Okay, good, they're communicating.

Sara is standing up, "I'll tell your mom. C'mon, let's go."

She puts my walker in front of me. I look up, "Can't."

"Can't what? Go?"

"No, can't tell Mom. My granddad is picking me up."

A smile—I mean, I don't mean for it to happen. I'm not that much of a butt, but it happens.

She folds her arms, "Fine. I'll email her later."

Great. Awesome. Something else to get bugged about. After the afternoon meeting, Granddad wheels up, checks me out, and we blaze towards the highway where we will, as is natural for a highway in Atlanta, only simmer.

Granddad tightens his grip on the wheel as we meet the bumper-to-bumper gridlock, "Polls show he's up on Clinton in Iowa."

My mind is drowning in the exhaustion of the day, "What?"

Granddad cocks his head, "You know, Obama. He's up on Clinton in the polls. You think he can do it?"

"Oh yeah. Of course. I think he can win. I mean, she doesn't have his charisma."

That's not original. I heard Shackleford say it in the TAG room today, but I'm not about to give someone else credit right now.

"I've never liked the Clintons, so I hope you're right."

The Republican in him can't bring himself to that; maybe, Obama can get his vote, but Clinton? Let's not get heretical. Though to be fair, I'm not even sure he is a Republican. More than anything, I think he just wants to not be in trouble. I feel that Granddad. I feel that.

After an okay diner at Panera, my parents bring me to the Roswell High School theater, a place I know all too well. My sophomore and junior years, I spent many a night, weekend, or afternoon, going over lines and blocking; though, today, I am seeing the play I should've been in, *Much Ado About Nothing*.

It's weird to enter these doors as a guest, but it's especially weird because no one else is here.

"Mom," I think. She is always worried about me and masses of people. I guess she's worried my presence will trigger a stampede of adoring fans? Screams, shouts, and then, I will be carried up to crowd surf. I'm sure this is her concern; it has to be.

A squeal, and I see her, a waft of silver hair, the jeans, the tucked in Roswell Drama Club long-sleeve shirt as she beams with joy, "Will Carter! I can't believe Will Carter's here!"

Ms. Ogle is the head of the theater department, a funny title because she is the theater department. She has always loved me, and it's mutual. She's quirky, weird, and as against the system as any seventeen-year-old can appreciate. But, the big thing, the most important thing, the major thing that will always put her down as one of the greats in my book is that she cares. She is in your corner, and she will fight for you any way she can. It's probably why she always looks tired; caring about people is exhausting.

She hugs me tight; I almost fall over, but it's good to see her.

"It's so good to see you up and awake," and she laughs, nervous maybe? No, I think she's just excited.

"It's good to see you, Ms. Ogle," I smile. My buzz cut shimmers in the bright lights of the theater lobby, and someone calls Ogle's name, and she looks to my mom and dad, "So good to see you," she smiles warmly as they exchange hugs.

"Good to see you."

Someone calls Ogle's name again, and she can't help but smile, even though I know she wants to scream as she calls, "I'll be there in a second!"

Then, a look to me, my parents, and we are ushered through the empty auditorium to a spot up front, marked for me, right in the first row, and we're there, alone in the theater. Anna comes in after a brief conversation with the stage manager, and I know she's annoyed; she's always annoyed when people try to hoard imaginary power over her. Soon, she's next to me, kissing me, and clasping my hand. She's always affectionate, even when I'm out of it. Tonight is one of those nights. People are coming up to me and saying hello, and I'm mostly smiling and saying, "Good to see you."

If this was the me before my accident, I would love this. I would feel so alive in all of this attention. I would feel a thousand stories tall. Now, I'm worried about those stories toppling over. I don't want too many people to come up, but I can't say anything. What am I supposed to do? Turn to Anna, and say, "Can you keep them away? I'm worried about feeling awkward. Also, it's late, and I'm getting sleepy. Have someone bring me a pillow."

No, I find myself so glad when the lights start to dim, and the how starts, and it goes well. I mean, sure, it's high school theater, but they honestly all do a good job. It's hard to watch Brian Rooney in the show I was supposed to be in; Benedict? I competed in ThesCon with a Benedict monologue, and now, he's got the part. I would be pissed if anyone else got this part. (He's the best actor we have at RHS, even I'm smart enough to see it.) But if it were anyone else? I'd be so livid.

Then, everyone is standing and applauding, and they return to the stage, and Brian, himself, does the honors, walking towards me down the stairs as the rest of the cast follows him.

"We'd like to take a moment to recognize a guy who would've been here onstage, you know. He put a great deal of work into Roswell Theater. I mean, who am I kidding? You know who I'm talking about. Will Carter!"

He hands me the flowers, and people are clapping, and I'm grinning ear to ear. They give me the flowers; they talk about how I made a difference to drama club, and how they're glad I'm back, and I smile and say, "Thank you."

I always feel like I'm bad at gratitude, like my outward reaction does not match my internal feeling because I might be grinning from ear to ear, but inwardly, my heart is a fireworks show. It means so much to be honored like, this, right? Though, it's weird that people are acting like they're proud of me, and I don't know why. All I did was not die and stay not dead. Seems pretty everyday if you ask me. Though, I guess it's a minor accomplishment when I should be dead, maybe?

When I get home that night, and we're sitting on the couch, Dad asks me, "You want to sleep upstairs tonight?"

"Yeah."

He smiles, his arm around me, "Good, because that's where I moved your bed."

We laugh. It's a good family joke, and as we climb the stairs that night, Mom ahead of me and Dad behind, both hands on the siderails, I can't help but feel this is the best way to close the night, sleeping upstairs in my own room like I used to.

We make it to the second floor, and Dad gives me my walker. When Dad opens the door with a creak, it's like I remembered it: blue walls, bed, nightstand, the two dressers, my bookcase, and my communist flag. Now, Uncle Johnny might have jokingly called me one, but I was no communist. I just thought it was a cool thing to have. I got it when I went on a mission trip to Moscow (that and the two communist officer hats). I mean, sure, I'm definitely on the politically liberal side, without a doubt, but don't worry, I gave no thumbs up for Vladimir Lenin.

"Feels good, don't it?" Dad says as he leans against the wall.

"Yeah. Feels good to be upstairs. I won't have to wake up to Shelby going outside anymore."

"Don't worry, you'll still hear her."

174

He imitates her whine and scratching, and it feels good to give a good normal laugh to a regular everyday joke. I like these moments because I feel like nothing is curated for me, like it's a laugh we would have before my accident. It feels more normal. Not normal is a moment away, but at least now feels more normal. Better.

The next week is a blur, a struggle, and every day, I'm just hoping to make it to the end. I wake up, eat my breakfast, pop my Ritalin, and with two hours before school starts, I work hard at my three classes, mostly physics. My physics test grade was a 73. A 73? It's passing, and yes, I want to pass, but I need to go to a good school; I need to have acceptable grades. I'm getting better, right? I'm getting back to my old self. . . I thought. I'm going to heal; I'm going to be that Will again. Right? But, no, this week has not brought that Will. This Will is tired. He goes to school, goes to therapy, comes back from therapy, does school, and goes to bed. Anna comes over, and she comes with my family as we get dinner. But mostly, school has swallowed my every thought. I'm struggling. Struggling bad. "Get me through today" is my prayer. You ever prayed that way?

Of course, you have. Everyone has. Everyone lives a moment in their life they want to get through. The trouble is not to let this become your life. Every day is a challenge, and every time you lie down in your bed with a heartbeat still in your chest is a victory. The day has been won, or at the very least, it has been accomplished. I don't know if I'm wining anything at this point.

The drumbeat of school and therapy bangs on. More work on vision, driving. Siri's talking about possibly getting me on a cane soon, which would be amazing. Sara and I are having our struggles, but I'm working on reading, memory, and organization. We did have a tense moment where she wanted me to work on my handwriting, "It's always been this bad though," I protested.

"That doesn't mean you can't improve," was her reply.

And, this is why I hate therapists. Okay, maybe hate is a strong word to throw at an entire group of people. Okay, maybe, I do not hate therapists, but I hate the presumption behind therapy that you should always be improving. If this is the case, then what is better? Better needs to be a location you can arrive at and enjoy; otherwise, you are always working, never achieving, always striving, never arriving.

For me, better is this cleft of rock in a cliff, a little cave on the side of a mountain that I must strive, strain, cut my fingers on stone to get to, sweaty, beaten, and bruised, but when I make it to better, I crawl inside this cave and rest in this better place as I watch the storms of life go past.

I'm not thinking about therapy today, only school, because today is Friday, and the best part about outpatient therapy? It's only four days a week for me. Friday is a great day, even though it's the day we take a practice test for AP lit, and I zone out reading the passage, have to read it again, still struggle to remember a single bit of what I read. The names—why can't characters in the stories we read have simple names like Joe and Sally? How am I supposed to remember Aristarchus?

I hope I don't have to talk about this. Please God, let us not have to talk about this. Please God, let her take this as a participation grade. Then, in physics, Mrs. Foss works with me the whole class, but again, I am still so gloriously lost that I want to ask her if we can pick this up again tomorrow. She tries problem after problem after problem with me, and all I can gather is that I know what fission and fusion are, and that's about it.

Fission is what happened to me. I am broken; I'm trying for fusion, to have the parts of me come back together, to make a complete, working me, like I was before, capable, sufficient, but I can't quite seem to do it.

I get in my dad's car a little bit more beat up this week than last. I hope he can't tell. I never want people to feel sad because of me.

After the conversation about today, Dad offers, "You're excited about tonight, though, right?"

Tonight. Tonight. Tonight. Wait, what is tonight? Don't ask that; then, he'll know you've forgotten. Pretend. "Sure."

"Sure, dang. I was hoping having your friends over would make you more excited."

Wait what, hold on. "Who's gonna be there?"

"Remember? Eric, Peter, Stephen, the whole gang. They're coming over for your birthday."

"Oh right. Wait, what day is it?"

Always a beat. I think Dad and Mom's hearts drop whenever I forget something so clearly, like they think I'm farther along than I am. I hate it. It hurts so bad to see them disappointed. I mean, I know they're not disappointed in me, but I still feel like the cause of their disappointment.

"Friday."

It's like they think I'm doing well because I'm on a walker, and even though I'm doing school every waking hour of my life, I'm still functioning. They get their hopes up that, maybe, maybe, I will get back to my old self, and I feel—not that they've ever said any of this, so it could be a complete fabrication of my mind—that I shatter that vision every time I forget something, like what the date is today.

Dad misunderstands me. I push my glasses up to the bridge of my nose, "No, I mean, like, what is the date?"

"February 1st."

"Oh my gosh."

"Time flies."

And it does. Days are meaningless to me. Mondays through Thursdays are the same: wake up tired, fall asleep tired, busy, busy, busy. Fridays are the end, less busy, better. I usually see Anna. Saturdays mean there's time to get work done. Still tired because my body has its own alarm clock, and Sunday? Sundays are church days; then, it's time to work on school.

As Dad takes me out of the car, he asks me, "Oh, by the way, what's your favorite U2 song?"

I give it a moment, a thought. "Sunday Bloody Sunday."

Surprise as he steadies me in my walker, "Really? Not Beautiful Day?"

We start the move to the ramp in the garage to the kitchen door, "Nah, Sunday Bloody Sunday is my favorite. Why?"

He follows me inside, "Just curious."

That night, there's Domino's hot, greasy, life-expectancy-decreasing, cheese circles they call pizza, Coke, Sprite, Mr. Pibb, and root beer, and, of course, we're eating it by the TV, playing video games. I do, and I don't like this. I want so badly to be liked by them again, especially Peter, my former best friend. I say former because it's not the same anymore. We can't really talk like we used to, make jokes like we used to, and I want to. I spend my time trying to think of something funny to say, some joke to make, something—anything to win their approval, but I'm mostly quiet. I play these games, *Call of Duty, Tekken, Halo,* and I can't. I can't do anything but get beat, and they're acting like this is normal, but I feel like a failure. I don't know what I want from them, but they're not giving it. They can't know what I feel. I mean, they're here, playing video games, eating pizza, and drinking soda, like we're fourteen again, and it's all for me. I know they want to be drinking or smoking pot; I'm not just being the dweeb kid accusing them; I know they do this because, in the summer, I started having to refuse to do this, and I know they want to. I guess I want to feel like they are hanging out with me because they want to, and God, how I wish I could be who I was. I just keep my mouth shut. I make one joke to complete silence, but then, I stay silent and play. I don't want to be awkward. It's better to be quiet than awkward, a lesson I have to learn every day again and again.

We go to open gifts, and there's a gift card here, a graphic novel from Peter that looks to a lower reading level than I was before, a gift card there, and Harrison gets me a pile of random junk from the dollar store, including two ribbons that go directly onto my walker: 2nd Place and Word's Best Grandma.

This causes great laughter, the kind of laughter we would have had all night if I wasn't brain injured, and that's nice. I'm thankful to Harrison for bringing it, but it feels like a party that your parents throw for you, so you don't feel bad. I'm thankful for it, but I hate that they are leaving at nine. I hate that I can't really converse or engage. I hate that they all leave like they have accomplished some duty. I'm grateful they came, but it's the worst, and I hate what this is, a broken boy with friends who want to hang out with the version of me from before but hang out with the me of today because they have to. Better. I need to get better, need to improve, heal, so that I can be the me of before, so that my friends will want to be my friends, so I can make jokes, can stay up late, can make Mom and Dad proud. Better is there; I know it. I need to focus. I need to buckle down; I need to finish therapy; I need to graduate high school. Then, oh yeah, then, I'll be better. I'll be somebody people want to be friends with, not someone people have to be friends with; I'll be someone worthy of being appreciated. Better. Better means people can like me, and then, I can like me.

As Mom cleans up the pizza and drinks, she asks with an upward lilt of hope, "Had fun tonight?"

I'm on the couch, sinking into the back, pizza stains riddled across my white RHS Young Democrats T-shirt, "Yeah. It was fun."

She smiles; I know that's what she wanted. She wanted me to get as close to old times as possible, "Good."

I can't tell her about my friends. I know she sees it. I know she notices how Peter is, how he's not the same Peter, how that high-pitched laugh he can get into when he's really laughing does not echo through the downstairs anymore. I know she saw how much of a passenger I was tonight. I know she hurts for me, and I don't want to add to that. They've put in so much, so much money for me, so much time for me, so much stress for me. I want to make them proud. I need to get better, so they can be proud.

The rest of the weekend involves the family, and it's good, but it's still people. I used to shine at family events, cracking jokes, destroying in dominoes, and I got so much attention, doing impressions and Brian Regan routines, and I loved it. Now, I'm trying, trying, but playing dominoes, I place a pink on a maroon, and it's met with laughter, the thing that shrinks my already raisin-sized ego and ignites my anger when it's not requested.

"Will, not quite!" Mom chuckles.

"A little rusty, I see," Roland adds.

I mean, I should be happy. Ball busting is what my family does to each other in any and all circumstances. This should be a sign that I'm getting back to normal. But I feel so small with the shriveling flower of my ego so quickly burned to dust over a game of dominoes. My face gets hot; my heart thunders against my chest; my vision goes double. I shake my head, clench my hands into fists under the table. I swallow, swallow, swallow. Make the anger go.

"We could never beat Will before," Granny lets out a little laugh.

"No, never. No one could beat Will at dominoes." Aunt Linda adds.

I look down. Breathe. Breathe. Swallow. Swallow. Swallow.

"He was the king, but hey, this game looks good for me," Uncle Roland chuckles to himself, his hand crossed atop his gut.

I swallow, drink water, get Dad's help to get to my walker to go to the bathroom, and then, I am okay. Though, I keep thinking on it. I need to have the redness in my face go away, to have my heart slow back down. I enjoy the presents, the ice cream cake, and the cozy feeling of my parents' couch.

I want to say something smart or something funny. Why? This is my family. They love me no matter what, but I guess I want them to view me like they used to, a seventeen-year-old with promise, a teenager whose opinion was worthy of listening to. But they love me at least. I guess because I've known their unconditional love before, it feels good now because it doesn't feel like their love is an act of pity. They would be here, no matter what state I'm in. They'll always be here, and we'll always make fun of each other, and I'll always get hot in the face, and then, we'll always laugh, and I'll always say something only Uncle Roland laughs at, and that's okay, and it's good. It's normal, well, normal for me. It's not better, but it's certainly not much worse.

However, these days are not my actual birthday. My true birthday is Wednesday. A couple "happy birthdays" in class, a hug, a kiss, and a gift of a scarf and a shirt from Anna, an announcement in the afternoon meeting, a dinner at Chili's, and then, it's the usual Wednesday night ritual: youth group.

The church I go to, the church I've grown up in, is huge, and the building for the youth group is the size of most actual churches in the U.S., The Bricks, as they call it, is two stories, a rock wall, video games and indoor basketball upstairs, pool tables, a little café; it's nuts, but it's where I spend every Wednesday night. They've taken all the kids into the auditorium, and I'm used to this; I know the deal—no crowds.

As I push my walker into the open doors of the auditorium, the drumbeat of "Sunday Bloody Sunday" starts up, the guitar joining quickly after, and then, Ryan, a guy his thirties with the haircut of a twenty-year-old (but it's okay because he's awesome), belts out the first line.

For me. Another night for me. It's a birthday party for me, a room full of kids, many who might know who I am, a portion who might not or didn't before my accident, but now, they're all here for me. Sure, David, one of the pastors, gives a talk about something not related to me, but this night is for me. I'm sat near the front, and I'm smiling, beaming; this is amazing. I can't believe that people are willing to do this for me.

Then, the real moment. They're talking about these yellow arm bands, like the Livestrong bracelet, everyone I know wears. They are for something, other than spreading awareness of Will Carter apparently. Kelli Bull, someone I've known since I was a kid, a friend starting in high school, blonde hair, button nose, capable of handling the spotlight well, steps up to the mic, "Now, we started this charity, these bracelets everyone has. We started this because Will always wanted to do something for Darfur. He was trying to set up a benefit concert, but obviously, Will was not able to do that. If you're not familiar with what's happening in Darfur, Sudan, the Arab majority is sponsoring the killing of the African population of Sudan. The Janjaweed is an Arab militia who is responsible for murdering thousands of Africans, many of whom are Christians. Through the selling of these arm bands, we have raised five thousand and sixty-two dollars."

Applause, and I'm, I'm just blown away.

"And we are giving all of it to Save Darfur to provide food, medical care, housing, and other assistance to the African people ravaged by this genocide."

There is applause, and I am in a daze; this doesn't feel like real life. Arms bands were sold, inspired by me, famous for being in a coma, and now, because of that, a group of people, suffering in Africa will get food, water, and medical attention. It's hard to stomach, the thought that I've had this much of an impact.

There is a cake for me, enough for a room of a hundred teenagers. It's passed around, and we eat, and I have a few nodding conversations, and I can't believe this is for me. I can't believe this moment is happening, and I know this wouldn't happen if I hadn't almost died. In some ways, it's good. It's good that I almost died, good I was in a coma, not for a birthday party but for the money for Darfur. That's all because I'm famous for not being dead. Thank God I'm not dead. Sometimes, I wonder why I'm not. Why did God choose to reach down and restart my heart? Why did God flutter my eyelids open? What is the impact of my life? What is the dent to measure the value of my existence? Will I simply ding the wall of life? Or, will I smash right through?

My mind wants to retreat to dreaming about tomorrow, about better, about the me who I will be, retreating from the me of today. Better. Better. Better. Yeah, but that was the impact of the old me, really. What about the new me? Better. Better. Better.

With Dad's help, I climb the stairs, brush my teeth, get ready for bed, and as he helps me transfer to the bed, he says, "Congratulations on officially being an adult."

A smile forms across my face, "Thanks, Dad."

An adult. Right. I'm an adult. It doesn't feel like it. I've never felt smaller than I do after my accident, but at least, I have this to chart towards forward momentum—I'm aging, and now, I'm no longer, at least in the eyes of the law, a child. I want to feel like an adult, feel like I have any semblance of control over my life. When I'm better, that is how I'm going to feel. I'm going to feel in control again; I'm going to go to college; when I'm better, people will respect me. I will respect me. When I'm better, everything is going to be better. Everything.

I'm not better yet, but one day, I'm going to heal.

This day is not that special; this is just a birthday, but that day? The day I'm better? That's going to be amazing.

14

PROM

S iri, now with red highlights, still the same spandex, has a lot more smile for me than the first day we met. I don't think she liked me at first. I don't think she got me. I don't think she understood my humor, and I don't know, maybe, sarcasm is associated with being a dick. Is that it? I don't know, but I feel like she gets me a lot more now, and I can drop some Steven Wright jokes, and she totally gets it. A week ago, I got my cane, and it was one of the best moments of my whole life. It went like this:

"Wanna try the cane?" She says, slowly lowering her larger figure to the edge of the mat I'm sitting on.

"Do I? Wait, you're serious, right? Of course."

And there's no crowd for this one. There's nobody really watching as she hands me the metal cane with the plastic rubber top, and we go for a spin down the hall. No thumbs up, no pictures, I thought there would be a different feeling. I thought I was going to feel like I was falling; I thought I was going to face what some call "a period of transition." But, you know, I guess these past couple months have been a period of transition, a period of waiting.

"You're going to heal. You're going to get better." I tell myself this. After each day, I am so exhausted, so tired of barely passing physics, so tired of being quiet in English class, so tired of creating awkward silences in conversations at the dinner table, so tired of me, so ready to be someone else, ready to be my former self again.

But walking around with the cane felt like normal, felt like something I could live with. It was independence, freedom of movement. The cane, at the very least, was a sign I was getting better, a mark on the wall to show my brain is healing.

We had gone out to dinner with Anna, and I was doing a Brian Regan routine, and I have a brain injury, and yes, I was tired, and yes, I shouldn't have been able to know it, but I did the routine verbatim, and I got shushed for being too loud. Now, this happened before my accident, and before my accident, Anna would be put her hands to her face in embarrassment, but it was kind of cute embarrassment, you know? Like, "Oh geez, that's my boyfriend," but now, I feel like it's real embarrassment, and my dad looks at me, "Shh, buddy, a little quieter, people are trying to eat."

Now, I don't know why, but this causes a vibration of anger to flow through my body; my left hand shakes a little bit, and my voice is a little loud, as I work on the most exaggerated whisper, "I'm so sorry. I'll try and keep my voice down. Is this better?"

Dad shakes his head; I know he's annoyed, but can't he see I felt small, and I was striking back at him for my feeling small? I ask where the bathroom is, and Dad offers, "Do you need me to take you?"

Mom hits his arm, "He's good."

And I am good. I get there; I take care of business no problem, leaning my cane against the sink, so I can wash my hands, and I open the bathroom door, and. . . where are they? No, I mean, I knew they wouldn't be right outside the bathroom because that would be weird, but how do I get back to the table? I remember coming in here, but I have nothing to draw on to get back to where I'm supposed to be. I look to the left, the right, and I. . . I really don't know. All paths look the same; all the tables look the same, and even the people, no face looks distinct. Something in my mind says the back right. Okay, let's head that way.

I continue scanning, looking for Dad, Mom, Anna, any sign of them, and I am walking through, having people move their legs, their belongings, "Excuse me," I mutter, as I continue moving.

I'm wandering and part of me wishes I was wearing sunglasses, so they could think I was blind, and it was a physical disability that was preventing me from finding my parents, rather than this failing brain, broken, beaten, bruised. I'm sure I look anxious as a waitress pats my arm, "Are you okay, honey?"

"I'm okay, just trying to find my parents."

I see my dad walking towards me, "There you are. We were worried you fell in."

That's the typical Carter line, but it's not funny to me right now. I hate it. No visual memory. None. I tried so hard to picture where we were sitting, tried to retrace my steps, but it was nowhere to be found. Nothing.

As we are walking back, Dad looks down, "Your fly."

Again, there's that little bit of frustration. I look down, pull my shirt and boxers through my fly, and give Dad a look like, "Eh?"

"Very funny, Will," he says in a way to let me know that he did not find it very funny, not even slightly funny.

We get back to the table, and I feel the need to explain things to Anna, "Got a little lost on the way back."

She wraps her fingers in mine, "It's okay."

The victory of going to the bathroom all by myself was ruined by the defeat of not being able to find the table. Independence? Not quite. The next few days are like a piece of WARHEADS candy. You know those? Crazy sour for a while, but there's a sweet core at the center, once you suck your way through the outer layer. That's what the cane is. It was supposed to be the thing that earned me my freedom, going anywhere I like, but then, it's not quite as sweet, and I'm still an eighteen-year-old kid with short hair, worse acne, and a brain injury. I know people tell me I am not my brain injury, but it sure feels like it when it shows itself for all to see.

Though, when I make it back to high school that Monday, I see Aaron, and he takes my backpack, smiling an exuberant smile, "Big day for you."

"Oh yeah. You like it?"

He laughs, seeing all the ribbons, "I see you kept your ribbons."

A grin creeps across my lips, "Especially the World's Best Grandma one."

A hearty laugh from Aaron as we make our way into the building to the TAG room, so I can finish up my econ, and before we head in, he says, "I know you're the comedy guy."

"Yeah, I know you know me."

He pauses, trying to remember, "God, I just had it."

It looks like forgetting things is a natural part of being human.

He snaps, lights on, "Have you ever heard of Hannibal Buress?"

My eyes go up, "No."

He gets kind of close, like he's telling me a secret, "Now, be careful with him. He's got some language, and if you tell anyone I told you to listen to him, I will drop this backpack so quick."

I sit behind one of the computers, my cane leaning on the chair next to me, "I got you. I got you."

And it feels good. Being asked to keep the secret that he told me to listen to an explicit comedian means Aaron trusts me.

Now that I have given up on trying to learn economics, and I use my book during the quiz, I am making my way through this. I know I will have to study for the end of course test, and I do. I study at home, after I've done the assignments that were supposed to teach the material to me, but I'm more focused on physics and lit anyway. I mean, I'm getting Bs in lit. I'm reading SparkNotes at home after I've read and reread what were supposed to read. I'm not trying to cheat. I'm not trying to slack off. I'm trying to stay afloat. College, remember? I don't just have to graduate. I need to get into college. I know my grades will affect my chances if I get waitlisted, and I can't do that. I need to go to college. If I don't go to college, the injury wins. The injury will win, and it will define me. It will defeat me. This cannot happen. I am going to get better, remember? BETTER. So, I wake up between four and five, and I study on nights and weekends. Anna has to tell me to be more active as her boyfriend, but can't she see what the stakes are?

So, when it's spring break, I can't get distracted. School's out, but therapy isn't. I focus on school, studying economics, physics, reading for AP lit. I am reading *The Great Gatsby*, and I am so thankful it's not *Heart of Darkness*. I mean, I still have nothing to add, but I am not nearly as lost. Still, I am reading each chapter twice, and then, once I finish a chapter, I read a summary of it online. I know when we get back, we're going to do a timed writing, and I can't afford to not do well.

College. College. College. College.

This is the chance for me to prove that this injury did not alter the course of my life forever. It is a bump in the road, not an iceberg in the water.

Later, the Friday before we go back to school, I'm in the car with Mom outside the Roswell Eye Clinic, and I know this is important because she got home to take me to a four o'clock vision appointment. Any teacher who can get home by 3:45 is on a mission. She looks at me, and she's got her low, serious voice on, "Caitlin highly recommends this. Promise me you'll go along with this. It's going to help you get back to driving."

I nod, looking down, not from sadness, more from exhaustion, "Okay."

And we go in through the glass door. The whole building feels like it's made of glass, smart move for an optometrist's office; though, the inside is more like a doctor's office, grey carpet, white walls, fluorescents. I've seen this all before, but I sit down in the black cushioned chair, and I wait for this next visit.

Soon, a smiley, curly-haired brunette woman in turquoise scrubs comes up and sits down, her hand out. I comply by shaking it and smiling, trying to match her positive energy.

"Hi, I'm Melissa."

"Will."

"Awesome. Nice to meet you."

I like the "awesome," an affirmation of the value of my existence.

"Nice to meet you."

"Come on back."

And we walk past the desk into a hallway, past the bathrooms, and into a little room with a table and two chairs on either side.

"Let's do a vision check," Melissa runs through the same

vision exam I did with Caitlin. Man, why can't all these thera-pists get on some social networking site and share information?

"You've got some vision loss in this left eye, huh?"

"Oh yeah, about a fourth."

This is the typical conversation, but she seems genuinely invested, and as she is testing me, she asks, "Who's your favorite musician?"

"Easy. Sufjan Stevens."

She stops, interested, "Who's that?"

I laugh, the little arrogant hipster in me loves this, "He's an awesome musician. He's doing an album for every state. He just did Illinois."

She stops, puts down her hands, and for the next ten minutes, we talk about music and comedians, and we don't do any vision therapy until she looks at the clock, "Jesus Christ, we have to finish this exam."

I laugh, and we finish it, and at the end of it, she uses the Brock string, this white string with the green, blue, red, and yellow beads on it, "Look at the red, focus your eyes on the red. See if you can make it double."

I focus, try and point both my retinas straight at it, and. . . nothing.

Melissa takes the string, "Yep. I see it. Your left eye shoots out. It's like it gets tired."

"Oh."

She sees my expression, "But don't worry. That's why we're here."

And I need to remember that.

She stands up, "C'mon."

And we go out to the front where she picks up a folder from the desk. We see Mom waiting and come over to her as Melissa hands her the folder but looks at me, "This has the exercises we practiced, the red and green glasses, the Brock string, and others. I want you to practice using the Brock string and the red and green glasses once a day for ten minutes."

Hitting my arm, Mom encourages, "Only ten minutes, Will, not bad."

"Yep."

Ten minutes? I don't have ten minutes. I have an economics end of course test in two weeks, a test in physics in a week, a timed writing for lit, and visiting colleges. Right, I need to check on those applications, and then, there are exercises for occupational and physical therapy, and I can't remember the last time I saw my friends. My mom keeps asking me if I've talked to Peter. What, is it my job to talk to Peter? I haven't had time to sit and breathe; I'm not talking to anyone. I need to get home and study.

When we do get home, and I try to study my economics, my mom is shocked, "Will, it's your spring break!"

I laugh, "Yeah. Break."

It's not the nicest response, but I feel the stress piling like bricks on my shoulders, stacking and stacking, and my back, my back is killing me. I want all of this to be over.

"Tonight, we'll go out for burgers?"

I nod, "Sounds good."

As she gets up, she says "Text Anna and see if she wants to join us."

It's like my mother is managing my social life for me. It's okay; I don't have the energy to manage it myself. I want everything that's not school to handle it itself. My plate is full. The bricks are stacking on my back, starting to crack and split, bits of red spitting in the air, as a fresh stack is dumped directly to my spinal column, and it is sore, so sore; my body wants to give up. Can't I just go back into a coma? This consciousness thing is hard. So tired. Always, every day, so tired.

Ritalin peps me up for a good four or five hours, and then, I crash. I think it's supposed to be six to seven; I say supposed to be because that's what my neurologist said, "It's supposed to keep you focused and energized for a good six hours."

Funny. I'm supposed to be healing too. I guess that I am? I don't know. The physical healing is easier. I'm on a cane now. That's something, right?

Have you ever written in pen on a paper and spilled water on that paper, and the ink bleeds all through the paper, so the words you wrote are now washed away? All that is left is this blurry blue splotch where your thoughts used to be. My days blur and blend like that into the same disembodied series of events that may or not be connected.

Going to get burgers is good at least; Anna likes to hold my hand, likes to rub my arm, and it's nice. Physical touch is a way to communicate without the fear of being awkward. I like to hug, kiss, and touch because I don't have to worry about remembering things, worry about whatever I just said; touch is the simplest, most universal form of expression. So, yeah, dinner is nice.

"Did you hear back from anywhere yet?" Mom asks her.

"Wait-listed at Emory. Still waiting on Tulane and UGA."

We've been talking about colleges for the past four years of our lives, striving, straining, pointing every action to this goal of college, and now, we're here. I fear, quite naturally, that all my late nights, all my hours in the theater, the debate team, and Model UN are for naught, my battleship of promise easily sunk by the brain injury torpedo.

Great.

Mom and Dad not only arrange my social calendar; they also fill all the silences where I don't have any words close to the trigger. Mom puts down her Diet Coke, "We're still waiting on Davidson. UGA, Wake Forest, Furman, and Oglethorpe. I think we should hear back next week."

Anna smiles at me, "That's good."

And, yeah, I mean, I've should've applied for more schools. Every day, I fear a letter is going to appear in my palms, my eyes fighting back the emotion, "Mr. Carter, we regret to inform you, you have been rejected by colleges. Had you not suffered your brain injury we would be more than happy to accept you. But, given your most precipitous fall from grace, we simply must reject your application for admission for all universities. Sincerely, admissions."

Why? Why would they accept me? My grades are nowhere near where they're supposed to be. I. . . I just can't. I'll let Anna and Mom do the talking.

"We'll go see colleges probably next week. Depending on where he gets in, of course. Right?"

She looks at Dad, who nods.

College. God. I don't want to even dream on it anymore. What if it's not real? What if this dream of college is set to crumble?

When we're home, Mom asks me, "If you don't get into Wake Forest, where do you think you'd want to go?"

"I don't know. Davidson? Furman?"

"We'll see. We'll pray."

Wake Forest. Number one. There weren't any other real contenders. I remember going to Winston-Salem and thinking, "This. This is where I want to be."

It looks like the college town from the movies, like the backdrop of every idealized vision of the future every teenager has in their brain for what culture has told us college is supposed to look like. I want that. I want the future I've crafted in my imagination. Before October 7, 2007, I used to believe my life had endless possibilities. Tomorrow is an ableist dream. You can only bank on tomorrow when you have no limits. It's a privilege no one talks about. Sure, I have privileges as a white kid that racial minority teens don't have, but if you've got a fully functional brain and a body still under warranty, you've got privileges too. Run through your dreams, and there's no limits. At eighteen, you've got the world ahead of you, but me? I've got roadblocks. My imagination has boundaries. I never thought this was a possibility, and now, I've got fewer possibilities.

Better? It's hard. I want to deny my injury, want to say it's a cold, and I'm getting over it. I don't know if better is coming. October feels like centuries ago. Is better coming? Or, is this just me? Is this who I am now? Shattered dreams?

At least now it's prom. I mean, I say at least, because it's a piece of what life used to be. The tux I get fitted for is just that, a simple black tux, clip on black bow tie, the full vest; the only difference from last year is the cane.

Dad is getting me dressed. Or, let me be clear, I put on my pants and shirt. I request his help with the buttons and clipping on the bow tie, and even with my teenage acne, missing a fourth of my left ear and sporting a cane, I don't look half bad in this thing.

We hop in the car, go to pick up Anna, who is in a red dress, skinny straps, her hair up. Pretty, she looks pretty. Soon, it's off to pictures at Stevie's house. I'm thankful Mom and Dad leave me. I love them, but I like when they let me live my life apart from them. Well, they looked like they were leaving, but they stand on the sidewalk, while we get set up for pictures, eight different teenage couples, girls in colorful dresses, different shapes, different frills, and the guys, we're the same carbon copy of high school prom—black tux, black bow tie.

"Okay, okay, now, let's have just the guys."

I shuffle over to these guys, my friends; though, William is probably the one I know and appreciate the most.

"Will! Get over here!"

And we lock arms; I pretend to hit William; he grabs my

cane and pretends to choke me; I pretend to choke him. I like this; the constant movement and activity takes the burden off me.

Then, of course, there's the limo. "Yes. This is my jam." R. Kelly's "Ignition (Remix)" plays throughout the car. Brian sings along, and he goes full diva, belting his heart out with his beautiful voice, which makes us all wonder why we started singing, and it's nice. I do my George Bush impersonation, and it gets laughs. I try to tell a joke, but I forget the punch line, and no one makes me feel bad about it. I hate myself for a solid five minutes, but no one's trying to make me feel bad about it. It's nice. Sure, there are some points where things are a tiny bit awkward. I'm getting a little too comfortable, "C'mon, Matlock, you know that Tosh routine."

A pat on my hand from Anna, "No, that's okay. We're good."

God, I know she's trying to be herself too and be like we were, pretend like everything's back to before, but I hate this. I hate being shut down; I always have, but after my accident? It feels like a knife in my side; I feel hot; I let go of her hand.

We get to prom, and you know what prom looks like. It's what every school dance looks like. There are silver decorations, tables for drinks, but you know, like soda or punch, people checking you in, and a dance floor, dark, smoky, and full of teenagers practically committing acts of fornication on the dance floor. And, what's worse than that is the circle of chaperones standing in a circle, nodding approvingly, "That's my daughter right there. Yes, the one shoving her buttocks into that young man's pelvis."

We make it to the dance floor, and to be honest, I've never been much of a dancer. I guess you could say it was nerves, two left feet, what have you, but now, I literally cannot be much of a dancer, as I am clutching a cane for balance and stability. I mean, what's good is that they start with a number of tracks designed to pump up the crowd, silly songs like "Who Let the Dogs Out," and "Bohemian Rhapsody." And I am thrusting my cane up and down like I'm leading the second line in New Orleans.

"What are you doing?" William laughs.

"Cane dancing, brother!"

"I love it!"

And I'm having fun. I'm enjoying being with people. I'm having fun with my peers, and I don't feel like everyone is looking at me. I'm not really dancing, and after a while, I need to sit down, and Anna and I go to a table where we are joined by Hattie, a pale girl with blonde hair, and her boyfriend David, who, sadly, has one of those forgettable faces. You know what I mean? Brown hair, everything proportioned well, but he looks normal and bland, so you don't really notice him.

"Tired?" Hattie asks.

"Yeah. Going hard on the dance floor."

"I saw that!"

We all share a laugh. I like this. Simple, easy. I guess since I know these people and like these people, but I don't know them really well, and I don't really think about them often (no offense to them), I'm comfortable.

See, I want Peter to like and accept me because he used to. Us not really hanging out, us not really talking, us not laughing and joking is not what it was. I want his approval because he is a key to before. He is a change. These people are fine, and of course, I want them to like me. Of course, I want them to think I'm fun or enjoyable to hang out with, but I'm not as desperate. It's easy to keep my mouth shut mostly and enjoy.

"Do you still do that thing?" Hattie asks me, leaning in close to speak up over the sound of thumping bass.

"What!?"

"That thing where you tell people you got into a fight with a bear!?"

I laugh, "Not as much. People aren't as curious about the cane."

She slaps my arm, "I thought the bear thing was so funny!"

And we're talking, hanging out, and it's nice. I hate the noise of this room; I hate how tired I am; I hate how much I am still in my head, but it's nice. It's refreshing to enjoy life and live it as an average teenager.

"Time After Time" starts, and we all get up. This is a high school prom must. So, we each find our partner and start the slow dance. Anna takes my hand, then sets my cane against the table, "Are you okay?"

Holding her hand, I check my walk, "I think so." And we go out for our slow dance.

"Let me know if you need to sit back down."

I nod, "Okay."

And we dance. She holds tight onto me, and I'm holding tight to her. I'm trying to enjoy this moment; my hands on her hips, cupped around them, hoping they don't slip on this shiny silk dress. I would put my hands on her butt; honest, I would. Hey, it's been a year, and she's smiling at me; her makeup sparkles even on this dimly lit dance floor. Her hair still looks so perfectly put together; mine has a few strands sticking up, and I want to kiss her; I do, but I might fall, and I can't do that. I can't; it's been a hard enough year, and God only knows how much worse that would make it. She pulls in closer, her head on my chest, steadying me all the while.

She looks up at me, "Thank you for breaking the rule."

It takes me a second, "What. . . oh, right, of course."

And she stops and kisses me, the whirling lights of a dance floor spinning around us.

Never has it been so sweet for someone to tell me they're

glad I'm not dead. We hold each other; to be fair, she's holding me more than I'm holding her.

A look to me, "You need to sit down?"

"Yes."

Thank God. My back is feeling the force of gravity. Is this what being old feels like? Dang, I guess for me to be old is going to suck. I'm so exhausted already. Blood. Is there blood in my brain? I'm so lightheaded, it's like the feeling is going out of my skull.

Before, I would've busted a move. I would be on that dance floor looking like a total dork; I'm talking *Saturday Night Fever*, Macarena; I'm talking dancing like Kevin James in [1]*Hitch* level dancing. Now, I'm sitting down, while the room stops spinning. It's past my bedtime.

Anna's holding my hand, stroking my fingers, and it's nice. A moment between us, and she is perfect in this moment. I knew I was never going to marry Anna Shults. I knew we were not meant to be; she's my best friend, well, she and Peter are. We're just best friends who kiss. I love her as my best friend, but right now, I'm enjoying being with her. I know graduation will come, and we'll go off to college, and we'll break up; I know for a fact, deep in my heart, that day is coming. Right now, I'm enjoying dating her, this moment, her pale, skinny fingers stroking mine, patiently waiting until I recover; I enjoy today, now, with her. I'm not thinking about school, therapy, college, or anything. I'm enjoying my hand in hers. She smiles at me; I smile back. I love this moment, and I love her in it. No, I don't love her romantically; I enjoy sharing right now with her.

Heaving heavy breaths and sweat dripping from his forehead, William Turner pops down next to us, no jacket, vest open, top button undone. I notice the song has changed as "Cotton Eye Joe" is halfway through. William is leaning back in the chair with the pose of someone who's just played a good game, and he's just finished the second half.

With his arm around my chair, "What's going on? You guys want to get out there?"

He's one of those guys who has definite dad energy. . . in a good way.

"C'mon, you guys want to dance out there with me? Stevie left me for the bathroom."

With the dance floor full, Anna looks to me, "Well? You okay?"

Deep breath. I find my cane. "Let's do this."

And as the beat sounds, and the fiddle sings a tune, we make our way to the floor; people scoot back to give me space. Whoever said teenagers aren't considerate?

With my cane jumping in the air, I dance what my little, crippled legs have left to give.

Anna lets out a laugh, as I jut out my lips, banging my head, my cane keeping time. Sweat collects on my neck as I focus on keeping my legs upright. If I stand in one place, I'm okay. William starts to dance around me, filling in as my Kevin James ridiculous dad-level-dancing substitute.

This is a normal teenage moment as Stevie comes back laughing, her head in her hands as she sees the exaggerated lip-bite her boyfriend is putting forth as he dances with his hands out, like he's making a pizza.

Anna's hands on her hips, pointing at us, "Boys. You guys are ridiculous!"

I get my lip-bite on, "You mean sexy!"

William gives a two-finger point in affirmation, "That's what I'm talking about!"

"Yeah!"

We're lucky to have our ladies; they both put up with a great deal of ridiculousness. Soon, the night must close down, and we're back in the limo, all sweating and tired, cuddling our partners on the seat next to us, and it's nice. This feels like high school; I don't feel like the crippled kid everyone felt sorry for. I don't feel like everyone is being overly nice to me, like I am a kid with cancer. I feel like me; for the first time in a long time, I feel like an average teenager, and I love it.

Outside of Anna, these people aren't my friends, not really. What I mean is, I like these people, but we're not in photographs together outside of prom; we don't really hang out. However, they made me feel good tonight, and I love them for it. William freaking Turner. He made me feel funny and fun, the way I used to feel, like the person I used to be. I'll have to deal with that later; my mom's told me that I'll always have a brain injury, but tonight, I wasn't really thinking about that.

Who knows? Maybe, just maybe, there is a future where I can be happy. Things might work out. I don't know. I'm trying not to enjoy tomorrow. As we make it back to Anna's house, and she drives me home, I try to stay present. Now is nice; tomorrow might be better, but let me hold onto tonight, now. I won't have this again, this moment. Living in the now is like trying to catch grains of sand with a sieve, but please God, I need to try. I haven't liked now for a long time, so this is a first. Let me savor it.

Dear God. Let me savor it.

15
GRADUATING PATHWAYS

Sitting at the lab table next to Mrs. Foss's desk, I know it can't be good. She asked me to stay after class for a little bit. "Will."

My heart is in my throat, flapping like a hummingbird on ecstasy, "Yeah?"

Mrs. Foss steadies herself on her rolling stool, opening her laptop to me, "Your grade right now is right there."

The flutter in my heart takes a healthy dose of lead as it falls to the pit of my stomach. 78.56, plain as day. "Ooh," I sigh, feeling my stomach crashing through the linoleum floor, breaking apart the foundation, tunneling deep into the center of the Earth, spewing dirt up in a fountain.

She pats my hand, "Now, that's not bad."

"What?"

Not bad? Not bad? I'm looking at a C in on-level physics. Do you think Wake Forest accepts anyone who makes a C in on- level physics? Do you think Davidson or Furman accepts average, regular high schoolers? C students? Are you crazy?

"All you need to do is get an 85 on the final, and you'll make it to a B."

"Okay." I send down a chain to bring my heart back through the underground tunnel.

"You can't make below an 85, but if you can do that, you got yourself a B."

I nod. I'm trying to not let anything out. I'm already rearranging my schedule in my mind to devote even more time to physics. Might not be able to leave the house this weekend; physics is what matters right now. Everything else is now in a box to the left.

She puts her hand on mine with a pat, "I'm proud of you, Will."

"Thank you, Mrs. Foss," I say, hugging her as best I can, "You've been a big help."

I mean it. She's never given up on me. Even when I have blinked my eyes at a question she's asked, even when my math abilities vanished into thin air, and even when I wrote "I don't know" for one of the word problems, she stayed true and worked with me.

It's nice for someone who's not family to be proud of me. I mean, I like that the people I'm related to are proud of me, but you know, they also kind of have to be. Hopefully, there's a reason for everyone else to be proud of me soon.

As I get in the car, Dad hands me three pieces of mail, reporting, "These came today."

"Oh. Cool."

I look down, and the envelopes are from Wake Forest, Oglethorpe, and the University of Georgia. My hands are sweating; my breath quickens in my lungs as my heart sputters up to a steady hum. "Is this what I think?"

Dad smiles, a hopeful look in his eye, "I think so."

UGA is my safety. I think, if anything, I should be able to get into Georgia, right? Right? Oh God, I can't even open it.

"Go ahead," encourages Dad, noticing my hesitation.

A tear, beat, pull the letter out, beat, unfold it, beat.

"Mr. Carter, we are pleased to offer you admission to the University of Georgia."

A clap from Dad, "Yes! That's awesome! I'm proud of you, Will!"

I can't believe it. Really, truly, I got into a college. Somehow, some way, God is leading. In my heart, I sing, "Thank you, God!"

Bricks are falling from my shoulders for a moment, breaking apart, red clay crumbling in the sun of blessing.

"Get the next two."

My hands are almost trembling, as I grab Wake Forest's envelope. Please God. Please God. Don't let this dream go. I'm not ready for that.

"We regret to. . . dang. . ."

A moment. A silence. A beat.

Dad puts his hand on my shoulder, "Hey. Buddy, I'm sorry. I know you wanted that."

Looking down at the letter, I read the words again, "Yeah."

I know the acceptance should drown out the rejection, but it doesn't. I spent the past three years pushing every fiber of my being, planning, plotting, grinding, fighting towards Wake Forest, and just like that, with those five little words, they dashed those dreams so easily, so carelessly, "We regret to inform you." You don't ever need to read beyond that.

Swallow.

Swallow.

Dad looks at me, "You've got one more."

Three years, working hard in all my classes, all my extracurriculars, getting SAT math tutoring, obtaining recommendations, receiving awards, writing application essays, fighting, planning, sweating, straining, and it's over. An admissions officer swiped away my work with a stroke of a few keys. I need a minute to kiss this school goodbye.

I don't know if I'll want to open the one from Oglethorpe now. Oglethorpe is the school I applied to because Mom said I should. They have Georgia Shakespeare, and hey, my aunt went there, and it seems like a decent enough school. It's not a school talked about among my AP crowd, so I'm less than excited to go there, but let's see, it would be nice to have options.

I notice a soft tap, as Dad nudges my arm, "What did Oglethorpe say?"

I look down at my lap, still one letter, thicker than Wake Forest's. Breathe. If it's a no, I might just open this car door and fall out. Anticipation building, I tear slowly, hearing the separation of each paper fiber.

"C'mon, c'mon," Dad is looking at me, believing good news. Well, at least that's one of us.

"We are excited to inform you of your acceptance to Oglethorpe University."

"Yes! That's great, Will! That's great!"

He hugs me, and I smile. Neither of these acceptances are to places I want to go. I mean, they were both schools I applied to just in case, you know? Wake Forest and Davidson were definite, "Please God, let me go there." Furman was a, "Okay, I could go there," but these two? Just in case. So, I'm happy, but I'm not as excited as Dad. It still feels like my life is not what it could be. I want to be able to get to the life I could've had.

Pathways is busy today; lots of patients are filling the waiting room; I guess we got here right at the worst time. As we enter, I see Chris, the guy who gave my dad the middle finger at inpatient, and he's walking without a cane or anything. Buzz cut, cargo shorts, and a T-shirt, he looks better now.

"What's up, Will?"

His speech is still kind of slurred; I think it's because of the stroke. He says it with a genuine smile. I guess he is one of the people from Shepherd whom I have known the longest.

"What's going on, Chris? Are you walking cane free?"

He stands up, turns around, his hands up, laughing, "Look at me now! Look at me now!"

"That's great!"

He laughs, and part of me is happy for him, but then, of course, the competitive side comes out. How did he get to walk before me? We went to inpatient around the same time. How is it that he is walking already? Is he more healed than I am? I express none of this, but I am thinking it, not saying anything, which is why Chris says, "You good?"

I shake my head to wake myself up to the present situation.

"Yeah. Sorry, I'm good."

Siri's form appears, leaning the doorway, arms crossed, "You coming or what?"

I can't help thinking about Chris walking before me. Look, I know this is a jerk thing to think, but I thought I was healing better than he was. I thought his injury was worse than mine. You know how when you're in a class, you might think, "That person's smarter than me, but that guy? I've got him beat." Now, it's not Christlike, or loving, or good, but you do it, you know? You do it anyway. Human beings are competitive animals, and I thought I had him beat. Turns out, I was wrong. Maybe, I don't.

I slump on the mat, and without realizing it, I sigh.

"What's the matter, sunshine?"

I would be mad about "sunshine," but I know Siri's cool. I know she doesn't mean anything by it.

"I want to walk."

Siri tilts her head, "How did you get in here?"

Without even realizing it either, my hands go up, cane sliding to lean on my leg, "No, I mean. You know what I mean."

"Without the cane." See? She's cool, "Yep."

She laughs, clapping her hands, "You must be some kinda psychic."

"What do you mean?"

She takes my cane from me in a grand gesture. Her energy threw me at first, but damn, I love how kooky Siri is, definitely not your typical physical terrorist.

Holding her arms opens, she smiles big, "You ready, Carter?"

Damn, I can't help but smile either, teeth brimming my mouth wide and big, "Let's do this."

She puts her hands on my gait belt as I steady myself, hands gripping the blue padding of the mat, a little slippery, but I clench harder. I look down and stand. No problem. I've done this before, but now? Here comes the hard part.

"Go slow, buddy. Don't you go running around here."

Snorting a chuckle, I focus on my feet, "Funny, Siri. Funny."

Her hand tightens a little bit on my gait belt, "I've got jokes too."

It was pretty crowded in here, but now, the machines are pretty empty. I see an older man on the leg press; I don't really know him, but he looks at me, gives me a thumbs up.

My eyes shift between him and my feet, and I smile and nod. Keep walking, you fool. Step, step.

"Keep your body upright," Siri's voice is behind me.

"Okay."

I thought I would feel like I'm falling, but I'm doing it. I'm walking. I mean, my gait is not pretty, but I'm doing it, even with stunted, broken steps.

Siri's voice is soft, "Let's round this corner, and then, we'll go back in the gym."

I'm walking. I'm walking! WALKING! ME!

I can't be excited outwardly though and risk falling. Then, they wouldn't let me walk 'til this fall, I'm sure. They've never said anything to that effect, but I know that that would be the case.

"I'm doing it," I say out of nowhere, as we round the corner.

"Yeah, buddy. Steady though. Steady."

Back in the gym, it's time for the typical debrief. Siri's on her stool, and I'm hopeful. I'm so ready to be hopeful about something, to believe in the possibility of good coming my way, but then, there's that dark thing that lives in my stomach, sloshing about, whispering that it won't. Failure, broken, a lost chance, a damn shame. It's not always the same volume, but of course, it's always there.

I guess I shouldn't be so dramatic. I'm just tired of it. I'm tired of feeling like this. I need good news, Siri, so badly.

She looks at me, serious face. Ooh, that's not good.

"That went really well. I think we can keep with the time-line of you graduating Pathways this week. We'll have to see, of course."

"This week?"

Wait. When did someone tell me that? Seriously, did someone tell me that? She said it like they had, so correct yourself before they change their mind. "I mean, dang, this week."

Great save, buddy. Great save.

Resting her head on her fist, Siri gives me one of those faraway looks that has all my panic buttons flashing. No, no, no, I remember; I swear I remember; it was an honest mistake. Please don't take it away.

"You want to walk out to the car? We'll give you the cane, of course, but I think you're ready."

"Yeah."

And we walk to dismissal, and when Dad comes, I walk out to the car.

"Whoa! Buddy!"

I smile as Dad puts my cane and backpack in the car. Siri is behind me.

"He's ready for walking. Please keep an eye on him. I would still keep some supervision on him, but his balance is good."

A good laugh from Dad, he slaps the top of his gold Camry, "Trust me, I always keep an eye on him."

As we drive off, Dad is happy. I like this. You know, it's like no matter how old you get, you want to make your parents happy, and I know I've made them so sad. Not intentionally of course, but I can see their weary faces and tired eyes. I'm done disappointing them and everyone else. The sun is shining bright, glittering off the back windows of the cars on the highway, the sky empty of a single cloud, and Dad is drumming his hands on the steering wheel.

"Great that you're walking, Will. I'm so proud of you, buddy."

Good. I'm glad my hope worked. "Thanks, Dad. I appreciate it."

The joy lasts for a second or two, and it's nice, smiling, not worrying, and then, it hits, crumbling on me like Sheetrock under strain, and my shoulders tense. Study for physics, do problems for physics, study vocabulary, do quiz for econ, do essay for lit, ask Mom about Davidson, do vision therapy exercises, before tomorrow, before school. Need to graduate. Need to get good grades. Cannot let this injury change my trajectory.

"You okay buddy?" Dad asks, drumming ceasing.

"Stressed. Worried about school."

I guess I need to tell someone. I can't keep holding it in. I mean, he knows. Mom and Dad tell me I look stressed, look tired; I don't really come out with it. I kind of assume they know.

Dad has this very soothing voice when he's listening. "What are you stressed about?"

I look down, my head feeling like the blood in my brain is pooling in my feet, "Getting it all done. I guess, I'm worried about getting everything done, and like. . . you know. . . I don't want a C in anything." I swallow. This is my fear, my greatest fear. I don't fear death; I fear this brain injury has made my life lesser; I fear there is a part of me that I loved and cherished, my abilities, yes, but also, the promise, the version of me that people thought might be successful, that part of me I had so much pride in, that part of me I had told myself was me. I fear I may never get him back. I fear I may never heal enough, never get better enough to get him back. They tell me I'm healing, but can I really heal to where I was? They're proud of me for walking, but will they be proud of me for the job I will have? I know they will be, but will it be the same? Or will it feel like that my accomplishments are always, "given his disability, we are so proud of him." I mean, it's not my parents. It's me. I want to live a life worthy of pride.

His hand grips my shoulder, "Buddy, no matter what, I am so proud of you."

I smile. See, I love this so much, but I also struggle with this. I want to do something worthy of pride, apart from this injury. I don't want to be broken. I snag the iPod cord from my dad and shuffle in my pocket for my Mini. Dad has always taught me to love music, and I give him something he will enjoy hearing as the guitar strumming picks up, and then, the drums kick in, "Take it Easy" by The Eagles.

We can't sing, but with the windows down, and the summer sky easing our mind, we belt it out for everyone to hear, whether they want to or not.

This. This. This. Now. Take it in. Take it easy. Breathe. I wish it was that easy, Glenn Frey. You and the Eagles had enough money, made it far enough in life, reached that stage where you were not in question. It was probably simple enough to take it easy by the time that song came out. For some of us, though? We've got a great deal of blood, sweat, and tears ahead before we can relax. Sometimes, I think relaxing will happen after I graduate high school, sometimes after college, when I am done with school, or maybe, after I get a job.

I limp into the house, holding my cane parallel to the floor to open-mouth surprise from my mom who is washing her hands at the kitchen sink. With her hands still wet, she unwittingly claps them, quickly realizes her mistake, dries them, and comes over to me, "Wow, Will! That's great! I'm so proud of you!"

An embrace, unsure at first, her not wanting to take me off-balance, catches me in the moment. What I mean is, I'm falling fast through this life—anxiety over work to be done, frets over what is incomplete, the possibility of future, and the fear of tomorrow—but Mom's arms hold me fast and keep me in this quick moment of joy. I rest into the hug, not for too long, but long enough to feel the embrace.

She pulls back, her hands on my arms, "That's so great, Will."

"Yeah."

I stand on my own, feeling a little unsteady, my shoulders sagging under the weight, but my heart feels light and free. I make my way to the couch, taking my laptop from the coffee table, and I get to work. We have dinner: fajitas; mom talks to Granny about my walking, and I get another, "I'm proud of you," and I love it. I wish I could take the night off. I so wish I was able to take a break, but now is not the time. No, no, no. Walking? Amazing. It's not full independence though. Mom and Dad still have to take me up and down the stairs. They want to be there when I'm walking, so you know, it's not full independence, but I get it. We've got this hard, white tile at the base of the stairs in front of the front door, and if I hit my head on that, it would be game over. I mean, I might not die, but I would definitely have to go back to Shepherd.

Every morning is the same routine. Get up at five, eat breakfast, study economics and physics. Thursday's the big day, and Friday's the bigger day. Supposedly, I will graduate Pathways on Thursday; I don't know; I kind of figure I'll believe it when I see it. Friday, though; Friday is the end of course test for economics. No book. No notes. I actually have to know how to answer questions about economics off the top of my head. I need to remember definitions; I need to know key figures and concepts. I need to have reading comprehension.

I can't help thinking about how, if this accident did not happen, if I did not have the brain injury, if I was not dependent on this tiny white Ritalin to supply me with all of my focus and attention, I would not be studying for an end of course test. Before, these things were a joke. Before, with literature, political science, world history, I found the final tests a meager comparison to the tests in class. Now, though, this is twenty percent of my grade, and I'm scared. I need to know how to define the differences between an open and closed economic system, between Adam Smith's, Karl Marx's, and John Maynard Keynes's theories of economics.

I used to have friends; I used to talk to my girlfriend; I used to be in a band, on debate team, in Model UN, and president of drama club, and I had somehow had time for things, but now, I have three classes and three therapies, and I am drowning. Two weeks. After this week, there are two weeks. Hold your breath; don't breakdown; don't scream. Hold your breath and keep working.

I surprise everyone with my cane-free limp down the hall. Aaron still carries my backpack, because the last thing we need is the miracle boy falling face-first on the high school linoleum floor, busting his face open in front of the other students. Aaron generally goes fast enough to keep them away.

On Thursday, as we're walking to lit, he offers, "I got a new one for you."

I stop, "Oh yeah?"

"You can be a little late, right?"

"I mean, do you know who I am Aaron? I do what I want."

A good belly laugh, as he reaches in the pocket of his orange polo to take out a folded piece of notebook paper.

I chuckle already, "Aaron, are we passing notes?"

With a furrow in his brow but a smile on his face, "See, I wanted to remember the name. Cause I know if I didn't write it down, I was going to forget."

The paper is perfectly creased and folded; I can see why he teaches math.

"Tom Segura. You know him?"

"No, I have never heard of him."

Aaron claps his hands victorious, "Yes! I got one you don't know!"

A good shared laugh; it's funny. If I saw Aaron, I would've never known how cool he is; I would've written him off as a jerk without ever talking to him. First, he looks like a typical Southern jock, but he's not at all. He's not. He's one of the nicest people I've ever met, but isn't that how it goes? You see the external (the polo, the college football hat, the muscular build, the buzz cut), and you go, "I know the box you belong in." Funny thing is, I hate boxes now. Damn. Hypocrisy sucks.

English is focused on the AP exam, you know, the one I'm not taking. I'm still working on my essay for *Catcher in the Rye*. As far as I can tell, it's about a jerk who thinks he's better than everyone else. Not going to lie, I hope to have that feeling one day, kind of. Now, I never wanted to be a jerk, and I don't want to feel better than everyone, just better than someone, you know? I hate the bottom. Here, doing my own work while the class prepares for the exam, I feel like the "special" kid, the one who's in class but not really.

I'm alone, aloof, adrift, and Ms. Colvin is giving the instructions for the timed writing, "Now guys, you will only have forty minutes per essay, so it's important to not spend too much time planning. Remember to read the question. Please."

Her usual charming, nervous laughter echoes as she pleads with the students. While everyone works on their essays, she comes over to me, kneeling by the desk, a soft voice, "How's it going, Will? You get me that essay, and after that, we will have the extra credit, but then, you will be done."

My vision goes double, as it sometimes does with my post-accident periodically lazy left eye, "Done?"

A smile, a laugh. She's got a good heart. I want to tell her how I see that, but I figure now's not the time.

"Oh yeah. I mean, after the exam, there's nothing really to do. That's what this whole class is working towards."

She shifts her weight in those thin black shoes that almost remind of me of ballet slippers. Her hands are in her cardigan; she wears a smile like a uniform. I think when she directs it at her students, she means it, but it's like there's some hard days under her usual glow.

I scrunch my bushy eyebrows, "So, what do I do?"

She puts her hand to her mouth, "Well, I figure you come here the day they're taking the exam, and you work on the extra-credit assignments they will be doing in class for the days after the exam."

And just like that, I saw my path to a B. Who knows, maybe an A. Ms. Colvin had told the class this, and at first, she was surprised I had forgotten, but she easily explained it again. The extra-credit sheet has all these creative little assignments, for example writing an imitation of JD Salinger and then, explaining how your work exemplifies Salinger's style. Each assignment was worth ten points added to your major assignment with the lowest grade.

Light from heaven, glorious mercy from God, a way out.

"That's awesome," I breathe, my shoulders relaxing.

"Oh yeah. You've got this, Will," and she pats my arm and moves to another student.

"Thank you, God," I mutter under my breath.

He's got me. At least for this class, I think my grade might be okay, salvageable, college worthy. Soon, Aaron and I head to physics, which, of course, is the only class I care about now, well, this one and econ. I cannot have Cs. Cs do not look good on a transcript. I haven't heard from Furman or Davidson yet. More importantly, the old Will would never get a C. I need to show them, everyone I am healing. I have worth. I will not be successful in spite of my disability. It will be an afterthought.

Or, at least, I hope it will not be mentioned as a qualifier to my level of success. Better, better, better. Must get better. I must show them I am better.

Physics does not help this feeling of better. We're reviewing for the final, and Mrs. Foss thinks I raised my hand, thinks I have an answer to the question. I didn't raise my hand. I have nothing, so when she asks me for my answer, I give the most honest answer, "I have no idea what's going on."

It gets a slight chuckle from Bryce and then a slap on the arm from Ashlyn beside him.

"We can talk after class. Is there a specific question you have?"

I am projecting fear in my eyes, not disrespect. Before, before all of this, I may have made some smart comment to try and get a chuckle out of my classmates, but I'm trying to make it so clear to her that I am honest and scared.

"Let's talk after class."

I appreciate this. She's thinking about me when she says it because she knows it will be worse for me if she tries to suss out everything I don't understand. That would take a long time, and then, I would have wound up feeling bad for dragging it out and wasting my classmates' time. After class is over, I limp up to her desk, when her phone buzzes, and she looks to me apologetically, "Dang, I need to take this. Is it okay if you come by tomorrow morning? Will that work?"

Aaron picks up my backpack, and stands behind me, as I confirm, "Sure. I think so."

She takes the call, as we walk outside.

"You still got that note, right?" Aaron asks as he waves to Dad's car.

"Definitely."

He takes off the backpack, as he walks to the car, "Do me a favor and don't listen to it around your parents."

"You got it."

Again, I appreciate this. I feel trusted. I mean, I guess he realizes my parents aren't the crazy type to call up the principal over me listening to a filthy comic, but you know what? Some parents are, so as cool as he thinks my parents are, he is taking a risk. Either way, I vow to not lose the note, and as we head to Pathways, I try to make space in my mental calendar to listen to Tom Segura when I get home from therapy.

Pathways is busy like any other day, and as I make it into

the therapy gym, I see Siri sitting on the edge of the mat, smiling at me, "Big day, huh?"

"I sure hope so."

She stands with the groan most people over fifty give when they have to move their bodies, "It is."

And with that, we walk to the stairwell.

Siri has her hand on my shoulder, "You're going to walk down and come back up."

"Okay."

And getting down the stairs is hard, but I concentrate, and my left foot starts to shake a little on the last steps, and I think, "Don't fall. Don't fall. You'll never get to leave today if you fall." And last step, and my left foot trembles as it leaves the corner, and then, with an uptake of air, I make it to the ground. Siri smiles.

"Good, now go up."

Up is no problem. I quickly climb back to the start.

"Good. Let's get on the treadmill."

I feel like she's testing me, and she probably is, and no, no, that makes my heart tremble and quicken to a sprint as I get on the treadmill. She starts me out slow, and I'm doing well. She increases the speed.

"Okay, I'm going to make it go a little faster."

I'm doing a faster walk, and then, she raises the incline, and then, she makes it a little faster, and my little heart is thumping like a shoe in a dryer.

"Great, Will, let's cool down."

And she flattens the treadmill, and I go to my usual sauntering limp as I catch my breath.

"Good work. Good work."

Then, she gives me a printout of exercises I can do on my own, and we go over them quickly; maybe, it feels quickly to me because I want to get to the end; I want to know this means I can graduate, at least graduate physical therapy.

"Alrighty then, I think it time. You need to get over to OT."

I give her a hug. We started off shaky, but by the end, she turned out all right; I hope she feels the same about me. "Thank you, Siri."

She sends me off, "Of course. You got it. I'll see you tomorrow."

"What?"

She waves me away, as her next patient enters, "Remember, with your parents? Now, go, Caitlin's waiting."

Okay, I do not remember that at all. Sometimes, I am told things, and almost immediately, they vanish. Puff, gone in a cloud of smoke.

Caitlin greets me with, "So, today's your last day, huh? Thank God."

I appreciate her trying for sarcasm as she quickly smiles and asks how I'm doing. Then, we get down to business. We start by sitting at the table. She has my folder open as we talk about my goals.

"Now, you said you wanted to improve your left-hand strength, right?"

I am thinking about what my chart says, but I nod, "Yes."

"And, you've done that. You wanted to work on your vision, which you're doing, and lastly, driving."

"Mhmm."

She pauses, and looks at me directly, plainly, "You're doing vision therapy which looks like it's helping. I think you need to continue that. Right now, I would not recommend driving, but after more vision therapy, you should be able to."

I nod. I don't want to think about not yet. Is she saying I'm not done? Is she saying I still have to be here? Her soft, sweet, twinge-of-Southern voice is encouraging, but I always worry her niceness is leading to bad news.

I put my hands on the table, "So. . .?"

"You've done what you can here, and I'm proud of you."

Another hug as I awkwardly stand; I thank her for everything, and I head over to my last and, possibly, most challenging hurdle, speech therapy.

As I enter, Sara is finishing with a client and gives me a plain and direct, "Please wait outside until I'm ready."

Not a good start. I swallow. One more yes, one more approval. Bad start. It's like a job interview; I'm tensing up; my head is light, and my thoughts are tumbling. What if she says I need to be here more? What if she says I need to not go to college? What if she makes me do like a summer course?

As an older man exits her room, I hear a commanding, "Will. Come on."

I stumble and fall into the chair like a ton of bricks. Sara gives a wide-eyed look, "That was a graceful landing."

Awkward smile, "You know me. Graceful."

She's got my folder too. She's got her hair tied back tight again, and I hope it's a good day for us. She hands me a pen, "You ready?"

"For?" I ask with a blank stare, confused.

"A test," she smiles, a cheerful uptake in her pitch, "You remember that test you took at the start of Pathways?"

"Oof."

She hands me a packet of papers, "You're going to take it again."

"Great."

And she starts the timer, and I get to it. Great. A test. So, now, it is clear to me that, if I fail, she'll have a good reason to keep me back. God give me the ability to do this. I have so much fear, such trepidation. This was so hard the last time I took it, but now, I'm actually. . . yeah. . . huh. . . this isn't too bad. I read over the questions again, but I think. . . I think I might actually be okay. And I have ten minutes; I check over my answers, and I give them to her, and she grades it quickly, as I sit there, hands tapping on my legs, heart playing percussion on my rib cage.

"Well, Will."

And I can just hear the bad news coming. She's going to recommend I don't go to college.

"You did great."

What?

She continues, "You got a 15 out of 30 the last time you took this. Here, you got a 29 out of 30. It's not perfect, but it is awesome—you did a lot better."

I sit there, starting to believe in good news, "Wow."

"I think you've come a long way. You've still got healing and work to do, but I'm really proud of how far you've come."

"Thank you for everything, Sara."

And we stand as we notice patients outside heading to the afternoon dismissal; she pats my shoulder, "You are welcome."

The meeting is packed as I can't seem to find a place to stand. Siri is up at the front, commanding the room with her large presence and booming voice, "And now, it's Thursday, so you know what that means."

"Candy!" Cody, a younger guy in his early twenties screams from his seat.

Siri laughs a little, before replying, "No, Cody. No candy."

This is met with an audible sigh from Cody, but Siri continues, "It means graduation. It means we are going to lose a few of you. I am happy to announce that Erin and Will are graduating from Pathways today. Let's give them a round of applause."

Now, it's a small room full of people I don't know, and the

applause is smattering and sporadic, but it still feels nice. I breathe a deep sigh of relief, deep from a place of deep peace as I start to believe, maybe, I am getting better. Maybe, I will be someone to be proud of. Maybe, this will work out. Maybe, I will go to a college I want to go to; maybe, I will be a success. Maybe I won't let everyone down. Maybe, my life is not a tragedy. Maybe, I am not broken. Maybe, this new version of me might be okay. Maybe.

16
VISITING COLLEGES

"Okay, are you ready?" Dad asks, and I lift my head enough to see he's carrying a stack of mail.

I'm on the couch, reading through my economics book again, hoping I can commit enough to memory, but my thoughts are traveling.

"What?" I pipe up, unsure if I've missed something.

"Last one," Dad says, tossing me an envelope, a terrible idea as it hits my stomach and falls to my feet. Dad should know I've got no hand-eye coordination, not now, not ever.

"Sorry, buddy," and he comes to pick it up, and I see what it is, white envelope with a purple outline, and the words Furman University clearly printed at the top. The envelope is thick.

"You want to open it?" He asks, as he points it to me.

"Can you do it?" I look up, my eyes flashing the sincerest hope. It's not that I can't open an envelope. I'm not saying I'm strong; I'm just saying my arms have enough muscle to rip paper, not to brag or anything.

"Okay, but then, we gotta go."

He tears open the envelope to reveal the letter, thick paper;

he steadies his eyes to read through his glasses, "Dear William Carter, we are pleased to announce. . . this is great! Proud of you, buddy!"

"Wait—"

"You got in!" he declares as he hands me the letter, "You're accepted!"

"Yes!"

I clap as he shares the news with Mom, and it feels good. One no, no message from Davidson, and three yeses. I can't believe it. Furman's a good school. People have heard of it, no offense to Oglethorpe. Depending on how you look at it, I should be happy with this. Dad is; he puts his hand on my shoulder, his smile wide and true.

"Doesn't that feel good? I mean, three out of four. That's great, Will."

"Yeah."

It all kind of swallows me as I think about Furman. Michael Chiu, my friend and the one who gave the talk that led me to Christ, goes there, and I remember liking it when I visited.

"What do you think? We gotta go visit these. I'll see what we can set up. Let's get to the car."

"Where are we going?"

As my dad explains in the car, the dinner is at Ippolito's, and it's going to be my teachers, my therapists, Mom, Dad, and me. I'm glad Dad is there. With all of those people, he will direct things, take the spotlight, and lead us past any possible awkward conversations.

When we arrive, we are greeted by a friendly blonde woman in her twenties wearing black pants and a black shirt, and she smiles and says, "Right this way," as she takes us into a room with big tables, and Mr. Irwin is sitting at one end already, Mr. Dodd next to him. Down the table, I see Ms. Colvin and Mrs. Williams, then, Mrs. Foss and Ms. Ogle. I see

Siri, Sara, and Caitlin crowded at one end. I see Mr. Cook and his wife.

I see Ms. Spradlin coming back to the table, and they all turn to look at us, "Will!" Dodd calls.

"The man, the myth, the legend!" Irwin adds.

And Mom and I sit down at the front of the table in those black metal chairs with the cushioned backs. Mrs. Williams, who looks like she could be making a business deal (blonde hair, tan, wearing her silver top and black pants), looks to Mom, "Thank you so much for this."

This, of course, is echoed by everyone there.

Dad takes the head of the table and brings his smile, charm, and commanding voice. He looks good in his blue shirt, jacket, and khakis, like a proper pastor, as he motions for everyone's attention, "Thank you all for coming to this dinner. We wanted to show you how much we appreciate how you have been there for Will and how you helped him succeed. Every single person here has done more than I could ever say. Debbie and I are so thankful for everything you have done. Your work has helped Will get to where he is today, and I can never say thank you enough for helping our son succeed." He swallows, clears his throat. He smiles at me. "Now, let's get to the important part."

He gives a good-natured laugh as he points to the food behind us: tables with three big bowls of salad and three baskets of breadsticks.

"We are happy to cover your dinner tonight. Salad, bread-sticks, and whatever entrée you choose are on us, as well as soft drinks, water, and a glass of the house red or white. Though, if you choose to go beyond that, it'll be up to you. Now, what do you say? Let's eat!"

He got a little choked up thanking them. I could tell. I love that Dad's an emotional guy, truly.

224

Spradlin pops her head out to see me, "So, what's the plan next, young man?"

"What do you mean?"

She laughs her usual big laugh and smiles; though she's older than my mom, she's got a youthfulness to her, "Have you decided about college?"

I bite my lip, "Well, you know I got into Oglethorpe, UGA, and Furman. Never heard from Davidson."

She waves points in understanding, "I asked Mr. Cook about that, and he mentioned they said they never received some of your documents. I know I sent a recommendation."

I nod. Her dark hair shapes her pale face as she speaks.

"So where are you thinking?"

I breathe. I try and relax my back, the small of my back is throbbing as it usually is. My head is flittering away with exhaustion, but I'm trying so hard to stay present, stay engaged, "I don't know. I . . . I think we are going to visit this weekend and maybe, the weekend after? You know me, though. I don't think I can go to UGA."

Spradlin points her hand with the big silver ring on it, which kind of looks like a finger amulet, at me, "UGA is a good school, but if you want my opinion, I see you at Oglethorpe. That's a beautiful campus, and you know that's where Georgia Shakespeare is headquartered."

"Yeah." I sip my water as she flags down the waiter to fill up her wine glass with some red.

Dad has some music playing; there's a beat, and then, the guitar and piano start, and Spradlin starts dancing with her arms as Earth, Wind & Fire's "September" pipes through the speaker.

"Yeah! This is what I'm talking about!"

I laugh; it's rare to see teachers exhibiting reckless abandon like dancing in public, even if it is while seated. Laughing, I ask, "Big Earth, Wind & Fire fan?"

Spradlin bites her lip as middle-aged people do and exclaims, "Oh yeah! I love disco! It is my jam!"

Mental note: Spradlin loves disco. I know it's weird; I don't know why I need to remember this, but something tells me that I do.

The dinner itself is quite lovely. Dodd and Irwin talk to me about the election. Politics was always our conversation of choice. They are quite a pair, Dodd has the body of a basketball player plus carbs, you know, the broad shoulders but the gut of a dad, and Irwin has the body of a basketball player minus the physique. I'm not saying he's skin and bones, but he is the definition, in my mind, of lanky, so it is quite the physical match up, but these two are the consummate pair of friends.

Irwin peers above Dodd's shoulder, "Dodd says he called it."

Dodd laughs his typical charming, belly laugh and turns to Irwin, "No, all I'm saying is I knew Obama was going to be a candidate one day. I didn't know he would knock Clinton out so easily."

With a raise of his eyebrows, Irwin corrects Dodd, "It's not over yet."

A laugh from Dodd, as he puts an arm around Irwin and looks to me, "Sure, and Waterloo wasn't the end of Napoleon."

We all laugh, and I love this. I've missed this. This used to be my regular afternoon banter in high school, talking with Dodd, Irwin, and Peter as we broke down the political events of the day.

Dodd puts his hand on my shoulder, "You got a plan for college yet?"

"I was telling Sprad I've got Oglethorpe, Furman, and UGA."

"Good list!" Irwin offers, as he adjusts his glasses. Like me, his spectacles always seem to need reorienting on his face somehow.

"That's great! Furman is a great school. UGA of course is solid, but I don't know if I see you there. I really don't know that much about Oglethorpe. Pretty campus though."

"I don't know. I think we're visiting, and then, I'll decide. Yeah, I'm not sure about UGA."

Irwin leans in, a stupid grin on his face, "Well, yeah, as big a football fan as you are, I always saw you at Alabama."

Good one. Good one, and Dodd laughs, as he pats Irwin's shoulder. They know me well.

I love these two men for something I can never fully express to them. Ever since October, since I was a skeleton with a heartbeat and a broken head, they have never spoken to me like I'd changed. They have never adjusted their tone, their speed of talking, or avoided cultural references. I haven't always under stood what they were talking about, but I love that they didn't calibrate themselves to the new me. They spoke like I had never changed. They always seemed happy to talk to me, like they had always been happy to talk to me. They visited the hospital with laughs and stories, and they never made feel that I had changed. I mean, of course, I had, but they always made me feel as I was the same person.

Soon, hugs and goodbyes are exchanged, and as we get back into the car, I feel the weight of the rest of my life hanging around my neck like a cinder block, dragging me to the ocean floor. Everyone wanted to know, "Have you heard about college? What are you going to major in? Where are you going? Who accepted you? What's the plan?"

Yes, every teenager has this millstone around their neck. Be kind to them. Stop asking them about their futures. But for me? I don't know. I don't want to be a narcissist, but I feel like it's an even bigger weight. Because, I mean, really, I went from standing on the edge of possibility to a coma to a miracle to. . . God. . . please don't let it be failure, and now, the choice is here. I don't know where I'm supposed to go. Honestly, I want to go to Furman because I think it's the best school I was accepted to, but I. . . I don't know. I need to visit it again to see. This is the rest of my life. I shouldn't see it that way, but that's how it's always been. I always had an answer to the questions: "Where do you want to go?" and "What do you want to do?"

"Wake Forest, maybe Davidson, and I'm going to major in international relations and work for the UN."

I miss that certainty; I miss that confidence in what tomorrow will bring. Right now, I see a crack in the clouds as I pray for no more storms.

As we get back in the car, Mom looks to me, "You know, Ms. Spradlin was the one who made sure you were set up to graduate."

"Really?"

She smiles big, remembering, "She was the one who set everything up with Spurka, so you could do English with Ms. Colvin in the morning, do economics online, and made sure you had all the credits you need. She's been a big help to you."

"That's great." I really wish I knew she cared this much for me. Like I said, I've always liked her, but I had no idea how much she did for me. I had no idea how much she was on my team.

"Yeah, she said to me 'Will will graduate,'" Mom says as she points out the turn my dad knows he needs to make.

When we get home, I climb the stairs by myself, Dad watching from the front door. He wants me to do it on my own; I know he's trying.

"I got it, Dad," I say, my teenage independence showing a bit.

"Okay, okay, go ahead," he says as he doesn't really move, and I climb the stairs to the bright blue bathroom and the white porcelain sink. I get ready, brush my teeth, wash my face, and I climb into bed. Soon, I hear Mom and Dad climb the stairs, and the boards creak like a dying animal, and I see them open my door, poking their heads in, "You off to bed?"

I put my phone on the charger, "Yeah. I've got the econ EOC in the morning." I know they want to have some more conversation, but my brain is empty. I normally have more words, but I am so tired.

"Okay. Night. We can talk in the morning about visiting colleges."

"That sounds great."

There's a linger, a pause. I smile, "Love you guys."

"Love you too."

I set my alarm for four in the morning. Maybe, maybe, I am being too much. Maybe, I am overly anxious, but I can't risk it. This is twenty percent of my grade. This is the difference between a B and an A. This is a transcript I can be proud of. This is the chance to prove myself. Am I getting better? Will I ever heal to the person I was before? Well, this test will help tell that.

In the morning, I roll over and check my phone, 3:58 a.m., great. Thank you, body. Oh, also, thank you for waking me up at 1:00 in the middle of the night to go pee. On the bright side, at least you didn't wake me up twice to urinate. After breakfast, I get to studying and more studying. Dad doesn't like for me to go down the stairs by myself, but I need to study. I have my note cards, going over the terms *gross domestic* product, *consumption, developing economy, mixed economy*. I reread the chapters or try to skim. *Capitalism. Mercantilism. Barter Economy.* At a certain point, it feels like gibberish, like these words have no actual meaning, just shapes on a page, and then, the words start to go double as my left eyes gets tired, and I have to put my head down on my book and do the only thing I feel I can. "God. God Father, please help me remember what I'm studying. Father, please let the test be easy for me. . . God. . . Father. . . please. . . please let me do well. I want to do well. . . please let me do well."

Dad comes down to make his Starbucks run, "How you feeling?"

"I hope I can do well."

He takes his keys from the table, "I'm sure you will."

I wish I had his confidence in me.

When he drops me off at school, I go into the Tag Room, and Spradlin directs me to the computer with a, "Good luck."

She knows I can't start yet, but she can see the fear in my eyes, and she lets me open my book and study. I appreciate this. I would spend my time talking to her and being nice, but I'm desperately hoping for a moment to get out of the conversation and prepare for this test.

Mrs. Rice enters with a coffee cup in hand and a shawl over her shoulders; her toucan nasally voice offers, "Oh Will, how's it going? You ready for the EOC?"

Spradlin comes to the rescue from her desk, with a loud blunt command, "Connie. He is studying."

"Oh sorry, you'll do great."

And she skitters off to her desk. The bell, the announcements, and I can feel my heart quickening. The pledge, and there's the patter-patter in my chest along with it.

Then, it's time. The drumbeat in my arteries is a crescendo, as I log into the test, and look at the first question, "Which of the following factors is used to determine a person's credit worthiness?

   1. Age

2. Wisdom
3. Yearly Income
4. Location"

Okay, well, it's not wisdom. You can't quantify that. This stuff is all about numbers, and I guess you could look at how many tattoos someone has, but that's not a wisdom factor for everyone because there are many people with no wisdom and no tattoos. Obviously, location is a problem as well. Age and yearly income. Age is definitely a factor; obviously, a five-year- old has no credit worthiness, but. . . I mean, I feel like yearly income is the one that makes more sense. Not too bad. Not too bad at all.

I'm going fast. I need to slow down. When I go too fast, as Sara said, I make dumb mistakes. I read things wrong, and I mess up. Slow down, read carefully. Careful. Careful. Surprisingly, this is actually pretty easy. I'm worried about how easy it is. Check your answers. Double check your answers. Triple check your answers.

And. . . my short response will be graded later. . . but. . . my multiple-choice. . . 92 out of 100. "Ha, ha!" I laugh out loud, and then, as the students and teachers in the room look at me. "Sorry, sorry."

I breathe. My shoulders soften. My heart slows down. I did it. I passed economics, and. . . I think. . . I think I got an A. I got an A!

I can't believe it. I am getting better. I am growing. I am healing. I am becoming what I want to be—capable, smart, a boy with promise. Ha, ha! Thank you, God!

I don't do it in person, but in my head, I am jumping up and down and singing and dancing for the Lord. Good, good, he is so good.

Aaron comes to the door, and I make my way to physics; EOC ate up my lit time. After getting the class started on a review activity, Foss comes by my desk.

"Let me know if you need any help. Remember, all you need is an 85."

We work through the class, and I try to not copy off of Kamran, but I can't get the 85 out of my head. Okay, I need to study every day for as long as I can. If I work hard enough, put in enough time, I can do this. Better is within reach. I know it. I can feel it.

Aaron comes to the door, "You ready, chief?"

"Let's do this." And we walk out into the May weather, and it's about as hot as you'd expect for Georgia.

Aaron puts his hand up to block the sun from eyes, "Jesus, it's not even one o'clock."

"No, my name's Will."

Stopping, not moving to my dad's car, he lets a smile creep onto his lips, "What did you say?"

Standing up straight, proud of my joke, I smile back, "You called me Jesus. I wanted to let you know you were mistaken."

A full laugh as we make it to my dad's car. Aaron runs his hand over his short blonde buzz, "I love it, Will. You're weird, but I love it."

"Thank you, Aaron." I think that's the honest compliment that I want.

Aaron comes around the gold Honda, puts my stuff in the back, and makes his way to my dad's window, "Big plans this weekend, I hear."

A short laugh, "Yeah, yeah. Heading up to Greenville, and then, we'll see UGA on Sunday, and I believe we'll do Oglethorpe the day after. You?"

"Grading. You guys enjoy."

And we're back home, and I'm at the dining room table

slaving over physics, and at some point, there's a break for dinner, and then, I want to study more, but I'm so tired that none of it makes any sense anymore. Distracted, I check my email, and there it is. A little boost, a little something to keep me moving and keep me going, "Horizon Theater Young Playwrights Festival."

"I forgot I submitted to that," I mutter to myself. I'm not expecting good news. You know? When you start to get used to disappointments, you guard yourself from getting your hopes up.

"We are pleased to announce your play *Anthropophagy* has been accepted into Horizon Theater's 2008 Young Playwrights Festival."

Beat. I can't believe it. What? Accepted? Me? I read it again; it must be a lie. No, it is one hundred percent true. I'm accepted. Now, that play was written by the me of before, but it's accepted, so I won't think about that part.

"Mom! Dad!" I want to rush down the stairs, but I know I can't afford another brain injury, so I carefully and slowly, step down, leaning on my strong hand, holding the unpolished handrail on the right.

"What is it, buddy?" Mom asks, washing her hands at the kitchen sink.

"I got accepted into Horizon's Young Playwrights Festival!"

She throws her hands, still dripping, up. "That's great!"

She is beaming, "That is so great."

And I am happy to get good news. I need a break, so I agree to watch *Princess Bride* with Mom and Dad. And, God, I love this movie. Then, I talk to Anna on the phone, and after the excitement of telling her about the festival, it's really just a "checking in conversation." You know—How's it going? How's school? What are you doing this weekend? And I know I used to be a more engaged boyfriend, and I wish I was, but I need to finish high school first.

In the morning after breakfast, we make the drive up to Greenville, and it's a nice, easy drive; South Carolina looks pretty in the summertime. It's weird; when you get outside of Atlanta, and you drive into the actual South (no, Atlanta is not the South, sorry), it's like the world gets brighter and greener. You start to notice colors in the landscape, the blue of the sky, the green of a field, the white of a magnolia tree.

Now, when you pull into the Furman campus, you see green. There is so much green, and there's the quad with a huge brown dome building at the end, and then a pond with a fountain between you and the building with other buildings on either side, and it's pretty. But then, I look at the people on the campus, and they're white. Now, this is not what bothers me. In case you somehow fell into a coma reading this, I will remind you that I, too, am white, but what bothers me is that it looks like they're all white. Guys in polos and khakis, girls dressed in the same pastels as the girls at my high school, and I swallow. Curious to see the tour, but this. . . this doesn't look like my scene.

We make it to the rest of the group on the tour, and a 5'11", shaggy brown-haired sophomore in cargo shorts and a purple FU polo stands on a bench, "Hey everyone! My name is Brent! I'm going to be your tour guide today! Can I get a woo woo!?"

I did not give Brent even a single woo, and I did not learn much of anything from Brent during the tour, other than I know for sure he has a Jack Johnson poster on his wall.

On the tour, I'm noticing the beautiful lake, sure, and yes, I am impressed by how nice their stadium is, and sure, I love all the options in the dining hall. Chick-Fil-a for lunch every day? Impressive. That's where we get ours for the day, but the whole time, I am thinking about Brent and Kayleigh, who we met on the tour, and no offense to either of them, but I know that we would not be friends. This is not better than high school. This is high school with a Chick-Fil-a and a worse football team.

As we sit in the car on the way home, Dad can tell, "Not your place, is it?"

I scratch the tiny bit of stubble under my chin, right next to a zit, "No. Too preppy."

It's nice to be able to head back home where I can get some good studying in.

Dad smiles, his sunglasses sparkling in the South Carolina sun, "Yeah, I could tell that from the moment we met Brent."

"Don't forget about Kayleigh."

We laugh, and I feel good knowing that I can cross Furman off my list, but then, I get a sinking feeling in my stomach when I remember there are only two choices left. The next day, Dad must run the service in the chapel, so Mom and I get in the car to go to UGA, her and Dad's old stomping grounds, and as we get in the car, Mom adds, "Now, I know you're not a huge UGA fan, but I want you keep an open mind. I think you'll love it."

"Yeah."

We start on our journey, and I know this is not the last sales pitch for UGA I'm going to hear today. She's been trying to promote UGA to me from the moment I started thinking about college.

"It's a lot cheaper than the other two. Think about that, Will, no student debt."

"Yeah."

I don't know what to say. I have no concept of student debt. She's not done, and she'll keep up the whole time, I just know it.

"I mean, your dad and I can help out a bit, but we can't cover that much."

"I know." I wish I wanted to go there. It would make everything easier.

"Just saying."

When we get to campus, we head to our tour, and we find a space in the parking deck and walk to the student center and wow. Just wow. Stone columns, four stories, a bridge to it, I don't know if this is my scene either. Students rush past us, and I see them swarming across our walking path. Now, there is more diversity; I am seeing nerds, dweebs, hardcore kids, the anime crowd, the homeschool group, and, of course, a fair share of Brents.

We hop on a bus, as our tour guide, Mandy, introduces herself via megaphone.

"Welcome everyone to our UGA tour! I hope you are doing fabulous today! And welcome to UGA, or, as I like to say, UG-Grrrrreeaat!"

I turn to Mom, trying my best at whispering, "If she's an example of who they accept, I'm going to pass."

She hits my arm, laughing to herself. The mom in front of us turns around, giving us a look.

"Sorry," Mom says and then turns to give me a "can you believe these people" look.

I mouth, "I know," and we let Mandy continue uninterrupted as she tells us all about UGA's football record, the different restaurants at the dining hall, how nice the dorms are, and then, a brief bit on academics. It's okay. I know where Mandy's priorities lie. Pretty sure we're in different social circles. For one, I think my group can make a circle.

We make it off the bus, and Mom puts her hand on my shoulder, "At least, let me take you to the Varsity."

And we hop in the car and drive to a white, rundown building with a big, red V outside, and as we enter, I can see it is bustling. It's not the kind of place with decorations. I mean, sure, there are a couple of framed photographs and some UGA memorabilia, but it is white walls with red trim. When you get up to the front of the line, they yell at you, "Whaddaya have!? Whaddaya have!? Whaddaya have!?"

And you need to be quick because there's a long line, and you can hear the kitchen, and you know they are expecting an answer, so you order your burger, Coke, and fries, and Mom says, "Oh, and two FOs of course."

"FO?" I ask.

"Frozen orange," is her reply.

"Okay." I don't know what the means, but let's do it, and we get our drinks and our food, and we make our way to a red plastic booth and sit down. The plate already has a grease stain, and we just got our food, but after we pray, we dig in, and I must say, it is one of the best cheap burgers ever.

"Whaddaya think?" Mom asks, as she sips her Diet Coke.

"It's good. Greasy and good."

"No, I mean. UGA."

It's time for some tough talk. The fluorescents in here are as a bright as a public-school classroom, and they light up all the red dots on my eighteen-year-old face as I break it down for Mom.

"It's. . . this is really big, and. . . I don't know. . . I wanted to get away from high school, you know?"

She nods, "Okay."

"And one of the things I don't like about high school is I know a lot of people, but I don't know them that well. I guess I thought a smaller place might be better? I don't know. I don't think I could feel like I was away from high school either."

She puts a hand on my hand, "It's okay. You don't love UGA. It's okay." Then, her hands go up to defend her point, "But you don't know what you're missing."

And we take a drive to downtown Athens, and I know she

wants me to love it, and I want to love it. I do. I really want to because this feeling is depressing. What feeling? No, not the feeling of disappointing my mom. No, it's the feeling of having only one option. Oglethorpe has to be great; otherwise, I'm settling, and I will never be able to get over the fact that it is my injury that is making me settle—that, if I didn't have this brain injury, my life would be better; it would still be on track; I would feel like I was going somewhere.

When we make it back home, Dad offers a hopeful face and is met with Mom's reply, "No, you gotta talk to him. He did not like UGA."

I'm a little bit behind, limping and all. "No, Dad, it's not that I hated it."

Dad lets out a laugh, "The beginning of a ringing endorsement."

I sit down on the couch with him, "No, seriously. I didn't hate it, and you know, if I had to go there, I would, but I don't think I like it better than Furman."

He raises an eyebrow, "I thought you said Furman was too preppy."

I'm cornered, but I can fight my way out, "It is, but I don't know. . . if it came down to it, I'd go there instead." Settling. I'm settling, but what options do I have?

"Well, one more, buddy. We've got one more."

One more, one chance. Please let it not make my stomach turn. Let it not be good enough for a handicapped kid. Let it be just. . . good. And as I lay in bed that night, I prayed, "God, Father, Lord, hear my words. God, I need you Jesus. I need you to make it clear where I need to be. God, bless our trip to Oglethorpe tomorrow."

I don't want to settle, because I know if I do, I am going to be so bitter. I am going to be so mad at God. I have no right to be, but I know I will be so pissed because the accident came out of nowhere, and he's in control. You're in control, right, God? Why do you want my life to be worse? What did I do that my life needs to be worse? I thought you had a plan and a promise for me. Didn't you say, "I know the plans I have for you, plans to prosper, not to harm you?" If I settle, I am going to feel harmed. And that harm is going to hurt me for a long time.

The next morning, I wake up, eat breakfast, study, get ready, study, go to school, study, study, study, and fear for my physics final, but mostly, I'm thinking about Oglethorpe.

When Dad and I arrive at the campus, it looks like Hogwarts, a green quad, trees throughout, and a castle-like look to the old grey, stone buildings. As we make it to the student center, I see a guy in jeans, a black shirt, and a conquistador hat; I see another guy with a cloak and staff. I mean, yeah, there are people in jeans and T-shirts too, but there are those more noticeable characters as well.

The student center, unlike the other buildings, is nothing to write home about, a bland brown brick structure that looks like it's from the fifties or sixties, dirty, but I'm looking at all the different people—the girl with rainbow hair, the guy wearing a picture of Nietzsche with dreadlocks with the words, "God is Dread," written on it—and I think I already love this place.

Our tour guide is this guy, Miguel, with jeans and a polo, tall, friendly, and very capable of talking and walking backwards. No bus for us; this campus is small enough to walk, and as we walk towards the quad, surrounded by trees, I keep looking at this glorious grey, stone, three-story building, and at the left end, there's this clock tower with the old, brass bells, and I feel like I'm at the closest I will get to studying at Oxford. I fantasize about being the modern-day J.R.R. Tolkien, and soon, I'll have to find my C.S. Lewis. This quad has these two large greys, stone academic buildings, the closest thing within reach to the Oxford of my imagination, and at one end, there's the gate, the entrance, and at the other, there's the library, but it looks more like a small castle, and as I'm gazing at this, I see a group of kids come out with brooms and lacrosse sticks.

Miguel encourages us to keep moving and explains, "This is the quidditch team. Now, I, myself am not a Harry Potter guy, but I do celebrate that these people take it seriously."

Dad and I follow at the back of the line as Dad turns to me, "They do know that it's not real, right?"

I look at them, running with broomsticks between their legs, "You might need to tell them."

We laugh, and for a moment, I feel better than someone else, but I also love it. I love that there is a group of Harry Potter nerds here, that this is the type of school to give up use of the quad to celebrate that.

Miguel keeps us moving and offers, "That's why we call Oglethorpe the island of misfit toys."

Sold. Hooked. What better place for me? I'm a broken toy. This will be perfect.

So, we continue our trek down to the theater, a building in the same style, a two-story building, and what looks like a building with a permanent metal tent on it, stripes of orange, red, and blue painted on it. I can see plays of mine being performed here, and yes, I am getting lost in my own grandiose sense of value. Yes, please! I haven't done this in a long time; let me have this one time.

Miguel is a charismatic tour guide who seems like he has given every tour with the same amount of grace and charm, and he stops here and lights up, "This is the Conant Performing Arts Center. As you can see, it is a large performing arts space, featuring offices for Georgia Shakespeare and Capitol City

Opera, both of which perform here. And get ready, do we have any Atlanta Symphony Orchestra fans in the house?"

Naturally, some shy hands go halfway up into the air, as most teenage arms do.

"You are in luck because Atlanta Symphony Orchestra performs here as well! What more could you want for your entertainment? We've got theater, opera, and music!"

It really is a charming space. It looks old, the theater outside, with the multicolor tent-looking roof appearing to need a touch up, but it's charming. I am debating about this. I go ahead with my question, "I have a question about academics."

Miguel stops, puts a smile on, and straightens up his tall body, "Sure thing."

I try and look as dignified as I can in my cargo shorts and Ramones T-shirt, "How is the theater department? And, say, what does international relations look like here?"

He laughs, steps back, stroking his chin, "Well, we've got a great politics and history department. Dr. Orme, Dr. Smith, and Dr. Maher are all phenomenal professors, and we do have some great classes you can take. Our school of business has a number of courses that pair well with courses you are taking in history. As far as theater goes, we have a great deal of opportunities. As you heard, we have Georgia Shakespeare who partners with Oglethorpe students in producing their shows as well as Capitol City Opera. Furthermore, the department puts on shows, and you have Rehearsal Room C, the student theater group which puts on performances as well. You have a number of great classes to take and a study abroad trip to Oxford to study Shakespeare."

I nod, "Thank you."

And he smiles, and we keep moving, and I have a lot to think about, "You like it?" Dad whispers to me, as we walk back up to the student center.

I whisper one little word I didn't think I would utter, "Yes."
He smiles at me; I smile back.

This is growth. I know this place has no real value in the game of comparison. Sure, it's a good enough school, but it won't impress any of my AP friends or any of the adults at church. But I think it's what I need right now, and somehow, someway, I think I will blossom here. The only hard part is giving up on my plan. I mean, this has been on my heart. I had wanted to do international relations, but it's not really my passion right now, but it was the plan, right? Theater would be great, and God, how I always loved writing plays, but there's no money in that, and how will I have a future in that? Oh no, anxieties creeping in. I like this place the most, but I can't think about this now. First, I must graduate, pass my classes, get at least Bs, and then, then I can have a positive outlook about the next step. We'll see, right?

17
FINALS

This is the week. This is when it all comes down. Finals. The proving ground.

My graduation is not on the line, but. . . my confidence is. My sense of self, my sense that I will be able to be the person I want to be, the dream that I will get better, hangs in the balance, right? The first two days are normal enough. Class schedule is normal.

Aaron is walking me to second period, rocking his smile, but it's brighter today, "Guess who got a full-time permanent position teaching math here?"

He takes my backpack, as I push off the desk to stand.

"Gosh, I don't know. Last I heard John McCain was running for president, so I am stumped."

A laugh, as he offers me a dramatic, fake punch, with a good-hearted laugh, "Close enough. I mean to be fair, I have definitely had my looks compared to his."

We walk out into the sunlight, bright as May mornings are, as I slowly make my way down the steps, gripping the side rail anxiously, "I would say you're more a. . . God what is his name. . . Diabeetus?"

A fully bell laugh from Aaron, "Wilford Brimley? Thank you, Will! I love you, too!"

Now that economics is over with, I can utilize first period to work on studying for physics and working on my AP lit extra credit. Mostly though, I'm studying for physics. The extra credit will get done, and I'll end up with a B (I hope) in lit. That's fine. There's seven points added to AP classes. It'll look like an A on my transcript, but regular physics? No special bump, no helpful boost. To be honest, I'm not really mentally present for either first or second period, thinking about my final for physics tomorrow. God, I can't get a C in physics. What will that mean for my recovery? How will I go to college? No, like, I mean I will go, but the whole time, I'll be thinking, "I got a C in regular physics. Maybe, I am really impacted from my injury. Maybe, the brain damage I suffered doesn't just affect my vision."

The bell chimes and there is the hurried rush of the students. The quick kiss from Anna disrupts my internal anxiety trip as I see Aaron appear in the doorway. The journey through the empty halls is weird. Students are, of course, rushing, late to class, but it also feels like I'm important. We see the occasional faculty and staff members. Coach Coyle was my AP world history teacher during my sophomore year, but now, he's an assistant principal. He's got cannons on either side of his shoulders, a bald head, and a resting face that says, "You didn't need me to tell you that I was in the military." But it's all an act. Having him as a teacher, I learned he really has a soft, caring heart, and when he sees me, he shakes my hand with one of his old man bear paws, "Good to see you, Will. So proud of all of you have done. You know where you're going?"

It's good for him to be proud of me; I always respected the

crap out of him, "Thank you, Coach. I'm deciding between Oglethorpe and Furman."

"Two great choices. Though if you ask me, you're probably more of an Oglethorpe guy, right?"

I laugh, appreciating the direct honesty, "Yeah. You're probably right."

He's already turning as he's talking, you know assistant principals, always on the move, "That's awesome. I'm proud of you, Will."

And we make our way to physics, and it's funny. Whenever men I respect tell me they're proud of me or show me respect, it makes me giddy as a schoolgirl. It's nothing weird. It's this feeling of all the glory you've bestowed on this person, and they're giving you a little sample of it. So, I'm beaming as I sit in my chair at the front of the physics classroom. Smiling and physics have never gone together for me, even when I was good at it.

"You ready for the review?" Mrs. Foss asks, brushing thin black strands of her hair out of her face.

"I hope so."

I'm as confident, as I can be. I have studied for four hours every day over the weekend. My mom had to frequently interrupt me with, "Aren't you ready to take a break?"

Not until this week is over, and then, and only then can I take a break, then and only then.

Foss tries her best at getting the class excited, but her short, plump body and quiet voice offer little to generate energy in the hearts of teenagers.

"Everybody, it's time for Jeopardy! Let's partner up."

I turn to Kamran who shakes my hand in camaraderie, "Let's do this."

He pulls out a perfectly flat and crisp piece of notebook paper and a finely sharpened pencil with no bite marks on the side, not even a scratch, and an eraser that's uniformly flat and still pink.

Foss hits the slide, and offers, "Two forces are acting on a 5.00 kg mass. One of the forces is 10.0 N south and the other is 15.0 N east. The magnitude of the acceleration of the mass is. . ."

With great gusto and focus, Kamran writes the question down and starts on the formula. My mind, however, is spinning, watching Kamran's writing, I try to follow along as well, but the board is starting to go double, the harder I focus on it, one eye staying straight, and the other drifting to the right. *Magnitude, acceleration of mass*, these words, what are these words?

I have an acceleration problem. Let's say two cars are traveling from opposite directions going 50 mph, and let's say one of these cars crosses the line. How long does it take the eighteen- year-old driving to feel like he can be successful?

I copy Kamran's answer. Maybe, maybe, I won't get a B in this class. Is that okay? Is that possible? Kids who are going to Georgia Perimeter Community College are getting an As in this class. What's wrong with you, Will? Did your accident take you below Georgia Perimeter? I mean, why bother going to college? If you're not above Georgia Perimeter students, maybe you should get a job at Target. Why set everyone's expectations up that you might, maybe be successful? Start them with a healthy spoonful of reality.

We finish Jeopardy, not in last place but not far off.

In the car, Dad looks up, "How'd it go?"

Looking down, I try to add some upward lilt of hopefulness that's not there, "It's. . . I mean, I want a B."

"Yeah."

He knows what I'm talking about. He knows I'm talking about physics because that's all I've been working on. Sure, I've done the extra credit things for it, but it's not like it is standing between me and the hope of better.

A raise of his eyebrows, he's going to offer some hope, "Jeff wants to get breakfast with you this week. What do you say? I was thinking after your second period on Thursday."

"Yeah."

Jeff is my youth pastor. I really like the guy, and we did breakfast or lunch a couple times before my accident, and they had always gone long, and they had involved laughs and serious pauses. I could use this. I mean, I need prayer for Wednesday, but I'll take it after, I guess.

As we are pulling onto our street, Dad drops, "I think Oglethorpe is probably the best for you. What do you think?"

My head is lightheaded; I need some lunch and my second Ritalin. It's been eight hours, and I can feel the molecules in my body starting to collapse in on themselves, "Yeah. I. . . I think it would be too."

Best for me? What does that mean?

It wasn't supposed to be like this, as though I were cutting a deal for my future. Peter is going to the University of Chicago. Anna is going to Tulane. Biplab is going to Northwestern. Eddy is going to Princeton. I'm not saying I was going to go Prince ton. I mean, Eddy is the valedictorian after all, but I was supposed to have good options, all good options. I was supposed to be someone to be proud of. That was the plan; that was the goal, but you know what they say about plans. I don't think God laughs; I can't live with that God. I do not accept that God; I believe God laughs, but I can't accept that this accident is just a humbling act. I cannot accept that God would seek to check my pride with a coma and twisted metal.

We get home, and I make myself a low-grade quesadilla: four slices of ham, two slices of Swiss cheese, a tortilla, and one minute in the microwave. I go right to the couch and shovel the lunch in my face, while I pour over my physics book. I hate this; I'm so tired, so stressed.

Did I take my Ritalin? Damn. Did I take my Ritalin? Did I take my Ritalin!? What's today? The 20th? The uh. . . God. . . the 20th? Thirty days hath November, April, June, and November. Okay, 60 pills. . . shit. . . what is it? I pour the pills out on the counter and they clack on the grey of the granite countertop.

Three of the pills fall to the floor. Shelby cocks her head up. "Ahh!" I fall to the floor, quite literally, but no, not in finals week. No! "No Shelby, no!" Her small black ears turn back, her head lowered, the soft look like she's about to cry, eyes of a lab, and I hear heavy footfalls, as Dad comes rushing downstairs.

"Are you okay?"

I'm picking up the three pills with my right hand, thinking minus. . . two times twenty. Dad sees me frantically getting back up to count my pills, my left hand shaking like a shutter in a hurricane.

His voice is soft but anxious, "Is everything all right?"

His hand goes to my shoulder, and he has that look in his eyes that makes me feel that seeing me like this hurts him, and I want to say, "I'm sorry," and I want to say, "I'm trying to get better," but I guess a part of me knows that will hurt him more, so I say, "Yeah, it's good."

He gives me a look to say, "you sure?" and then, he pats me on the shoulder with, "Okay," and goes back upstairs.

Ritalin twice a day makes it harder to keep up, makes the math harder if I get off by a bit. I feel so tired and sluggish, like my head is weighed down by millions of metal beads, sinking back to the back of my skull, as though my head might topple back by its own force of gravity. I must not have taken one yet. I must not have. I take one, put the pills back in the drawer, and I wait to see if maybe this is my third of the day; I don't know what I expect will happen if I take one extra, a seizure maybe?

Nothing happens, and I get back to studying nuclear fission, fun. I never knew I could find physics so relatable. The molecular makeup of an environment coming apart at the seams? Ditto. I feel that. Am I absorbing any of this? What did I read? Am I even studying, or am I just looking at words? I am scanning the pages. What did I just read? What is the formula for nuclear fusion? What is an isotope? I wonder how many multiple-choice questions there are. Is it all multiple-choice? Will I have time to check my answers? Wait, what is an isotope? Where was that formula? The throbbing in my lower back pulsates as my shoulders harden into cement, and I feel the stress pressing, pressing me down. I wish it would marbleize me, crush me into the most refined form of myself, but it keeps pressing to no resolution, and what have I studied? I can't begin to think, begin to remember. What is an isotope? Screw it. Take a shower. Yeah, I'll take a shower. Something to help me refocus, clear my mind, give me energy? I shower, and then, get dry, put my clothes back on, head back to studying, confident the shower will help me focus, give me the strength to read without distraction. It's a lie I believe and need to keep believing. I need to think there are things I can do to do better, but when I sit down on the couch again to read my physics textbook, "Wait. What is an isotope?"

I guess I'll never know.

I need to take a break, need to do something different. I think back to Spradlin, the former disco queen, the woman my mother said made it clear, "Will will graduate." She's been in my corner so much since the accident. I log on to a music torrent site I used before my accident, download a couple disco compilations, splice a number together, do some research on disco classics, and soon I'm bopping to Earth, Wind, & Fire and the Bee Gees. I have a pretty awesome set of tracks.

I pop in a blank CD, burn it, title it Spradlin's Disco Mix with a Sharpie, and I get back to studying, before Mom comes in the den, "Hey, how was your day?"

I didn't even hear her come in. How long has she been here? Did she just get home?

"It was okay. We reviewed. I'm. . . I'm studying for my physics final."

I try not to be too much of a teenager; I really am so thankful and appreciative of everything my parents have done for me, but I really, really, really need to focus. Okay? It's not like I curse her out or scream. I'm trying to tell her to stop talking to me in the politest possible way, but I can tell I've kind of hurt her as her shoulders fall, and her voice flattens, "Oh, okay, just wanted to check in. We'll get dinner soon."

"Good."

Back to the books, and I want to be done. I want so badly to be done. One more hurdle. One more stupid test before I'm done being tested, having to prove I have not beaten or broken beyond the hope of a comeback; there is one more fight I have to fight. Once, I graduate high school, I will prove to everyone who thinks this accident was the end of me, that it smudged my perfect future into a distortion of shitty possibilities and broken plans, that I am okay. They will be silenced, and I will have physical evidence that I am enough. This is what I tell myself because I need to.

This is a checkpoint on my way to better, and I need to cross it because, if I don't, I will have to accept that I might not heal to the point that I want to; I might have to deal with the possibility that I will never be "smart" again, that someone at the table might never say, "Well, hold on, I want to hear what Will thinks." If I can't cross this finish line, if I can't get a B in physics, if I can't do that, I might have to accept I will always be this person that I hate. I may have to swallow my inability to focus, my struggle to understand, the awkward silences I've created, the loneliness of struggling silently, as not a bug in the software to be fixed but the makeup of the software itself.

I had so many plans, and if I can't get a B in physics, I might as well give up on all of them. I know this sounds too much, sounds like I'm being an emotional teenager and "a bit dramatic," but everyone creates artificial finish lines for themselves. If I can date her, I'll be okay; if I can get into this school, I'll be okay; if I can get this job, I'll be okay; if I can get a 4.0, I'll be okay. If I can get into college, graduate school, marriage, two kids, three kids, a damn subdivision—what are these finish lines? They are all freaking arbitrary! It's part of how we survive, but is it good? No. Is it of God? No, but it's part of how we sinners and broken people get through the day. Do you ever look at the clock and try to make it to the time you can leave? Then, you understand what I'm talking about. This B in physics is my end of the day, my getting married before thirty, my getting the apartment in the city, my three-bedroom house in the suburbs, that moment when you get the promotion, the arbitrary finish line you need to reach in order to be okay.

But I really need this.

I need to feel like I'm not stupid, that I'm not broken, that my life might actually work out. Dad comes through the door with two big Chick-Fil-a bags, and to be honest, I didn't know he left or how long he's been gone, but I am always happy to have Chick-Fil-a. I cock my head up, a speckled acne-laced smile, "Chick-Fil-a?"

Setting the bags down on the table, he collapses in the closest kitchen chair, "Thought it would be easier than going out somewhere."

"Thank you, Dad."

He smiles, "Of course, buddy, I'm proud of you."

I scratch what has become a full head of hair, "Thanks, Dad."

He stands and walks into the den, the afternoon, almost summer sun hitting the back of his salt and pepper head in a haloed glow. He smiles at me.

"You know, you're my hero, Will. I always tell everybody that. Will's my hero. You've worked so hard."

A silence, as this hits me, and yeah, it feels good. "Thank you, Dad."

Mom comes out of the bathroom, talking, never a moment wasted, "Let's go ahead and eat, so we can make it to group."

Dad looks to me, "You okay home by yourself?"

"Of course. You've got group."

And Dad gives me a hand to help me off the couch, and I limp over to the black square of our kitchen table as Mom hands me a glass of water and herself a Diet Coke. Once the food is distributed, Dad bows his head, and then, we all do.

"God, Father, Lord over all, we come before you with gratitude," eyes closed, a smile blows over his lips, "Thank you for bringing Will here. Thank you for helping him get better, for helping him graduate Shepherd Center and high school. Thank you that he has the same personality, the same drive and motivation. God, I pray you will bless him with memory and focus. God, bless him with a good grade on his physics final tomorrow. Most of all though, Lord, bless him with your spirit. Bless him with peace. Remind him, God, that you love him, and you have a glorious plan for his life. Bless this food to the nourishment of our bodies, and in your name, we pray. Amen."

And we dive in, grease, peanut oil and, according to every Southern churchgoer, the Holy Spirit, and yes, these fries are serving as nourishment and medicine for stress relief.

Mom is dipping a fry in ketchup, "You ready for your physics final?"

That's a loaded question. I try my best to answer, "I still have a lot to read."

A quizzical look from Dad, "You've been studying all day."

"I know. I know. It's a lot, ya know? It's the whole semester, yeah? And, there's a lot I need to read over, and. . . I don't know, I'm pretty stressed about it."

There's a silence, and then, Dad offers a soft, "You've got this, Will."

I wish I shared his confidence as I take three healthy bites of my chicken sandwich, the golden-brown crust of the chicken crunching then dissolving in my mouth. There's a silence that I feel somewhat obligated to fill, but the gears in my brain feel rusted with exhaustion, close to coming to a halt.

Dad leans forward, his soft, inviting face looking into mine, "You look exhausted, buddy."

"I am."

I wish I could offer a piece of positivity, wish I could charm the conversation, rebut with a joke, but every part of me wants to crumble into a million tiny specks of dust and be blown into the wind, scattered wherever.

Mom picks up the wrappers, the used napkins, and ketchup packets, tosses them in the Chick-Fil-a bag, all the while sending sad looks my way, "You going to bed?"

"Probably while you're at group."

Mom grabs her purse off of the chair, and she stops, "If you go to bed early, make sure you leave the light in the kitchen on. Love you."

"Love you, Mom."

And they're off, and I'm here alone, which, honestly, is for the best. I love my parents dearly, but I don't think they realize how hard it is for me to focus, how much noise and talking to me throws me off at every turn, and then, getting my mind to tighten back and find the concentration is a challenge all over again.

I need to go to bed. My eyes are falling with the force of gravity that creates a giant, gaping black hole.

My phone vibrates with a text from Anna. "You free?" I wish I was my dear. I wish I was, but I am searching for the strength to make it up the stairs, so as heartless as it may sound, I do not have the strength to talk to you. I don't send that. I'm thinking that I need to the lock the back door, the front door, turn off the lights, and then, I am upstairs, brushing my teeth, getting ready for bed, and when I lie down to sleep, my phone rings. It's Anna. "Oh crap."

I wait till it stops vibrating, I send off the text I meant to send, "I'm sorry I need to go to sleep. Physics final tomorrow. Can talk tomorrow. Love you." I feel a twinge. I mean I think I love her. Of course, if I did, wouldn't I be willing to talk to her now? Shouldn't I have answered the phone instead of texting her? I can't. So close to the finish line, so close. I close my eyes, and did I set my alarm? Check that. Is my volume on? It's on full. Do I have a second alarm just in case? And a third one? Do I have a copy of my study guide? Is four early enough to wake up? Do I need to wake up at three? I'll be so tired if I wake up at three. But if I don't wake up at three, will I be able to finish all my work? Don't I need to wake up at three?

I set the alarm for 3:30 a.m. I need this. I hope Mom and Dad don't say anything about me waking up at 3:30. They tell me I get up too early, tell me I need to sleep. And sure, yes, I know they care about my health, but right now? All that matters is getting a B in this class. I'll make up the sleep later, right? Time enough for sleeping when we're dead, right? Though, I tried that, and I did not wake up rested.

The brain keeps knocking, "What if you fail?"

"Shut up," I whisper, closing my eyes tighter, trying to fight my mind to sleep.

"You don't even know how to do half of the problems."

Close my eyes tighter. "Think about nothing. Think about blackness," I tell myself, shifting to my side, pulling my Mickey Mouse comforter with me. I cannot let this brain keep running; I need to beat it to sleep. . . figuratively of course. It can't afford any more bodily harm.

I don't remember falling asleep, but I know it happened at some point. I know my mom cracked the door, and I wasn't asleep yet, and I know she closed it quick, and I know it took a long time after that, but at some point, I fell asleep. Now, my phone is buzzing, and I feel no rest at all, and my head is throbbing, and it's dark. You know, three-in-the-morning dark? Yeah, that kind of, "what time is it even?" kind of darkness. Willing myself out of bed, I shuffle down the stairs and prepare my bagel with butter. I'm so tired and stressed about this test that I don't even turn on the TV. I want to eat, take my pills, and study. I need to study. I must get more physics into my brain somehow; even if it does not want to fit, I will cram it in. I will make it stay.

I start to read. I open my book, and it's just a series of symbols. It's Chinese calligraphy, and I keep trying to make my eyes focus on one thing, but they keep skipping down the words, and I can't focus. I can't get my stupid brain to stay on track; it's a game of Pong in my head, grey matter bouncing back and forth between the rounded corners of my skull. And AHHH! Why won't you focus? Focus! FOR ONE SECOND!

I almost hit the table; I almost throw the book on the floor. I almost break down. I put my head on the table. I seem to know the feeling of this cold, wooden dinner table against my cheek a lot more recently. If I could cry, I would. I want to, but it's like the stress of working in overdrive has burned my tear ducts dry, and the only thing I feel is the pressure of the steam building up in my back and chest. And it's exhausting. Why can't I have caffeine? If it were before my accident, I would stop by QT to pick up a Monster energy drink, but that won't be able to happen for a long, long time. Crap. I need to take my Keppra, and... damn... my Ritalin.

I just wasted... looking at the orange numbers on the stove, "4:30." Well, great. One hour wasted. Great. Maybe, I'm meant to fail. Maybe, I will have a great life as a failure, working at some bag boy job or something. I think back to the children's coloring books and toys people brought me in the hospital as though I had been knocked down to half of my age. That's what you will be; you will become exactly what people think you are.

No, no, no, no. I go to the drawer. I find my Keppra, the yellowish oblong, and the little white drop of Ritalin. Swallow. Wait, I will need to take the second Ritalin at school, right? I don't know. I put one in a Ziploc baggie and put it in my pajama pants' right pocket just in case. You don't want to be without the fuel you need. If my limp wasn't so pronounced, it would look like a problem, a senior in high school walking around with a pill in a baggie.

Okay. Back to work. Holding onto the grey granite countertop, I slowly pull myself to the table. I may not need the help, but I'm feeling woozy, so dizzy from being so tired, and feeling like nothing more than a balloon with a few puffs of air. It sounds dramatic, but I am dead. My mind is a solid metal crank being pushed by a cricket, and I collapse in the kitchen chair, and I open the book, and I push my eyes through the pages.

Wait. The formulas. Let me remember the formulas. Didn't she give us that?

I run my hands through my backpack, pulling out a mess of crumpled papers, and I find it, hole in it, the shape and structure of an accordion, and I flatten it out by slamming my physics book on it, and I try and memorize. *Mass. Distance. Velocity.* These are words, and they have no meaning, and I look like a crazy person, hunched over the kitchen table, muttering to himself, "Distance equals initial velocity times time plus point five times acceleration times time squared. Distance equals initial velocity times time plus point five times acceleration times time squared. Distance equals initial velocity times time plus point five times acceleration times time squared."

If you saw me on a Marta bus, you'd be like, "Whatever happened to that guy was bad."

"Distance equals initial velocity times time plus point five times acceleration times time squared. Distance equals initial velocity times time plus point five times acceleration times time squared."

I breathe out. I think I kind of know what that means. And I pray I don't forget it.

I hear a few creaks from the steps, a thud, a thud, a whine, and the clattering of dog claws on the wooden steps as Dad stumbles down the stairs, being led by the small forms of Jack and Shelby, not affected by the early hour, a religious devotion to food propelling their bodies forward. Dad is tired. He's in his black Nike sweatshirt and grey sweatpants, a uniform to match his level of exhaustion.

He looks at me, his eyes thin, "Why are you up this early?"

The dogs whine, scratching at the garage door. Nodding to my book, I remind him, "Physics final."

He opens the garage door, steps out to grab two cans of dog food, "This early?"

A nod, "Last day."

The food drops in the dogs' bowls, and it's like they haven't eaten for weeks as they begin quickly devouring the chunks of meat and slurping down the brown liquid.

A sigh from Dad, as he comes to the table, "You're almost there. Proud of you, bud."

"Thanks Dad."

While I appreciate this, I'm so afraid of failing this final.

"Okay. I'm off to Starbucks. I'll get you some Chick-Fil-a? A biscuit?"

"Sure."

The sound of whining and scratching. Dad lets Jack and Shelby out to the backyard, and he grabs his keys from the little rack next to the door.

"I'll be back soon."

There is the closing of the door, the loud buzzing of the garage door, and the rev of an engine. I can hear him back out because our driveway has cracks and a big piece of concrete kind of sticking out.

I need to focus. Read the book. Read through the sections on the final.

Thermodynamics, nuclear energy. Just read. A couple sentences, and the bouncy grey matter starts again, "What if you can't remember anything? What if you get a zero on this? What if you fail the class?" I throw my head from side to side. Shake your head clean. Shake your brain right.

Focus, Will. What if you—DAMN IT, WILL, FOCUS! Back to the book. Try to absorb what's in the book. Try to skim through, checking the important details; maybe, just maybe, something will stick. And pretty soon, I hear the dogs at the door, scratching and whining. I let them in, and they want to jump on me. I'm a little scared of falling, so I quickly sit down until they calm down. Then, I hear my parents' door crack open and the softer thuds of Mom coming down the stairs. Blue housecoat and slippers, she looks at me with tired eyes similar to Dad's, same early morning hoarseness, "What time did you get up?"

"3:30."

She stares wide-eyed, "That's too early."

I shrug. I don't know what to say. It's too early if you don't have a brain injury. It's too early if you aren't worried about failing a final. It's not too early if your whole identity is based on getting a B in your physics class. She shuffles off to make her poppy seed bagel, her everyday breakfast.

I close my book and start to head upstairs. I know I should stay and talk, but I can't really focus without a shower. Yes, that's it. I need a good, hot shower. I find myself in this position a lot, not sure of how to end conversations and just retreating because I have a task to complete. Though to do so, I lie to myself; I tell myself, one day, I won't be so busy.

So, I shower, brush my teeth, get ready, and I'm back downstairs on the couch with my physics book, and I am trying to cram a whole semester's worth of material into my cranium, and I... I can't. I just can't.

When Mom comes back downstairs dressed in her blue North Face jacket and khakis, she looks at me with sad eyes. I guess she can see how exhausted I am.

"Good luck, sweetie."

She gives me a hug, holds me tight, "I love you, and I am so proud of you."

"I love you too, Mom."

A final squeeze, and she's off to work. And it's me, and I'm alone with my book, and there's not a noise in the house, and I can't. I close the book. I bow my head. Stillness, silence.

"God. . . I want to get a B in this class. . . Please, God. . . help me get a B in this class. . . I'm so tired. . . help me remember. Help me remember." Lights, tires over bumpy concrete, the slow buzz of the garage door, and soon, Dad enters with a white and red Chick-Fil-a bag, and he drops it on the kitchen table, "You ready?"

And we're in the car, and I have that silver foil on my lap, and I am shoveling the biscuit in my mouth as I drop the butter crumbs like spittle. I remind myself to take my Ritalin when I get to school.

We're in the circular driveway of the school, and I'm anxious to get out and get to class and try and review before the test. Dad puts his hand on my shoulder, as he sees me looking for Aaron.

"Can I pray for you?"

"Of course."

There's a drip of silence as we bow our heads, and Dad's soft soothing voice knocks on the doors of heaven, "God, Father. . . we love you; we worship you. God, we thank you. . . thank you for what you have done for Will. Thank you that he is alive. Thank you, God, thank you for how you have healed him, and God. . . God, we pray you will help Will. God, we pray you will enable Will to pass this test. We pray that you would help him remember. . . God. . . we pray you would give Will a B in this class. God, you say whatever we ask for in faith we shall receive. And Lord, I ask in faith you will give Will what he needs. In your name, we pray. Amen."

The morning looks brighter, May in Georgia is bright and blue. And as I see this, I see the buzz-cut head of Aaron, waving and smiling a goofy grin.

"Morning!"

Dad gets out with a handshake, "Last time Aaron."

He returns the handshake and goes to the trunk to retrieve my backpack.

"I know. Crazy how fast time flies."

I open the door and scoot out, "The big day has arrived."

Dad smiles and nods and looks to Aaron, "Thank you again for everything."

He adjusts the straps on the backpack, "Of course. Happy to," looking back at me, "For this guy? You got it."

I shuffle over to them, "I'm assuming you are talking about how great I am."

A good morning laugh from Aaron, "Or how much of a benefit it has been for you to know me."

I start to hobble onto the sidewalk, and pause as I try to think of something witty; I don't want to let there be a silence, "It has been an honor to be your role model."

A good laugh from Dad and Aaron as Aaron starts the walk, "I am going to miss getting taken down a peg every morning."

I look back at Dad, smiling, "Love you."

"Love you, too."

And we're in the school, and it's quiet as students are pouring over books in the halls, furiously scrambling through note cards, and otherwise, doing their best to do all of their studying moments before their final exams. I try to focus on walking, avoiding making eye contact with anyone. Normally, I would be happy to give a hello or a smile, but today, I need to get to Mrs. Foss's with no distractions. Eyes forward, Will. We're past the main entrance point, moving onto E Hall, and then, it is over to H and Foss's room, and Aaron is trying to keep me engaged, "Any plans over the summer?"

I never want to ignore Aaron; I'm happy that a guy who was probably pretty popular in high school wants to talk and make jokes with me.

"Mom signed me up for a stupid study skills course, and then, I guess. . . I think I have like stuff for Oglethorpe. You?"

"Oh yeah, buddy. Got to teach summer school and then run a basketball camp."

He claps his hands and spins, a grand way to show how

exciting summer school and basketball camp are. It kind of feels like he's showing off, with the spinning I mean.

We make our way to H Hall, as Aaron follows behind me, "Glad you're going to be starting things at OU. That's huge. You must be happy."

I smile, "Yeah, wasn't my first choice, but I'm looking forward to college."

He claps again, "Man, OU is awesome. Looks just like Hogwarts."

I almost roll my eyes, "That's what everyone says."

And we're there, H105, and I'm feeling my pulse rising, my head feeling light and my breath becoming short.

Aaron grabs my shoulder, "You've got this, buddy. Remember, you got this. I'll be here to pick you up after, but you're gonna rock this, okay?"

I look up at him, stern, serious, "Yes. I'm gonna rock this."

"That's the spirit!"

Aaron leads me in, waves to Mrs. Foss, and drops my bag off at my desk.

In the doorway, he points at me, "You're gonna rock this."

I straighten up in my chair, "Yes, I am."

And it's me, Mrs. Foss, and two other kids on the other side of the room. Honestly, I would be lying if I said I knew who they were. It's not an arrogance thing, more of a brain injury thing.

Mrs. Foss looks up from her laptop, "Will. You wanna go ahead and get started?"

For a second there, I forgot about my extra time, "Yes."

"Okay, grab a Scantron sheet, and here's a copy of the test," as she hands me a one.

I take one and go to my desk and flip open to question one, "Assuming 1 kg = 1,000 g, a 5 kg object has less inertia than an object with a mass of. . ."

Okay. What? I know what kilograms are, and I think I know what inertia is, maybe, kind of, but what? Slow down. Think, Will. Think. Let's star it and skip it. And, that's what I find myself doing for a number of questions. I can remember the definitions; I can remember how things connect or disconnect, and I'm happy about that. I can even remember some of the history, and I stop and look up to thank God. I am happy to have that, but these math problems are causing my world to start spinning. What is happening?

Focus, Will. Focus.

I get through the test with a number of skipped questions, and I've got thirty minutes, or I've got thirty minutes until the class is over. I'll still be taking the test. Back to the inertia question. I try to figure out inertia. The formula is one half mass times the radius around the object twice. But I don't have the radius. How do I get the radius? Do I have a formula for that? Is there a way to get that from the mass? If I don't have radius and I don't have inertia, okay, so wait. . . is there a mass that's less than the other ones? That should be easy. Let's see answer choices. . . are. . . ah, they. . . no, this one has less, so. . . I'm looking for more, and they are all grams and the kilograms are less. Dang. I mean, what do I. . .? And then, I see it, "6,000 g." That's 6 kg, which would make it more, so circle it.

The next several math problems are. . . well. . . I scribble and scrabble, try formula after formula, and I get some answers that are close, but none of my math really comes out exact, and then, the bell rings, and I see my classmates get up. I hear, "Have a good summer, Mrs. Foss! Have a good summer, Will!"

And, I offer a quick, "You too!" while I keep taking my final. Time to check every answer, as Aaron comes in and stands at the blackboard. I look up, "Hold on—"

He puts his hand up, "Take your time, buddy. Take your time."

I go through the questions, and I don't know about my answers, and I don't know if I should know, but I've taken about twenty more minutes, and I swallow, and I hand it to Mrs. Foss.

"You done? She asks, looking up from her computer. I nod.

"Okay," and she takes it and compares it to the answer key, and each strike of her pencil on the Scantron is like a punch to the gut as she strikes through wrong answers. She holds it up, and does some math in her head, muttering to herself, and puts in the grade book. As she hits enter, her hands go up, and she shouts, "Yes!"

"What?"

I don't know what I think she's saying yes to. I'm hoping it's my grade, but I don't want to get excited yet. I don't want my hopes dashed. She looks up at me with her doe eyes and beckons me over, "You want to see your grade?"

Do I? Do I want to see my grade? I stand up, my left hand shaking a bit, rattling against my leg, as I limp over to her desk to look at the computer. She points one of her fingers at the screen, "Right there."

And I gulp and look, and I see the numbers, "81.95."

"Does that mean?"

She grabs my hand, a smile sparkling on her face, "You got a B, Will!"

I hug her. "I got a B!"

Aaron claps, not slow or sarcastic but genuine and excited.

"Way to go, buddy!"

"Yes! Thank you!" And for this one, sweet moment, I feel like everything is going to be okay. I give Mrs. Foss another big hug and make my way to the car.

Aaron puts his hand out, "It has been a privilege, sir."

"Put that away," I say, as I give him a solid hug. He laughs and returns it.

"You've got my email. Please keep in touch."

"Of course. Thank you again, Aaron."

He wipes the sweat off his head and smiles, "Of course, Will. Of course."

I get in the car as I see Aaron walk back into Roswell High School, and I can't believe it.

I'm done. I'm done, and I get in the car and look at Dad who gives me a, "Well? How'd it go?"

I smile bright, confident, "I got a B."

He grabs my hand, "That's awesome, Will! That's awesome!"

And, it is, and as we drive home, I can't believe it. I thank God. I can't believe I did it. It's funny, I guess; before my accident, I would have been furious to receive a B in physics. This year, I can't believe I did it. I can't believe I did it.

I've got today, and then, I'll be here nice and early to prepare for the graduation ceremony people are surprised I'm attending; I mean, I guess I had always mostly believed I would graduate. I don't know if I'll ever be myself again, the smart one, the one with promise, and it's almost silly, but now, I feel like I have a little bit of my shine back.

My dad smiles. "That's great, Will. I'm so happy you ended with a B. Glad you can rejoice with Jeff tomorrow."

I look up at him, the early summer Georgian sun hitting my eyes and almost blinding me, "Jeff?"

My dad is focused on driving, as we make our way down Holcomb Bridge, "Jeff Summers. Remember, you are getting breakfast tomorrow."

"Oh, right." I had totally forgotten about that. Everything that was not related to the physics final had sort of dissolved into the middle distance. Now, the non-physics part of life is coming back to me. I have so much to tell Jeff, so much I want his opinion on. I keep thinking about the Playwrights Festival. I do love to write, but can I really afford to get a degree and fall flat on my face? What if I major in playwrighting, and I end up working at Steak 'n Shake because my writing never really took off? What if I no longer have the shine? What if my brain injury took my ability to write just like it took my intelligence? What if the creativity got beaten and battered, leaking out of my skull like so much blood?

Am I crazy? I mean, let's be real, could I even write before my accident? I mean, I had written a couple of short scenes for church, but I wrote my first play last year. Did I make the right choice for college? I mean, Furman has a better international affairs program. What if that's where I should've gone? I mean, even if I don't work for the UN, I can probably find a job doing something? If I can get a decent job, I can ward off the mark of failure, but if I dive head first into writing, it is either sink or swim, and I am so tired of sinking. Sometimes, there's that fear that I have anvils tied to my feet now, so swimming is a thing of the past, my cries for help drowned out in the air bubbles of my inability.

When I wake in the morning, I am not thinking about graduation. I am not thinking about anything other than this idea of what my life could be, what I want Jeff's advice on. I want him to tell me to go one way, and I'll do it.

When we pull up to the IHOP, I see him, gut like my dad, younger with a brown goatee, a suburban guy military haircut. He's standing out front, and he lights up in faux frustration.

"Come on guys, I've been out here for a whole minute!"

He gives my dad one of those handshakes-to-hug deals and turns to me, "We have much to catch up on, my friend."

There are two kinds of IHOPs—bougie or gas station; this is one of the bougie ones, shiny black and blue booths and freshly vacuumed carpets. A smiling waitress in her early twenties welcomes us and leads us to our table.

"I'll get your coffee and water, and then, Samantha will be right over."

We sit down, and Jeff's face hasn't lost the positivity. He's a youth minister, and he's got the same youth minister peppy energy, but it's genuine, and he likes sarcasm, so we've always enjoyed each other. And we do the normal catch-up things. We talk about the semester; I throw him some Demetri Martin lines, and we order our food, and after we pray, Jeff gets right to it, "So, what is on your mind?"

There's stillness. I kind of don't want to say because if it's just in my head, it seems almost easier to deal with, but I see him staring at me, his shoulders turned in, an almost interrogation stance that lets me know he's listening. I swallow.

"Well, you know how I always wanted to work for the UN? Like go to Wake Forest and major in international relations?"

Jeff smirks, "Well, I always thought you would do something in politics."

I may have said some controversial things in youth group, like it's okay to be a Christian and vote for a Democrat (actually, at seventeen, I probably said that Christians should only vote Democrat).

"Well, that was the dream all of high school; that's what I was working on, debate team, Model UN; in fact, the day after my accident, I was supposed to retake my SAT to get into Wake Forest, but. . . I don't know, I got into this playwrighting festival, one that I went to last year."

He nods, sipping his coffee.

"And, I feel like I'm cheating myself."

He pauses, a little coffee drips on his goatee, "What do you mean?"

I breathe. "Like am I majoring in international relations because I'm scared, you know? Am I scared of majoring in playwriting and going out there and failing miserably? I want to get married, and I want a family, and you need money to do those things, and what if I never make it? You know? Like what if I never get a big play?"

Jeff smiles as he puts his coffee down.

"Look, Will, I understand. You're scared of venturing out and believing it will work out. Did I ever tell you what my mentor told me about God's will?"

I shake my head no.

"Well, he told me there's a way to determine God's will for your life—and, let me say, it is by no means a perfect formula, like it's not like you can do this, and it works perfectly. It serves as a good guide."

I nod as the waitress checks on us. I give her the thumbs up. No food yet. I need to hear this.

Jeff continues, his big arms gesturing as he talks, "Desire, ability, and opportunity. You want to go where you have all three, but if you got two out of those three, you are good to go. And when it comes to writing, you've got the ability; I've seen your stuff. You've got the ability, and, you've got the desire. You're waiting on the opportunity, which you have to trust God to provide."

I remember to nod; I tell myself, "Don't forget this, Will. Remember these words." And, we talk about Oglethorpe, what my summer will look like, and I feel good. I feel the warm, caramelly, buttery peace that fills up your whole body. I don't know how to explain it; it's something you can't control, but when it hits you, it hits you, and you know that things will be okay. Now, I may doubt, and scramble later, but in this moment, I can only breathe in and breathe out and know it will be okay.

After a hug and a number of sarcastic jabs exchanged, I get back in Dad's car, and he turns to me, "How was it?"

I smile, "Really good. I know that I want to major in play-writing."

A pause—even though he has never done anything but support and encourage me in my creative pursuits—I half expect him to offer disappointment or antagonism. Pause. Thank God my doubts are nothing but fear.

His lips curl in a smile, "That's great, Will. That's great."

And I want to sit in this space forever, this space where I feel like everything's going to be okay, this space where the world works, and I feel like it works with me in it, where it feels like there is something I can add to it. I feel good now, and I want it to stay that way. I'm not thinking about my injury or getting better; I'm not worried about tomorrow; I'm not fretting the social panic attack that will be graduation. I'm a dinghy drifting on the breeze in a quiet ocean of possibility, and I love it.

This moment, now, I want to stretch it out like taffy, pulling it out across my life, but soon after I think this, Dad looks at the clock and then looks at me, "We need to get back home and get you to school for graduation practice."

The taffy snaps. Shoot.

Let's get on with it then, and as we make it home to get ready for graduation with so many people and so many moving parts, I pray that the sweet, melty peace returns. Please God, let it return.

18
GRADUATION

Graduation practice was a complete waste of time. I mean, I didn't think it would be helpful, but I had hoped I wouldn't be doing the thing I find myself doing in moments I want to get it out of: counting down from one hundred in my head waiting for the moment to change. However, soon, we're all in the gym, and we're tired, hot, and ready to finally walk across the stage and get on with it. Then, the word comes, and we make our way onto the football field with green grass and the blue and amber sky of a typical Georgia day in May. The lights from the football field are blindingly bright, and we march out to our seats as the band belts out "Pomp and Circumstance."

"Don't trip. Keep up. Don't trip. Keep up," I think to myself as we march. I'm not enjoying this moment. I'm not even in this moment. I want to make it through this moment without looking stupid, and it's almost over, this journey. Keep an eye on the person in front and try to keep up. I almost trip, and I fear the worst, but I catch myself, and the sound of applause is barely noticed against the noise of my insecurities.

We're sitting down on the field in our folding chairs, and Dr. Spurka takes the stage, "Roswell High School's graduating class of 2008, we are so proud of you!"

There is the sound of applause, and I almost forget to clap, but I finally remember to slap my hands together. And with that, graduation commences as the speakers go one after the other: Spurka, a state senator, and then, Eddy, the valedictorian, a small guy with a big brain, "Thank you Dr. Spurka, our great and powerful leader."

It's a good start, and he keeps hitting, "I know we're all sad to see Roswell High School go, especially all that great food. Who knew there were so many ways to prepare cardboard, am I right? And of course, the portables, the best of learning environments; there is no better place to study in Georgia than a sweat box with a broken AC."

So, this guy who I met as quiet and shy is delivering jokes that have the crowd hollering and clapping. I'm not going to lie; I am kind of jealous, but I am mostly happy for him. Sure, I would love to be up there delivering zingers, but I am happy to see the guy who had not always carried himself with social confidence, the guy who was looking for a friend group to call home, crushing it up there tonight. He gets applause, and he deserves it, and now, it is time for the main event.

So, the awarding of diplomas begins, and we stand up and start moving, and it's a slow line; I mean, the school is bigger than the college I'm going to. I keep moving, "Don't fall down. Don't trip. Don't do anything stupid." And, I'm not even conscious; I'm just moving forward, limping steadily ahead as the football lights with their alien beacon level of intensity shine down on us. I'm not paying attention to the crowd; I don't even know what is going on. I just know that I keep moving forward. I know that if the black robe in front of me is moving, I need to be moving. Listen for your name and keep moving.

The stands are full, I think. There are almost seven hundred of us graduating, so honestly, the field is pretty full of chairs too, I think. Again, my vision is tunneling, so I can survive getting my diploma. My heart is a bullet train, aflutter with not looking stupid. One limping foot in front of the other, Will. And I hear my name, and I go to shake Dr. Spurka's hand, and he's smiling wide, "Congratulations, Will."

I don't even know it. I am so oblivious to it; all I hear is the noise. I almost miss it. Everyone is giving me a standing ovation. Whistles, cheers, applause, and I don't even really know it. I mean I know people are clapping, but I don't get that they're all standing for me, but I raise my arms in excitement anyway. The stadium of parents, the sea of students, they know about me; they've been pulling for and praying for me since October. Maybe, some of them are wearing the wristbands for me; maybe, some of them have sent meals to my parents. Some of them have me on a prayer list at home or read the Caring Bridge updates Dad writes for me. There is this overwhelming ocean of people who are swelling with support, and like a wave, it swallows me; I feel this moment of joy. I did it. I graduated. I have a piece of paper that says I am, even by the smallest of margins, better. I have a piece of paper that puts me back, if only in a small way, on track, and underneath those bright white, other worldly spotlights of the football field, I feel, for a drop of a second, true joy and true hope.

And with my arms raised, I limp off the stage, the black robe I was following, well advanced beyond me, so I walk off, and the wave of joy has been swallowed back out to sea as I scramble. I don't know where to go; I don't know which seat is mine. I don't know which row is mine, and I'm lost, and they all look the same. Like a cornered animal, I don't know where to go, so I shuffle towards black robes, and a soft hand touches my back. It's one of the counselors, who's been standing on the perimeter, "Need help?"

I'm sure I look frightened, and all I prayed for was to not look stupid. All I wanted was for this to go off without a hitch, and I failed.

"I don't know where my seat is at."

With a smile, soft voice, (I can see why she's a school counselor.) she says, "Let me take you."

And we walk over to a row that I know is not my row, but there is an empty seat, and I sit down. My heart is racing; my head is light, and I hate that this moment of better has been swallowed by the effects of my injury. I want to swim back to the ocean of before, but this is now, and I have to stay in this moment as we wait on the rest of our classmates to be called, and again, it is a long one. I am counting the graduates; I know it makes me sound like a guy with a beard, a semi-automatic, and a manifesto, but counting is a good way get through a moment you just want to get through. Waiting is one of the hardest parts of life, but there I am, in my head, "One hundred one, one hundred two."

And I see the last of my classmates' trickle across the stage, and Dr. Spurka moves to the front of the stage. He's tall with cut features, like a man from stone, a powerful nose, and an athlete's build which is visible even through the flowing, black drapery of his graduation robe, and like a master showman, he peers out at the crowd, pausing ever so briefly, before announcing, "I present to you the graduating class of 2008!"

With that, there is thunderous applause, and everyone stands. The girl next to me, gives me her hand, as if to help me up (which is awkward, because I am much better at standing up by myself) but I don't want to be more awkward, so I let her help, and she almost falls, steadies herself, and I'm standing.

I'm standing, and I have a diploma.

I graduated high school. I'm going to college. I can walk. I can talk. I can think. I can live.

On the field under the clear, black, Georgian summer sky, I am.

I am here. I am okay.

I have a brain injury, but I am okay. There has been pain; there has been disappointment;

I have shed tears. My soul was weary and my body tired, but I am here, and I am still me. I am a different kind of me; I am a new version of me, but I am still Will Carter, and I will continue to be so.

At this moment, after all of this—after the surgeries, the coma, the diaper, the wheelchair, the walker, the cane—I feel so proud to be alive. I feel so proud to be me.

EPILOGUE

The search for better did not end after graduation, and I continued to attempt to recover a more desirable version of myself. I went to Oglethorpe University for my Bachelor of Arts in Playwriting. Excitement and anticipation quickly gave way to depression and isolation since school was a great deal harder than I could manage with the same kind of night-before level work I offered before my accident. After failing my first paper, I dedicated all of my time to schoolwork. I struggled to make friends, and I found myself back in the place of wishing to be someone else, dreaming of sliding back to the smooth skin and confident grin of my former self. I longed to graduate college, to drive, to be married. I spent my days wishing my life away into the future.

Eventually, I found a great group of friends, and I healed to a point where I was accepted into honors and leadership fraternities. More than that, I was blessed to be accepted into Boston University to obtain my Master of Fine Arts in Playwriting. This—I thought—would make me feel healed. This would allow me to love myself and not feel disabled. Graduate school. I thought graduate school would make all the difference.

Then, I was in the same boat as before. I was in graduate school, and I was sleeping four hours a night, still waking up at four in the morning, surviving on Red Bulls and carbohydrates. I had three friends, and I struggled to write anything that didn't get massacred during the readings in my playwriting classes. Depression crawled back in, hollowing me out, replacing me with a tired, empty version. "This Year" by the Mountain Goats became my theme song again. I went home for Christmas, and I had nothing to offer those who asked me, "How's Boston?" How I wished I could give them a good word or a sign of an accomplishment.

Then in the spring, I got to teach a college creative writing class as part of a teaching fellowship. It was a class of twenty undergraduates, and I was the sole instructor, responsible for teaching them the craft of writing short fiction and playwriting. I was incredibly excited; could this be the thing? The previous fall had sort of crushed my hopes of being a playwright, and I didn't have the same excitement and joy while writing a play, but for the first time in a while, I was looking forward to waking up. Is it Tuesday yet? Do I get to teach again? Do I get to read students' writing? Do I get to conference with them? Do I get the joy of offering encouragement? I was anxious about if I was doing well, but the students kept telling me how they loved the class. Soon, I was waiting for every day that wasn't Tuesday, my class day, to be over, so I could get back to teaching.

"I've found it," I thought. "This is what I will do for the rest of my life."

So, I had another year and a half of graduate school, and they were hard, like wreck-every-aspect-of-my-life hard, like I didn't have time to sleep or time for friends. I was not in a good place. I didn't feel confident in myself, and I kept looking for something, anything to help me like who I was.

That last year and a half was hard, but I made it through. With the help of the friends that sought me out and the ever-present, overflowing grace and mercy of God, I graduated. I have my Master of Fine Arts in Playwriting. Then, I was blessed to get into a teaching program, teaching inner-city high schoolers in Louisville, Kentucky. I was accepted into the University of Louisville to receive my master's in teaching. This, I thought, would be my future. I would teach high school. I would get my second master's, and I would find a woman in Kentucky, settle down, and start making bluegrass babies. However, that did not go according to plan.

My first year, I was hired to teach English, but I was moved to theater and humanities. It was a challenging year, and I struggled to control the class and learn the humanities content well enough to teach it. To my surprise, I was rehired, but I was not hired to teach English. Instead, I received an offer to teach theater and humanities again. If I accepted this contract, I could not get a certification in the same subject area my master's was in, so I was transferred to another school. After a month of waiting for a position at this school, helping another teacher, I was moved to the ninth-grade classroom of a recently removed teacher. It was so incredibly challenging, even harder than the year before, that I felt as though all I was doing was failing. Day in, day out, all I did was work, and none of my work was going well. I struggled to manage my students and teach, and while working so much, I became so tired, so stressed, felt so low. My teaching evaluation did not go well, so I decided Louisville and the inner city were not for me, and I started applying for work back home in Roswell.

Soon, I got hired at the high school I graduated from to teach ninth and tenth grade English. I moved back home, and over the summer, I received my master's. Life was going well. Soon though, it returned to the usual case of shattered hopes and downward spirals as the semester brought about a Hindenburg-like fate. My girlfriend at the time broke up with me. My boss wanted me to read and write reports on a professional development book, observe and write reports on veteran teachers, submit lesson plans a week ahead of time and do a million other things to improve as a teacher. The mountain of work felt like it might topple over.

However, all was not lost. See, I started dating this great woman. She's a nurse at Emory, and while she was a little shy at first, she soon opened up. She's sweet, considerate, happy to see me and talk to me, willing to let me go on about things that do not interest her, and wants me to be around her more, talk to her more. She encouraged me when I told her I wanted to quit my job teaching high school. So I did, and we started dating, and eventually, she encouraged me to pursue my dream of teaching college, so I did, and I got two adjunct teaching jobs.

I realized that I love this woman, and I wanted to spend the rest of my life with her, so after six months of dating, I proposed. We were married in January of 2019, and eventually, we got pregnant, and we had our daughter. And after four years of working hard at it, I am blessed to be writing these words as a Lecturer of English. Furthermore, my wife and I recently welcomed our second child. Life did not go according to plan, It went better.

Truly, my wife that helped me see that all of this was worth it. Life is full of so many seemingly wandering threads; some are weathered and worn; some look twisted and tangled; some are knotted as though they will never be free, but they all— whether today, tomorrow, or an inevitable eventual in eternity —work out. It took finding someone who loved me as I am, a brain-injured, weary soul, someone who filled me with the confidence to write my story. It took me twelve long years, but I finally found my form of "better." I had to realize that "better" does not mean that I am the version of me from before my accident or that I wake up every day happy with who I am. Better is accepting that the me of today is as beautiful as God says I am. Better is believing today's me is enough. Now, I am someone new, and as I heal and grow, I will change into a daily version of the most authentic me necessary to live a fully present life of today.

ABOUT THE AUTHOR

In October of 2007 when Will Carter was a senior in high school, Will was in a car accident and suffered a brain injury. After an almost three-week coma, Will awoke and went to the Shepherd Center for therapy. In May of 2008, he was able to graduate Roswell High School, and then, four years later, he graduated from Oglethorpe University with a Bachelor of Arts in Playwriting. He went on to receive his Master of Fine Arts in Playwriting from Boston University and his Master of Arts in Teaching from the University of Louisville. Will's work has been published in Brain Injury Today, The South Florida Poetry Journal, Inn Parentheses, The Calderwood Press, His View from Home, and more. Currently, Will lives in Georgia with his beautiful wife, Ashley, and their two wonderful kids, Ellie and Alexander. He teaches full time at Kennesaw State University. Will has gone from seeking to hide his brain injury to joyfully writing and speaking about his brain injury and stroke.

ACKNOWLEDGMENTS

I would like to acknowledge the extraordinary debt I owe to writers who have given me advice, encouragement, and direction, Anthony Grooms, Jessica Hander, Aaron Levy, Christopher Martin, Ronan Noone, and Kate Snodgrass. At different points and in different times, these writers have given me encouragement, advice, and direction. They have given me mentorship and friendship. This work would not be possible without all they poured into me. I would like to thank my glorious wife, Ashley. She has encouraged and supported me throughout all my writing. I would like to thank my parents, Bob and Debbie, my brother, Andrew, my sister, Anna, and my extended family as well. They loved and supported me through my entire healing process. I would not be where I am today without the love of my family, my church, and my wife. Thank you, God, for the life I have and the ability and opportunity to write this book.

Running Wild Press publishes stories that cross genres with great stories and writing. RIZE publishes great genre stories written by people of color and by authors who identify with other marginalized groups. Our team consists of:

Lisa Diane Kastner, Founder and Executive Editor
Cody Sisco, Acquisitions Editor, RIZE
Benjamin White, Acquisition Editor,Running Wild
Peter A. Wright, Acquisition Editor, Running Wild
Resa Alboher, Editor
Angela Andrews, Editor
Sandra Bush, Editor
Ashley Crantas, Editor
Rebecca Dimyan, Editor
Abigail Efird, Editor
Aimee Hardy, Editor
Henry L. Herz, Editor
Cecilia Kennedy, Editor
Barbara Lockwood, Editor
Scott Schultz, Editor
Rod Gilley, Editor

Evangeline Estropia, Product Manager
Kimberly Ligutan, Product Manager
Lara Macione, Marketing Director
Joelle Mitchell, Licensing and Strategy Lead
Pulp Art Studios, Cover Design
Standout Books, Interior Design
Polgarus Studios, Interior Design

Learn more about us and our stories at www.runningwild-press.com

Loved this story and want more? Follow us at www.runningwildpress.com, www.facebook.com/runningwild press, on Twitter @lisadkastner @RunWildBooks

NOTES

1. THE COMA

1. "I Don't Know What It Is" is a single by Canadian-American singer-songwriter Rufus Wainwright, released in a slim-line jewel case format on July 26, 2004.

2. SHEPHERD

1. Jones, Chuck, Artist. Road Runner and Wile E. Coyote / Chuck Jones. [Between 1949 and 1963] Photograph. Retrieved from the Library of Congress, <www.loc.gov/item/2004679156/>.

6. LAST DAYS OF SHEPHERD

1. Michael Gerard Tyson is an American former professional boxer who competed from 1985 to 2005. Nicknamed *Iron Mike* and *Kid Dynamite* in his early career, and later known as *the Baddest Man on the Planet*, Tyson is regarded as one of the greatest heavyweight boxers of all time.

7. THE SKULL FLAP

1. The Mountain Goats. "'This Year.'" *Sunset Tree*, John Vanderslice, Prairie Sun Recording Studios, California, 4 Nov. 2004.

8. GOING HOME

1. Chechik, Jeremiah S., director. *National Lampoon's Christmas Vacation*. Warner Bros, 2003.
2. Mickey Mouse is an American cartoon character co-created in 1928 by Walt Disney and Ub Iwerks. The longtime icon and mascot of The Walt Disney Company, Mickey is an anthropomorphic mouse who typically wears red shorts, large yellow shoes, and white gloves.
3. *Jeopardy!* is an American television game show created by Merv Griffin. The show is a quiz competition that reverses the traditional question-and-

answer format of many quiz shows. Rather than being given questions, contestants are instead given general knowledge clues in the form of answers and they must identify the person, place, thing, or idea that the clue describes, phrasing each response in the form of a question.

4. *The Price Is Right* is an American television game show where contestants compete by guessing the prices of merchandise to win cash and prizes. A 1972 revival by Mark Goodson, and Bill Todman of their 1956–1965 show of the same name, the new version added many distinctive gameplay elements. Contestants are selected from the studio audience: the announcer calls their name, invoking them to *Come on down!*, the show's famous catchphrase.

9. CHRISTMAS EVE

1. *A Charlie Brown Christmas* is the eighth studio album by the American jazz pianist *Vince Guaraldi* (later credited to the Vince Guaraldi Trio). Coinciding with the television debut of the Christmas special of the same name, the album was released in the first week of December 1965 by *Fantasy Records*.

10. TUTORING

1. Robert James Gronkowski is an American former football tight end who played in the National Football League for 11 seasons. Nicknamed *Gronk*, Gronkowski played nine seasons for the New England Patriots, then played his final two seasons for the Tampa Bay Buccaneers.

2. George Timothy Clooney is an American actor and filmmaker. He is the recipient of numerous accolades, including a British Academy Film Award, four Golden Globe Awards, and two Academy Awards; one for his acting and the other as a producer.

11. PATHWAYS

1. Dan Wilson. *What a Year for a New Year. Maybe This Christmas*, Darin Harmon, Nettwerk Records, 5 Nov. 2002.

2. Regan, Brian. *I Walked on the Moon*. Performance by Brian Regan, The Brian Reggan Company, 2004. Accessed 2 Nov. 2023. https://brianre-gan.shop.musictoday.com/product/3BDD02/brian-regan-i-walked-on-the-moon-video-download?cp=781_66102

3. *Operation* is a battery-operated game of physical skill that tests players' hand-eye coordination and fine motor skills. The game's prototype was invented in 1964 by University of Illinois industrial-design student John

Spinello, who sold his rights to renowned toy designer Marvin Glass for $500 and the promise of a job upon graduation, which was not fulfilled. Initially produced by Milton Bradley in 1965, *Operation* is currently produced by Hasbro, with an estimated franchise worth $40 million.

The game is a variant of the old-fashioned electrified wire loop game popular at fairs. It consists of an *operating table*, lithographed with a comic likeness of a patient (nicknamed *Cavity Sam*) with a large red lightbulb for his nose. On the surface are several openings, labeled with the names of fictional and humorous ailments, that contain plastic pieces. The general gameplay requires players to remove these plastic objects with a pair of tweezers without touching the edge of the cavity opening

12. FIRST DAY OF SCHOOL

1. *Ride the Hatch Shirt*. 2006. *Sufjan Stevens Avalanche – Ride the Hatch*, Asthmatic Kitty Records, https://asthmatickitty.com/merch/avalanche-ride-the-hatch/. Accessed 2 Nov. 2023.

14. PROM

1. *Hitch* is a 2005 American romantic comedy film directed by *Andy Tennant* and starring *Will Smith* in the title role, along with *Eva Mendes*, *Kevin James*, and *Amber Valletta*. The film, which was written by *Kevin Bisch*, features Smith as Alex *Hitch* Hitchens, a professional *date doctor* who makes a living teaching men how to woo women. Unfortunately, while helping his latest client woo the woman of his dreams, he finds out that his game doesn't quite work on the gossip columnist with whom he's smitten. *Columbia Pictures* released *Hitch* on February 11, 2005, and was a box office hit, grossing $371.6 million worldwide. The film received mixed reviews from critics.